SECRETS & WISDOM

Other Works by Ian Gouge

Novels and Novellas

On Parliament Hill - Coverstory books, 2021
A Pattern of Sorts - Coverstory books, 2020
The Opposite of Remembering - Coverstory books, 2020
At Maunston Quay - Coverstory books, 2019
An Infinity of Mirrors - Coverstory books, 2018 (2nd ed.)
The Big Frog Theory - Coverstory books, 2018 (2nd ed.)
Losing Moby Dick and Other Stories - Coverstory books, 2017

Short Stories

Degrees of Separation - Coverstory books, 2018
Secrets & Wisdom - Paperback, 2017

Poetry

Selected Poems: 1976-2022 - Coverstory books, 2022
The Homelessness of a Child - Coverstory books, 2021
The Myths of Native Trees - Coverstory books, 2020
First-time Visions of Earth from Space - Coverstory books, 2019
After the Rehearsals - Coverstory books, 2018
Punctuations from History - Coverstory books, 2018
Human Archaeology - KDP, 2017
Collected Poems (1979-2016) - KDP, 2017

Anthologies

New Contexts: 3 - various authors, Coverstory books, 2022
Making Marks in the Sand - various authors, Coverstory books, 2022
New Contexts: 1 - various authors, Coverstory books, 2021
Triple Measures - Tom Furniss, Ian Gouge, K.M.Miller, Coverstory books, 2020
Oak Tree Alchemy - various authors, Coverstory books, 2019
Play for Three Hands - Tom Furniss, Ian Gouge, K.M.Miller, 1981

Non-Fiction

Shrapnel from a Writing Life - Coverstory books, 2022

Ian Gouge

Secrets & Wisdom

TABLE OF CONTENTS:

Angela...7

The Interview..23

The Bay Tree...43

Welshman...68

Evening Class..73

Hester..79

The Glove...92

My Dear Polly..112

Westminster..118

Recommended Books 130

Vinno..134

Anne 146

Hobart..160

Fourteen 173

Twins 184

Old-Age Travellers 187

When It Happened 189

Candles...193

How Does It Start? 199

A Strange Kind of Map......................................242

Stanley Grice...260

Angela

"My friends call me Angel."

It had been her favourite line, delivered with a slight tilt of the head and a playful smile intended to lay bare the lie, to seed the notion that she was - if they played their cards right - anything but angelic. She had stood before her bathroom mirror and rehearsed, her smile fed by a panoply of memories harvested from the past rather than any anticipation of her immediate future.

And now, having made the decision to get off the tube two stops earlier than she needed to, and standing by the door as the train pulled into Green Park station, she saw fragments of that same reflection whisked away by the bright lights of the platform. Such mirrors offered by the Underground were fleeting and rarely flattering.

Her favourite mirror adorned the large mahogany chest of drawers in her bedroom; a gift from many years ago which would make a suitable heirloom had she someone to whom she might pass it. Its wooden frame - a little like the rest of the piece - was beginning to show its age with slight discolouration and uneven patina. And even though the mirror itself was beginning to bloom a little under the glass in the corners nearest the window, it had always been faithful to her - as it had been that morning when she sat before it once again to apply her rouge. It was an almost religious certainty her old and trusted friend offered, one which allowed her to dismiss the windows of the Victoria line with such ease.

She left the station to the northern side of Piccadilly more out of choice than habit - even though both former and latter had become so closely intertwined across the years. Angela had always been quite clear-cut about Piccadilly: one could only walk along its north or south side, not both; crossing half way was an endeavour bordering on pointlessness. Her preference for the northern side arose through trial and error during the days of her youth, later confirmed through sheer practicality. She had come to navigate by landmarks towards which she initially felt she might have an affinity, and after that, to those where she had actually established some kind of connection. She preferred, for example, to be able to see and admire The Ritz and Fortnum's when walking, eschewing immediate proximity in favour of taking them in. Hence north over south. In the case of the RA the opposite was true, proximity winning. Indeed, though she admired its interior (with the exception of one room in particular), she despised the external facade with a passion, so getting past without having to look at it was a victory of sorts. In terms of practically (or habit), all those years ago she had found herself most often around Berkeley Square, and so that too made leaving Green Park on the northern side of Piccadilly the only option that made any sense.

Standing on the edge of the Berkeley Street pavement, waiting at the lights on for the green man, Angela looked away up the street trying to transport herself into her past as if the surrounding throng and the hubbub of speeding traffic were not there. There was an Audi showroom just behind her and, about half-way up the road, she could make out where they sold the most expensive Range Rovers. Yet momentarily she was projecting herself beyond these to where Berkeley Square itself started and the Jaguar showroom stood.

How old had she been when she first went in there? Twenty-one perhaps? Twenty-two? They had let her sit in the front seat of their pride a joy - an E-Type that had ostensibly not been for sale - and even though its red leather clashed dreadfully with the peach of her light summer frock, she swore she had never been happier. Dicky Johnson bought the car outright, there and then, in spite of what the Manager had said. Dicky told her he had never seen anything so beautiful, her sitting behind the wheel of an E-Type. Jaguars still meant something in those days; they were special. And of all the cars in which she had ever sat, that memory was the most precious.

Over the course of the next few years she went back into that showroom on more than one occasion. Once, after yet another sale had been concluded in her presence, the Manager (Charlie, as she came to know him) gave her a large bunch of flowers. She was his "Good Luck Charm"; that was what he had said. Cars were different now - Jaguars especially. Someone once described them to her as "a Ford in a skirt". She had thought that terribly unfair. Charlie - who was probably close to retirement by now - would have hated it. But perhaps - as the green man suddenly appeared and she was thrust out into the road - it was just another sign of how times had changed.

Ahead of her, two girls walked, their long straight hair hanging outside short black leather jackets. Leaning their heads slightly towards each other, they were laughing conspiratorially. It was the laugh of youth, of blind confidence. They were wearing tight black leggings and shoes whose inappropriately high heels only accentuated the movement of their buttocks beneath the straining lycra. Angela watched the hypnotic and rhythmic motion for a moment. She could see how men were drawn to such explicit displays. Of course, in her youth she'd had to work harder. Such a rhythm could only be suggested and not made explicit beneath the sorts of fabric available then. It was easier in the spring or summer when lighter dresses would cling more readily, but nevertheless there was still the walk to perfect, the cadence to master. It was a skill she had learned and believed she still possessed, and as if to prove it to herself, for a few steps exaggerated her sashay. "This is how you do it, girls", she thought to herself.

Across the road The Ritz whispered to her, magnetically drawing her gaze away from the young women, on through its pavement arches, and then - in her mind's eye at least - beyond its windows and into bright golden rooms. For an instant her recollection made her feel as if she were there once again, being ushered through its splendid doors by footmen in pristine uniforms, and then into rooms where the carpets felt three inches deep. The pavement upon which she now trod was suddenly soft and full of spring, and she recalled Lord A••• who had been the first beau to introduce her to the refinements of High Tea. She knew she had blushed far too often, bewildered by the silver, the smallness of the sandwiches, the brightness of the cutlery. They had treated her like a lady - only because of her companion - but she had revelled in it. Determined not to let him down, she had watched his every move, copied him faithfully, took cake when he did so, sipped tea as he sipped tea. At one point he had laughed at her antics, which only made her blush even more, causing his Lordship to take her hand and kiss it in spite of himself.

She shook herself mentally and the pavement became hard once again, her heels clicking in a distinctively satisfactory manner as she walked. The two girls had disappeared - presumably up Dover Street or into some shop or other - and Angela tried to concentrate on making progress. It was a studied kind of disinterestedness she tried to practice; giving the air of being nonchalant, relaxed, of not caring in the least who saw her or what they thought of her - whilst all the time the entirely opposite was true.

Ahead, just across Old Bond Street, the facade of the Royal Academy loomed obliquely in front of her, its dark grey mass as formidable to her as it had always been. Today it was sheathed in scaffolding - either for cleaning or repair or the preparation of materials that would allow it to boast of yet another exhibition, another triumph, another season. She checked her watch in an involuntary movement to re-locate herself in time, not so much the time of day but - if it were possible - the time of year and the proximity of the Summer Exhibition. Even though it was still a long way from June, she knew from her only exposure to the process, that preparations started so much earlier, and that even in April the cogs of the RA machine would be turning.

She had met Jack when he was tutoring a Life Drawing class in Wimbledon, and even now could only think of their meeting as fate. A few weeks earlier she had cried off work in the perfumery section of Debenham's in order to go racing at Sandown Park with two of her girl friends. As bad luck would have it, she was spotted by one of the less pleasant junior managers from mens' wear, and the following day when she returned to the store she had been summarily dismissed. Part of her was secretly pleased to see the back of the store; she had not set foot in another Debenham's since. It was like a badge of honour. Having never been that good with money, she soon came to realise how much she had been living hand-to-mouth, and how much she needed a job. She could survive for perhaps a week, maybe two, but that was all. As she searched for permanent work, a young woman not yet twenty, she had spotted an advertisement in a Newsagent's window seeking models to sit for an art class. It was only two evenings a week and it paid next to nothing, but Angela was in no place to be choosy.

What struck her most about him - initially, and even now in remembrance - was the way he taught and the way he drew. In a few seconds his hand could move across the surface of a sheet of paper to leave behind, as if by magic, foundations of perfection. His lines were fluid, full of energy and motion, challenging the eye to follow them, to dance with him. And he seemed to achieve all of this unconsciously and without calculation. Oh, he dressed casually like an artist and wore his hair long, but his eyes, just the hazel side of brown, had a depth and intensity that only truly fired when he was at work. But of this he was largely innocent.

Jack's class was almost entirely comprised of women. As Angela sat in the middle of the circle, a stole or cape draped around her (she was never truly naked!), she watched as they called to him, sought his advice, needed their imperfect attempts corrected. One evening, after they had finished, Angela suggested to him that some of them deliberately made mistakes to ensure they captured their paid-for share of his attention.

The ladies assumed that she and Jack were an item. At the end of the second week, he asked her if she would sit for him. Once again he wanted to try for the Summer Exhibition and had been searching for a subject that could inspire him sufficiently to bring out his best. Even though he did not regard portraiture to be his forte, he told her that she might just be that subject. Would she mind just one sitting, just to see?

Even though Angela knew Jack's request had been nothing but professional, her first visit to his study - a converted back bedroom in a top floor flat near Putney Bridge - was one she undertook with some trepidation. He had arranged a seat for her in the middle of the room and simply asked her to sit in it and look out of the window. For an hour he drew rough sketches. His hand flew, his eyes fixed upon both her and the paper; and yet it as if she wasn't there at all. When he moved away from his easel five sketches lay at his feet.

She remembered the way he had said "Coffee?" before leaving the room. It was another diffident connection that could as easily have been addressed to the postman. She had walked over to where the sketches lay on the floor and stared at them. There she was, captured in duplicate, her image and form portrayed in a way she had never thought possible. She was hugging herself as he returned with their drinks. He put them down on a small side-table laden with brushes and tubes of paint, and came to stand next to her. Even then she could tell he wasn't happy. Though she had never seen anything quite like it - nothing quite like herself depicted in such a way - she knew that it was not good enough. Not for Jack.

Perhaps it had been that sudden sense of needing to help him, to offer him more, that had prompted her to kiss him. Whether she was walking past the RA, or shopping in the supermarket, or sitting on a bus, it was a memory that still made her smile. He had been taken aback for a moment, but that was all. A hour later he returned to the bedroom with his sketch pad and drew her as she lay there, tired, newly satisfied, somehow more complete, and she watched as his eyes fired again. Later, with his fingers made multi-coloured by the pastels he had been using, he smiled and turned the pad towards her. It was the most beautiful thing she had ever seen. And Jack was still smiling. They were getting somewhere.

Two days later, she'd had an interview as a receptionist in a legal firm in the city and landed the job. The following Monday, after spending the entire weekend with Jack, sitting for him, walking along the river and on Wimbledon Common, she started work. She had expected to find it easy, but the environment was a pressurised one; a lot was expected of her. She struggled at first, and the days wore her out. Jack was forced to run his art classes with another model - and to work on refining his piece for the RA without his muse.

On the third Wednesday - Angela remembered it as a dark and foreboding day - the Head of Chambers asked her if she would accompany one of the firm's most important clients, H••• R•••, to a social event the following evening. He was, it was explained, only in London for a few days and the reception concerned had come up at short notice and he didn't want to go alone. She had been flattered; after all, she had been with the company less than a month. She knew they could have chosen any of the other Secretaries or Personal Assistants - but she also knew that she was the prettiest by far.

The firm gave her an allowance to buy herself a new dress and it was in this, a shimmering blue full length gown, that she greeted H••• when he arrived at her flat to take her into town. The taxi ride was short enough, but strained. Had she been with Jack or someone she knew well - someone with enough of a common background - she would have found it easier to make small talk; but H•••, impeccably attired in his dinner suit, seemed from a completely different world.

Once they were in the hotel (a hotel she would be walking past very shortly, in fact) she became swept up in the grandeur of the event. The meal itself was formal and a little stiff for her liking - after all, wasn't she a girl who was dating an artist and liked horse racing and dancing?! - but the splendour of the ballroom, the brightness of the silver, the sound of the small orchestra playing in one corner, all contributed to the newness and magic of the evening.

After dessert and coffee, H••• rose and very properly asked her to dance. On reflection - on perpetual reflection - she knew she should have politely declined. But even though her head was beginning to swim a little because of all the champagne she'd had poured for her, she felt obliged to accept; after all, wasn't she there as a representative of her company? A little while later, as the twirling on the polished ballroom floor seemed to gain pace, she swayed a little too far and almost stumbled. At that, and to one or two nearby gasps, H••• swept her up and in her relief that she had been rescued, she closed her eyes.

When she next opened her eyes she found herself lying under the expansive and soft covers of a large bed. She knew she was naked. In front of her she saw H••• fixing his tie at the mirror by the door. Sensing her movement, he looked at her in the mirror, a slight play on his lips not quite making it to a smile. From his jacket pocket he pulled out his wallet and then, without a further word, took something from it, dropped it onto the dressing table, and left the room. She had lain there for a few minutes, almost paralysed, and then, holding the bedclothes tightly about her as if the room was full of people she didn't want to see her, moved to the side of the bed and stood up. She could see it was money H••• had left there, and undoubtedly it was intended for her. Instantly she felt angry and cheapened. How dare he! And then she suddenly realised that the notes he had left were not five pound notes but fifty pound notes, and the bundle she was instantly counting in her hands was not only the most cash she had ever seen, but the most money she had ever possessed.

Old Bond Street had initially triggered the memory: that and the combination of the Royal Academy and Fortnum and Mason's just across the other side of Piccadilly. Angela had always wanted to be able to shop on Old Bond Street. Influenced by her mother, she had grown up having it represent something legendary, as if it inferred a quality on the people who shopped there. Unconsciously perhaps, in her early youth it came to represent what could only be regarded as an unattainable goal.

She chose not to return to work the following day, nor any day after that. How could she? She had been compromised totally. They had all been compromised in a way; her, the firm, H***. She knew almost immediately - perhaps even before he had left the room - that she was of little consequence to him. She knew he would probably never think of her again, and that the episode would fade into a vague memory of a long-ago London triumph to be shared at all-male dinner parties.

And instead of immediately going back to Jack, she returned the following Tuesday to the Meridien - there, just ahead of her now - and stared at its facade from the other side of the road. It was just a big inconsequential building. London was full of them. In that moment, she dismissed it as irrelevant and headed up Old Bond Street where, with a very small portion of her new largesse, she bought a simple t-shirt from one of its boutique stores. That would be her trophy. And then, on a less of an impulse, she walked back to Fortnum's and ordered a small hamper as a surprise gift for her mother.

Since that day, both Old Bond Street and Fortnum's had enjoyed her patronage on multiple occasions. She had - against one measure at least - 'arrived', and that felt good. Now, crossing Sackville Street and Swallow Street and striding confidently past the threshold of the Meridien once again, she remembered those initial forays into a world from which she had assumed she would always be excluded. Doing so aroused a degree of pride she would now never exchange - even though, at the time, it had come at a terrible cost.

She next saw Jack the day following her shopping spree, the Wednesday. He immediately sensed that something had happened, that something significant had changed. She had tried to deny it, then to be vague about it. He knew of the planned evening at the Meridien, and faced with her evasion and in the absence of anything concrete, allowed himself to speculate and draw conclusions. On one level these were close enough, on another…

As a taxi hooted its horn somewhere nearby and caused her to jump slightly, Angela wondered if she had ever truly measured the price she'd paid. What if Jack had been a boy she could have really loved? What if they could have had a future together? That Wednesday they had argued and she had left him. It was an inconclusive parting as far as she had been concerned. In those days she still believed in the healing properties of time, and she recalled feeling confident - perhaps in a way she never had previously - that she would always be able to go back to him.

Two months later, as the Summer Exhibition opened, Angela walked confidently into the courtyard of the RA, joined the queue, and waited patiently to buy her ticket. She had heard from someone who still modelled for Jack's drawing class that this year he had finally been accepted. She was convinced she knew what he had submitted, and had built a scenario where she would find his portrait of her, where people in the gallery would recognise her standing beside it and gasp, and then Jack would suddenly appear and they would fall into each other's arms to the smiles and applause of the RA's patrons. Wasn't that how it was supposed to work? She smiled at her naivety even now, at her last vestige of innocence.

The exhibition was relatively quiet; she had chosen the time to visit carefully. Purchasing an exhibition guide (an expense which would have been impossible to contemplate just a few weeks previously), she found his name and made her way to the room in which his painting was hung. He had named it 'Call Me Angel'. As she entered the small, darkly painted space, she did so with the image of that pastel drawing in her mind. That was what she was expecting to see transferred into oils and made even more spectacularly beautiful.

There were perhaps two or three dozen paintings in the room. She scanned them quickly, but her painting was not there. She wondered if there had been a mistake, so she checked the catalogue again. Chamber Seventeen, it said, and that was where she was. And then, returning the guide to her bag, she caught a glimpse of his painting. It was not the pastel image made heavenly, but one of the rough early sketches turned into a dark, menacing, nightmarish, evil thing. The woman who stared back at her - a woman unmistakably her - was hard and harsh. It was the face of a woman who you might cross the street to avoid. There was no love in the painting, only hatred. Had she been able to study it, she would have seen the quality in the work; that Jack had indeed painted it brilliantly, and finally found a subject which had forged passion with talent and given birth to something remarkable.

But it had killed something too. It had destroyed Angela's dream, her fantasy. As she turned on her heel and walked quickly, head bowed, from Chamber Seventeen all the way to the exit and back onto Piccadilly, she left not only Jack behind but unwittingly any future aspiration for love too. She had not seen it then - and might not recognise it even now - but perhaps Jack had seen something of the new Angela, an element of the woman who glanced up at the statue of Eros as she reached the Circus itself.

Had she walked this way after her disastrous visit to the RA? She struggled to remember. If she had, Angela was certain she would not have consciously understood how, in those few preceding tumultuous days, she had experienced the polarities of love - nor how doing so had forced her to align her future to one of them. If Eros was to be her Pole Star (and in her heart-of-hearts, she knew instinctively this was her fate), then her direction of travel, as certain as her footfall on the Piccadilly pavement, would frame the meaning of love in such a way as to lead to Dicky Johnson and Lord A⁕⁕⁕. And yes, back to Old Bond Street, and Charlie's showroom, and Fortnum and Mason's more than once.

Waiting for the traffic to pause, she reflected - as she often seemed to recently - how those heady cash-rich early months had allowed her to move out of the cramped flat, funded through her late father's limited estate, which she had chosen primarily to be free from her mother's clutches. Out and into something larger and more central. And how, since then, she had relocated not once but twice until she had become comfortably holed-up in her attic apartment in Pimlico, settled in a building which demanded respect and, she trusted, conferred a kind of respectability on its residents.

It was a respectability that had become increasingly important to her as she had grown older. To a certain extent age conferred it of course, bestowing something upon her that the young could only aspire to - assuming they could recognise it at all. Yet there had been a peak, a zenith, beyond which, as age became ever more vital, other things began to feel a little less 'reliable'. She had been forced to abandon her carefree nature in terms of the clothes she chose to wear. Some colours were suddenly a challenge, and it had become impossible to carry off just about anything. Achieving the desired effect began to take a little more planning, a little more craft. She knew that there was something essential that she would never lose - it just became a touch harder to find it, and increasingly difficult to mine.

As she moved across the Circus, she was as certain as she could ever be that she still had 'it', that undefinable thing. After all, hadn't she shown those girls in the leather jackets - and anyone else who had been looking - that she still had what it took?! But somewhere there was a line drawn she had been forced to cross, much in the same way as she now crossed to the other side of Piccadilly and left Eros behind her; a journey that in her prime she would never have contemplated making. Time had eroded many boundaries.

The one building which epitomised the decline of Shaftesbury Avenue was The Trocadero. As she hurried past it, conscious it had taken longer to get here than she had anticipated, she wondered if it had ever been successful at anything. Although not a site she had ever frequented, Angela knew it had tried its hand at a number of things, adopted various disguises. For her it had always failed - and it was a failure proving inevitable and endless. Not only that, but its foundering had been very public with the building unused - almost derelict - for large swathes of time, like a wound that could not be healed. Perhaps it was not the building itself; indeed, she knew little enough about architecture to make any kind of pronouncement in terms of 'merit', or style, or functionality. Yet it seemed a construction which sat uneasily in its environment, not through any fault of its own but because of where it was. To walk in this part of London - this side of the Circus - was to accept grime and dirt, to condone an absence of colour from life.

Oh there were bright spots of course, and colour too if you knew where to look; yet this was colour in the practical and not emotional sense. It was colour that lacked subtlety, more often than not too vibrant and too harsh. She had an attachment to the more royal hues of Piccadilly and its local spurs. Those streets held promise and opportunity, and were representative of something more acceptable. But here, where the bundles of cardboard and rags in doorways started, there was little that was positive, little hope.

Ahead, the lights of the Lyric Theatre were starting to glow brightly now that the sun was beginning to fade. There was colour, she thought. The Lyric remained one of her favourite London venues - in spite of its Shaftesbury Avenue location! - and it was there she had first been introduced to the capital's theatre, held spellbound by spotlights and aura and a youthful Michael Gambon before his big break on television. Perhaps it was because the Lyric had been her first cultural experience that no other theatre had been able to come close to it. Perhaps it had been because that evening had been so special, enhanced for other reasons... She shook her head slightly and smiled to herself, unable to recall who it had been who had taken her there.

As she headed towards Wardour Street and the uniqueness that is Chinatown came into view, Angela checked her watch. She would be perhaps ten minutes late; but that was acceptable wasn't it, even these days when it was no longer quite so fashionable to run slightly behind schedule? There was colour in Chinatown too, provided you liked red - and Chinese food. She struggled with the brashness of both. She knew places like Wong Kai's or the Noodle Factory were popular, but preferred to offer her patronage in a more subtle and refined way.

Mind you, this was becoming increasingly difficult, all things considered. It had been fine to be choosy and ever so slightly snobbish a few years ago; those years when she never needed to contemplate going anywhere near the Circus, when her boundaries were framed, almost literally, by outposts like the Meridien and Berkeley Square; by Burlington Arcade, Curzon Street, Park Lane and Pall Mall. Park Lane! She smiled to herself again, allowing her mood to lighten a little as it had become darker and sullen in the last few minutes. In her pomp she would have navigated along the expensive side of a Monopoly board, and no mistake!

And then, suddenly it seemed, there she was, already across Dean Street and turning the corner into Frith Street. She paused to validate the address she had written on a slip of paper and kept in her coat pocket so that she would not need to risk opening her purse in such savage surroundings. She knew the building numbers well enough now, and that she was heading towards the Soho Square end of the street. She checked her watch. Perhaps closer to fifteen minutes late, if she was being generous. It wouldn't be a problem, she was sure. It never seemed to be.

A short while later she stood in front of a nondescript, darkly painted door. There was - as there seemed to be with all doors these days - a small panel of buttons and associated nameplates. She knew the number (not the name) from her little slip of paper.

She pressed the appropriate button on the intercom.

After a short pause, a click, then a man's voice, tired and lacking joy.

"Hello?" Was that a promising voice? A kind voice?

"It's Angela," she said - and she rehearsed in her head, "My friends call me Angel".

The door buzzed open.

The Interview

His excuse was "I'm dying".

I had asked him why the interview, why now?

"We're all dying" I said in response as we sat sipping wine on the patio overlooking his Tuscan garden. He looked in ridiculously rude health.

"Ah," he smiled, as if I had discovered some incontrovertible truth that in turn justified him and his well-publicised desire to 'break boundaries' - though at that moment I had no idea what that might mean. In the trees some way below us, far beyond the swimming pool and small orchard, I could make out people moving, their dark blue uniforms punctuated by flashes of white; one or two had been forced into shirt sleeves by the heat - and I inevitably wondered what, if anything, those figures might have to do with his breaking boundaries.

"I had it installed a couple of years after I moved here."

He thought I had been looking at his swimming pool. From the surface of the water, between the occasional leaf that had somehow found its there from the fruit trees, the sun bounced irregularly in our direction. His pool avoided the predictable and ubiquitous blue that seemed universal; its random mosaic tiling of interspersed reds, yellows and green giving it something of a patchwork quality.

"I found I couldn't live without one of course," he continued. "During the first summer I took advantage of Leandro and Vicki's offer to use their pool whenever I needed it, but... Well, it wasn't really private. And I couldn't entertain."

I turned my eyes towards him, allowing the hand that had been shading my eyes to find its way back to my wine glass. It was three in the afternoon and I was already beginning to feel the effects of the Multipulciano Bruno.

"Entertain?" I queried. There was something in the way he said the word which seemed to lace the generic activity to which he referred with a certain significance. It was a uniqueness in his speech I could not help but notice. Had it always been there I wondered, this ability to invest extra layers of meaning in simple words and phrases?

He smiled, and I sensed he was amused by my inept probing, as if I were some kind of treasure hunter waving my linguistic metal-detector in his general direction with the faint hope of hearing the machine beep.

"As I began to know people," he explained, "and as they began to know me. At first it was mainly Leandro and Vicki's friends I purloined. Not all of them; just the choice ones. The ones that fitted me best. And as I began to know people from the town, to make acquaintances in my own right... Friends even, over time."

"You were popular then?"

"Not at first," he said, laughing. "At first I was another strange Englishman; an interloper who spoke none of the language. Someone who had invaded their domain and was desperately trying to pass himself off as one of the locals. Some were more hostile than tolerant."

"It must have been difficult."

"Fun, actually. Or rather a challenge." He paused, glancing beyond the pool, the orchard, and the trees towards the hills in the distance. "Perhaps it was difficult at times, too. But then the painting helped. Or" - and here he corrected himself quickly - "it was rather those hills, this landscape."

For all his renown, this was an air of self-deprecation which struck a discordant note. His desire to wave away his contribution, his talent, had a falseness about it that seemed unnatural. Unbelievable, in fact.

"You're too modest," I ventured.

"About my daubings?"

"Hardly daubings."

Unable - or unwilling - to summon the energy to restrain him as he leaned forward to top up our glasses, I watched him weighing his response; a conflict perhaps between a private assessment of his talent and that of the wider world. As he offered me the replenished glass there came a distant shout from the far off olive trees.

"Perhaps I was lucky," he suggested, ignoring the muted vocal intrusion. "You must remember that I had never really painted in my life before. Let alone - God forbid! - possess any misplaced or mad notion about having talent or being some kind of artist."

"But you did," I suggested.

"Did what? Have talent - or harbour the secret notion that I might think I was capable of becoming an artist? The two are most definitely different. Perhaps after a while the thought might have crossed my mind."

"Which one? That you had a modicum of talent?" I played down the scale of the suggestion to try and make it palatable.

"A 'modicum', yes." He smiled. "I guess it was only natural. If enough people start telling you something is true then sooner or later, no matter what you might start out thinking, you have to come round to believing it yourself. Salut!"

He took a sip of wine with the air of a man who, after all this time, still found the whole experience - sitting on a warm Italian hillside drinking good quality wine - breathtaking. I followed his gaze. From the trees below a figure had emerged and was beginning to make the long march back up the hill towards us.

"You were lucky to find this place," I said.

"My first real slice of luck was when Alex offered to try and sell some of my landscapes in his gallery," he corrected. "Even now I don't really know why I agreed. Perhaps I was flattered. I met him when he arrived for dinner with Vicki one day, when Leandro was away on business."

"Was that here?"

"This place was my second piece of luck, remember. I used to rent a hovel on the south side of town. It was small and vaguely appropriate; quiet enough. There was a lake of sorts nearby, and in the spring it was an amazing place. When I started painting I thought I was Cezanne!"

At this he let out a huge laugh; the kind of laugh I had not heard from him before. As he played it out, he seemed to be pinching himself inside, as if he still couldn't believe how things had turned out. Clearly the notion amused him too, and I could see that it was not self-deprecation after all, this dumbing down of his ability, but a genuine lack of understanding as to why people should appreciate him in the way they did. Or that he even had any ability worthy of appreciation in the first place. It was almost a by-product rather than an end in itself, as if a stranger had tapped him on the shoulder one day and given him a lamp complete with resident Genii. He could neither refuse the lamp nor prevent the Genii from escaping the bottle.

"I stayed there about a year - which was long enough," he carried on. "It actually ceased to be appropriate, partly because Alex was selling my paintings almost faster than I could turn them out - and at ever-increasing prices too. He must have been some kind of magician! Under those circumstances - and with a much more healthy bank account, not to mention a growing reputation to support - the hovel and I had to part company." He laughed again, back to restrained amusement.

There was an interesting mix here; the notion of Genii and magician, balanced against the vaguely industrial process of 'turning out' paintings. I had seen some of them, of course; vibrant and daring, his landscapes seemed to both define and defy the countryside around us. That they had 'taken off' was no surprise.

Away down the hill the small figure appeared no closer even though I had little doubt they had remained in motion throughout our conversation. As I looked, I could feel my host's eyes upon me.

"You asked about my entertaining," he prompted when I returned his gaze.

"You mentioned it," I replied. "It had justified the pool, perhaps. Or at least been linked with it."

"I said as much?"

"Implied - though I'm not exactly clear what you meant. 'Entertaining' could be anything from dinner parties to whist drives."

He smiled. It was a game, our conversation. Or perhaps a joust, intellectual and largely innocent.

"You've come this far," he suddenly said, putting his wine glass down on the low table between us. He rose. "I wouldn't want you to go away empty handed - metaphorically at least."

Accepting his invitation, I got up and followed him as he walked across the patio and back into the house through the large glass doors that comprised half his sitting room wall. Having started our meeting there some two hours previously, I already knew the views from inside were spectacular; yet even so, in spite of this certainty - or perhaps because of it - I paused to glance back out across the terrace, the orchard and the fields to the purple hills beyond.

Ahead of me, he had paused in the hallway at the foot of the stairs.

"One of the big draws of this place for me," he said as he began to ascend, knowing I was firmly in tow, "was the potential of the loft. It had dawned on me that I had to decide whether or not I was going to take myself seriously at this new game I had discovered. Alex's success on my behalf forced the issue really. I had come to Italy with a vague plan, and suddenly the plan had borne fruit - and more." He paused on the first floor landing. "It would have been relatively easy to carry on the way I was going; after all, I was earning enough to live on now. I had two choices: just get a slightly better hovel or go 'all in' and burn my bridges."

"You chose the latter? I can't see you as a perpetual hovel man."

He nodded.

"There was some money back in the UK from the sale of my place in London. It was my nest-egg, my parachute, in case things didn't work out. I took soundings from my friends - who were all terribly supportive and enthusiastic, of course - then got the money over here and bought this place."

"So there's no going back?"

"Would *you* want to?"

I looked around his first floor landing, glancing through the open doors: his bedroom, a guest room. Everywhere was bright, light and simply furnished. Yet there was a touch of class about the house; unfussy but measured. There were some nice pictures on the walls here and there, but - and this I realised with surprise - none of them were his.

"I got that from Alex," he explained in response to my momentary gaze at an abstract but fetching collage that hung outside his bedroom. "I get most of my things from him; some paid for, but many as gifts. He has taste."

Turning, he moved towards a door at the end of the short corridor and opened it. There was another staircase beyond. I followed him as he led me upwards, this time without explanation. After six or seven steps, there was a small landing where the remaining stairs doubled back on themselves - and here was the first flood of light.

He paused on the last step, hesitating. "Not too many people come up here you realise".

The space was enormous, clearly mapped over the entire footprint of the house. Not only were the walls painted white but the vaulted ceiling too, on each side of which were inset four large windows. The room embraced light, drawing it in and then bouncing it around joyously. All around were the tools of his unexpected trade: easels, canvases, paints, brushes, furniture, props, ornaments. Leaning against the walls at various points around the room, canvases in various stages of completeness. His canvases. It was a treasure trove.

He said nothing as I began to edge my way around the room, my eyes darting from one item to another, from one image to another. This was why he had nothing of his own on display elsewhere in the house. As I paused before a large painting of a lake, he drew alongside me.

"That's the lake near the hovel," he explained, "or at least how I remember it. Of course the colours aren't quite right, so in the end I abandoned it."

It was stunning. I told him so.

"These are largely old pieces; landscapes mainly," he said, taking on the role of the museum guide. "The most recent is - what? - maybe twelve or fifteen months old."

"Why did you stop?"

"Painting landscapes? I haven't really; I've just moved on. It was time to try something else. Like this."

Placing his hand on my arm, he turned me towards the opposite wall, half way along the studio. There, stacked in three neat groups, were portraits of young women. They were staggering. I had seen examples of this new style in London of course, but to be this close... He had transferred all his natural vibrancy into these incredibly subtle depictions of female beauty. It was perhaps several seconds - more than I could ever have imagined - before I realised that all the women were naked. Yet it was a subtle nudity, without crassness or crudity; celebratory rather than voyeuristic.

"In a way these were Alex's idea. He thought it would be good to experiment. His instinct told him that if I could turn my hand to something completely different, then that might just prove something."

"Your modicum of talent?" I suggested.

"As you say," he smiled. "I had no confidence, no self-belief - not to begin with at least. But after a while... Well, you can see for yourself."

"May I?" I asked, venturing to sort through the stacked canvases.

"Be my guest."

Image after image had something sublime about it, as if it attempted to transcend the merely two-dimensional. While they boasted more artistry than craft; there was passion of the most intimate variety there too.

"That's Sophia," he said as I bent over one particular painting. "There are a few of her."

I stood up, in my hand an immaculate portrait of a woman on the cusp of life, possessing extreme beauty and serenity. Yet despite her nakedness - or even because of it - there was a modesty in her pose.

"Sophia?"

"The girl they're looking for."

He said it with a lack of feeling that belied the painting I held, as if a world of distance existed between artist and subject.

"Do you know where she is?"

"If I did, I'm not sure I would tell them," he said, "after all, it's none of their business."

"They seem to think otherwise; that's why they're here." I thought of the blue uniforms at the bottom of the hill.

"They think they'll find something because of these," he gestured to his paintings. "Because Sophia came here and I painted her - just as I painted a number of other girls."

"But this one," I looked again at the one I held, offering it to him as if he were able to look at it for the first time, "this one is different. The style is so much softer, more mature, more…"

"Romantic?" he offered.

Whilst the word sounded right, it did not seem to do the picture justice. It was too common, too shallow; it had echoes of cheap gestures, and there was clearly more than that here. He took the painting from me, studying it himself.

"She would arrive relatively early in the morning," he said. "Well, early for Italians anyway. I preferred to paint then. We would drink coffee and talk for a while. In the beginning this seemed to help her relax; it was important she was at ease with me. Then we could come up here and I would begin. Depending on how the session was going, I could work anything from an hour to four hours. Afterwards we would have lunch, often sitting outside as we have today. The pool was being built when Sophia first started coming here. Once it was finished, sometimes she used to swim."

Just for a moment he seemed to be overtaken by a memory, an image. I looked at the woman in the painting and tried to draw the scene for myself. Romantic? Idyllic? Whatever the word, to some inherent idea of manliness it was sublime. I wanted to comment but had no idea what to say.

"As you can see, she is truly beautiful. Inevitably perhaps there was a bond between us, because of these," he gestured again to the canvases leaning against the wall. "Artist and model. Picasso and all that! We had no secrets. I remember the first day we made love. She climbed out of the pool, her skin wet, shinny in the sun; her hair like perfect long brushstrokes against her back and shoulders. It was not planned, nor engineered. Like many things, it just happened. It seemed a natural extension of our relationship. We fell into a routine: painting, swimming, making love. And then one day - don't ask me why - we made love as soon as she arrived. It was different, more impulsive. And the paintings after that… This one, for example. You've noticed the difference in style, the greater subtlety and softness. I guess there is a kind of intimacy about it; something more immediate."

"I've seen one of these in London; I'm sure I have."

He replaced the painting against the wall and motioned for me to move on.

"At the Cromby and Giles Gallery, perhaps? Alex has a connection there - though how he persuaded them to keep a small stock of my work I'll never know. We get such a ridiculous amount of money for them!"

He was correct. I had visited Cromby's as soon as I knew I was coming to meet him. Theirs was the only gallery I was aware of that regularly displayed his work, and so it seemed the logical thing to do. But his revelations now left me with a question.

"The painting I saw in London…"

"Yes?"

"The same style, most definitely - that softer, intimate feel about it."

"But?" It was not difficult for him to sense that there was a question to follow.

"Unless my memory's playing tricks with me, I'm sure it wasn't Sophia."

We stopped by one of the large, low-set skylights and he showed me how, from a certain angle, the window framed the mountains in the distance.

"This is ready made," he said. "I haven't painted it yet, but when I return to landscapes I'll pick a day when the clouds are gathering in the distance and rush the colour onto the canvas in a huge and dramatic sky with the land cowering beneath it."

"And will that be soon?" It seemed to be such an immediate and real image to him that I could not see its execution being very far away.

"Perhaps sooner than we both think."

Between the portraits and the far end of the studio there were various half-finished canvases. Some, neither landscape nor portrait, appeared to be the end products of experimentation either in style or subject. It was only when I reached the workbench at the far wall - a bench littered not with painting materials but a small range of chisels and woodworking tools - did he speak again.

"It wasn't Sophia. Of course it wasn't. Neither your memory nor your visual acuity have failed you."

"But the style?"

He let my poorly formed question hang for a moment, then chose to answer it with one of his own.

"Do I need to paint you a picture?"

It had been said without any attempt at being clever, demeaning, or insulting, nor as an attempt at humour; but once what he said had sunk in - for me in terms of content, and for him in terms of the sheer appropriateness of the language - we both laughed.

"There's something else you need to see," he said, beginning to walk back across the room. As he did so there was the sound of someone rapping on one of the downstairs windows and a shouted greeting rose up the stairs to us.

By the time I joined him in the lounge he was already shaking hands with a Carabiniere.

"Roberto", he said, introducing me to his new, blue-uniformed guest.

"Signori," as we shook hands, "my English, she bad."

The two men exchanged a few words in Italian.

"I'll just be a few minutes," said my host, "perhaps you'd like to wait by the pool."

As I left the house their conversation began, the rapidity of it dispelling any residual notion I might have had of him being an awkward Englishman abroad. If those first few months had been difficult, it was clear that one of his mitigating actions had been to throw himself headlong into the language. This kind of fluency - mastery of another tongue - was not something that could be obtained by accident; it demanded focus and dedication. I wondered whether the image of being a laid back character who just happened to get lucky was not a little disingenuous. If he applied himself to his art in the same way as he evidently had to the acquisition of language, then it was more than just Alex's acumen which had led to his success. The notion of trial and error, experimentation and disappointment, work and more work, was not one I had seriously entertained to this point. I recalled the workbench, the half-finished canvases. Perhaps assumptions that there was something 'special' about artistic talent which rendered workaday labours less relevant, said more about my preconceptions than anything else. Perhaps - and this as I returned to my unfinished Multipulciano - he might also have been something of a genius.

I had been watching the light dancing on the surface of the water for a few minutes when the two men emerged from the house. Roberto offered me a short salute then disappeared round to the front of the building. Instinctively I looked down the hill towards the trees.

"They've all gone," he said, seeing the direction of my gaze. "Roberto was apologetic - he's a good man who plays a wicked game of backgammon! - but said that they had to look."

"To look?"

"To see if they could find anything."

"In relation to what, exactly?"

"Sophia's disappearance. Or at least that's how they choose to frame it. Obviously someone is very worried."

"And knows she came here," I suggested.

He laughed.

"Everyone knew that Sophia came here - after all, how could she suddenly appear in my paintings without doing so?" He too picked up his wine glass and emptied it. "According to Roberto, it appears that not everyone has yet accepted me…"

"Your Italian is very good," I offered. It was a loose connection, but I felt obliged to say something.

"It's important - for them as much as me."

"He seemed more like a friend than a policeman."

"Roberto?"

"Yes."

"That's how I would prefer to regard him. And, I hope, that's how he regards me. Friend first, potential criminal second." He laughed.

"They didn't find anything of course."

He paused before replying.

"No - and yes." Another pause. "Come."

It was said in English but somehow I sensed that it had more than a touch of the Italian mentality behind it; closer to an instruction that an invitation perhaps. We walked alongside the pool and then down a few steps onto the slightly scrubby land that spread out before us. All of this - perhaps fifty to a hundred yards either side, and then much of the expanse down into the olive grove - belonged to the house. I had already established as much. Once in the trees, the border was a little less well defined.

"Certainly a significant part of the orchard would be mine. At least fifty metres I would say. After that it gets a little hazy."

"What does your neighbour say?"

"The trees actually go on for a reasonable distance - and they spread out too. It looks a narrow expanse from here, but as the land drops away the wood fans out to either side. As for neighbours? Depends exactly where you're standing when you ask the question."

We walked on for a short while, covering the ground towards the trees more quickly than I had imagined - though the hills in the distance appeared as far away as ever.

"Sophia stopped coming probably two or three weeks ago," he suddenly said, as if in response to a question from me. "She was jealous. Some of my other models, you see. I realise now that I had been making certain assumptions about our relationship - about my role, if you will. The Artist and the Model. I had assumed that there were certain rules... Or, more precisely, an absence of certain rules. There were privileges that went with the territory and which, being a reasonably hot-blooded male, I suppose I didn't stop to think about or question."

"She had invested meaning in your relationship that wasn't justified?"

"Perhaps. Or perhaps she recognised it for exactly what it was, but had assumed exclusivity. It was not something we talked about. There seemed no need. I thought things were just working fine as they were - at least in terms of our relationship."

I took my eyes away from the uneven ground for a moment to look at him.

"So something *wasn't* working? Such as?"

He carried on walking for a few more strides, eyes focussed on the first trees which were now just yards ahead of us. Then he stopped.

"I told her I wasn't going to paint her any more," he said. "She was shocked. Before I had a chance to explain, she became upset. She began to accuse me of all sorts of things: betrayal, lying, lacking any talent… Anything she could think of in fact! Perhaps some of it was true to a degree, but it took me a while to explain."

"Explain what?"

"I had begun to feel the paintings weren't working. Certainly they succeeded on a certain level; perhaps they still managed to capture her beauty two-dimensionally, but I began to feel that might not be enough. Or that they had taken a step backwards. There was just not enough in them to satisfy me any more, and no longer enough to do her justice."

"But they are splendid," I countered, somewhat confused, "how anyone could be dissatisfied…"

"You haven't seen the last ones. No-one has." This he said with some finality. "It was Vicki who gave me the idea. We had initially been talking about money; and then the subject had meandered to possessions and then experience. She made some comment about 'not being able to take it with you': the suggestion that there was no longevity; that we should enjoy what we have now; that no matter how we try, there would come a point when the lights went out and nothing would matter any more. It gnawed away at me for a while, this idea, this truth. That dying meant the end of things. I came to the conclusion that perhaps the two dimensional portrait wasn't enough, that it was fulfilling Vicki's notion of impermanence. And that didn't seem right to me. It didn't seem right that I could care as much as I did about someone like Sophia - and I do care about her - and yet despite my best efforts, still fail to preserve her in any true sense. Don't get me wrong, I love my work; I'm proud of my paintings and what I've achieved. But under certain circumstances… Which is why I decided that I couldn't justify painting her any more - and when I had the idea."

"Idea?"

"Come," he began to move again, "my last little surprise."

As we stepped across the threshold of the trees I immediately sensed the ground beginning to fall away exactly as he had said. The breadth of the wood became immediately apparent.

"Where Caesars walked," he murmured.

I stopped.

"Sorry?"

"Legend has it that there was once a trail that ran right through here. A path from the old town down through the mountains. Probably to Rome, who knows? It was part of the story the estate agent sold me, but Leandro says it might be true."

"It's a thought," I offered.

"Something to cling to, perhaps." Saying this he too stopped then motioned me onwards. "Just a few more metres. I'll wait here."

"A few more metres to what?" I was a little confused.

"You'll see."

I walked forward - more slowly given it was evident I should be looking for something. It was quiet and still, and the canopy of branches overhead made the heat a little more bearable. I glanced behind me. He was motionless. Over his shoulder and in the distance, I could see the villa on the crest of the hill.

All around me there were nothing but trees. Not densely packed, but for the unwary close enough together to induce a sudden sense of being lost. Alternately, I looked down at the ground then above me, not knowing precisely the location of his 'last little surprise'. And then, glancing to my left, something caught my eye. A pale shape, upright against the darker bark of the trees. I moved closer, inadvertently holding my breath. Then, suddenly: Sophia! But it was not Sophia in flesh and blood, but her image, every bit as magnificent as her portrait, carved into the living bark of the tree. A small three dimensional rendering of her, beautiful and perfect. And then all about me I noticed other trees and other carvings, some clearly fresh, the wood pale and untarnished. Others - such as Sophia's - already bore the tint of nature's discolouration. It was a living gallery!

"What do you think?" He had arrived unnoticed at my side.

"I'm amazed," I said - my amazement existing on many levels.

"You can see why, when you asked me if Roberto and his men had found anything, I said 'No and yes'?" He said this with a slight smile, more pleased perhaps by the linguistic twist than anything else.

"But why?" I said, looking back at Sophia. "I mean…"

I did not know what I meant, nor which question I should ask first.

"Vicki's idea," he reminded me. "About not taking it with you. About the failure of the two dimensional. The deadness of painting, in a way. I wanted to see if I could do more; to leave an image that wasn't frozen in time, but one which grew and - to some extent at least - lasted. I don't know where the notion came from exactly, but it seemed worth trying."

"To carve Sophia - and the rest - in wood?"

"No, my friend! To carve them into a living tree, so that as the tree grew my models would be growing also. To ally my depiction of them, my art, with something that carries on, that lives. It's like a heartbeat; a real heartbeat."

"But surely the trees will die? After what you have done to them, they must do."

"One day the lights go out?" He smiled. "Probably - but not yet. Not for a little while at least. And in the interim I feel as if I will have done justice to my models; to Sophia - even if she never realises she is here. Its as if I have given them all a chance to live beyond the canvas. And while she lives here she will change; she will age as we all must age. And yes, eventually she will die as the tree must die - but isn't this something more profound than simply putting paint on canvas?"

✳

Eventually I wrote my article as commissioned - and eventually it was published as expected. Word about his tree sculptures began to leak out of Tuscany - after Roberto's find I dare say it would have been the buzz of the town within hours. My article was just about simultaneous with the news breaking generally, which for a while earned me some recognition for having achieved a 'scoop'.

I did not hear from him directly again. Oddly enough I had a letter from Alex (via the gallery in London) which suggested he was happy with what I had written - and particularly my highlighting the irony that the sculptures were commercially 'worthless'. I allowed myself the gratification of knowing he had taken the trouble to read the piece. I tried responding via both the gallery and Alex, initially without success. A few weeks later came another note from Alex which suggested things had gone somewhat downhill - even after Sophia was located alive and well in Milan.

A final communication informed me of his leaving his Tuscan villa for pastures new. Whether voluntary or not, Alex refrained from saying. He also made no mention of his destination - although I was certain that, in one way or another, it would boast mountains and a 'hovel' in which he could entertain.

The Bay Tree

The sound of steam hissing from the cappuccino machine roused him; he had been watching the bay tree outside in the courtyard leaning in the wind. A woman dressed in an apron of narrow pink pinstripes held an empty mug uncertainly beneath one of the steaming nozzles and waited. The coffee-maker looked new - as did the uniform which, as yet unscarred by innumerable Sunday afternoon battles to come, hung a little stiffly on its wearer.

The café was obviously doing well: it had begun a rather unpleasant Sunday morning on the cusp of Autumn and still the place was full. Indeed, he had only managed to get a table by waiting on an elderly couple as they rummaged through some coins to check their change before leaving.

Perhaps it was the location that was the attraction; after all, 'The Bay Tree' was only yards from the shoreline of a sedate south coast harbour popular in summer with swimmers, sailors and walkers alike. It was possible the café had gained a reputation for something. He had seldom eaten there, but it would not be unreasonable to suggest that they perhaps enjoyed a degree of recognition for the excellence of their Viennese Slice or Black Forest Gateaux.

He checked his watch. It was a little after eleven. If he finished his coffee reasonably quickly he could be halfway home by twelve o'clock providing the traffic was okay.

The far wall of the café was filled with paintings of the bay, yachts, and various views of the sea. There had probably been a similar number when he had last sat in 'The Bay Tree', and he wondered whether some of those he could now see might also have survived the last eleven years. There was a small white card alongside each picture, and neatly and uniformly typed was a title, the name of the artist, and a price. He scanned for little red dots stuck to the cards but found none. It was, he had always assumed, the universal symbol that a painting had been sold and its ongoing exhibition was temporary and arranged through the generosity of its new owner.

His view was momentarily blocked by a sea of pink as the waitress, walking past his table, paused before she moved on. Instinctively he looked up to locate what had obstructed her smooth passage and found himself staring at a tall man.

"Excuse me," the newcomer said, smiling, "this appears to be the only vacant seat. Would you mind?"

Chris looked quickly about the room to verify this statement. It appeared to be true.

"Please." He opened his hand towards the chair, offering the place.

"Thank you."

After a moment the waitress appeared again.

"Tea - with lemon, not milk, please."

Chris looked towards the coffee machine and wondered whether the woman would be pleased that this new order would not require her to further her acquaintance with it. As he looked back towards his own drink, the new man caught his eye.

"Unpleasant out, isn't it?" he offered.

As a matter of policy, Chris's normal tack at a moments such as this - trapped into conversation with a complete stranger - would be either to make it clear that he was not interested in striking up any kind of rapport (without being rude, of course!), or to keep his reply as brief as possible and make a run for it at the earliest opportunity. For some reason, neither seemed appropriate in this particular instance. He studied the face that awaited his response. The calm smile was understated and relaxed. There was something benign in the man's eye too which seemed to suggest the absence of any ulterior motive. It was almost as if he were actually interested in the fact that it was blowing a gale outside and that his café companion might feel that way too.

"An hour ago it was much worse. Raining too."

"You haven't been here an hour, surely!"

The notion of spending an hour drinking coffee in 'The Bay Tree' made Chris smile.

"No. Walking, mainly."

"Ah." The arrival of lemon tea broke the response in two. "But I think it should brighten up a little. Perhaps the wind might ease - with the tide, possibly."

It sounded credible enough; Chris hadn't given it any thought.

"I put it down to Autumn," he suggested, somewhat blandly. "It's what we should expect, isn't it?"

A clean hand with well-managed fingernails was offered across the blue and white check of the plastic tablecloth. Chris looked at it, then up to the face of the man to whom it belonged.

"Angel. Matt Angel."

Matt's features seemed to match the quality and tone of his manicure. His hair, receding slightly, was reasonably long but groomed and neat; the strands of grey that punctuated the dark brown gave the impression that they had always been there, having arrived as a result of knocks, set-backs, and the general accumulation of life. This sense of worldliness - once Chris recognised it - was there in his eyes and smile too. Perhaps Matt had managed to find a balance in his life which allowed him the freedom to actually be interested in the weather.

"Chris."

He took Matt's hand. The shake was firm yet unthreatening. Chris noticed that Matt was not wearing a watch and found himself checking his own.

"Going somewhere?" Matt enquired.

"Oh, only home. In a while."

"You don't look like the sort of man who's in a particular hurry to go anywhere, to be honest," said Matt. "Almost like you belong here."

Chris laughed at the thought.

"I'm sorry, I didn't mean to be funny."

"No, no; that's ok. I used to live around here a few years ago, that's all."

"I see. So you know the area well then?"

"Reasonably. And you?"

"Me? No; I'm just visiting. Today only. I like the sea. Oh, and the church. I want to take a look at the church."

Chris looked out of the far right-hand window. In its top corner, just beyond the swaying trees which bordered the car park, he could make out part of the stone bell tower. It was, he knew, one of the oldest in England.

"But you've come back."

"I'm sorry?" Matt's words pulled Chris back from his study.

"You've come back. To 'The Bay Tree'. Doesn't that mean that you belong here?"

"I don't think so."

Matt lifted his tea and took a sip, his pause seemingly designed to give Chris a chance to elaborate. He did not.

"You might think it's a little naive, or that I'm a trifle, well… But I tend to think that people generally only choose to go to places they really *want* to go to - and that they do so because they have a specific reason or because they belong there. Take me. Why am I here? Generally because I want to see the church, because I'm interested in…history, shall we say? Let's be broad! And I'm in 'The Bay Tree' because I was thirsty and wanted a drink before I visit the Norman chapel round the corner. Simple, isn't it? But then that fits my theory. I don't belong, but I'm here because I have a reason and I choose to be. Does that sound fanciful?"

Chris had finished his coffee while Matt had been talking. There was an eloquence in the way Matt delivered his short monologue that seemed in keeping with the rest of him. Perhaps he was charming. Chris always had difficulty in defining an individual's characteristics. Often someone would make an observation about a mutual acquaintance which would take him completely by surprise. Although such insights would help him 'round' the person in question, they often involved some kind of recalibration too. Matt seemed particularly open, however, and Chris felt vaguely reassured that if he was indeed charming, then at least he had been able to see it for himself.

The pause grew too long. He laughed nervously.

"You want to know why I'm here, is that it?"

"I'm interested. Oh, and please don't get me wrong; I do generally find people interesting. Think about my theory;

please, just for a second! And from my point of view, too. I get a certain sense that you belong here. You say that you do not - perhaps you used to, but not any more. In this case, my theory tells me that you have a reason for being here - and for at least an hour too! The walking, perhaps; but not the best of weather. And you do not live nearby; I suspect that too. So I play this little game with myself; that's all." For a moment his smile left him and he placed both his hands on the table, leaning forwards slightly as he did so. "I do not wish to make you uncomfortable; and of course you can simply tell me to mind my own business..." And then the smile returned. "But I would appreciate it if you could satisfy the curiosity of an over-inquisitive stranger..."

Chris looked away briefly, taking in again the window, the pictures on the wall, and the small space between the last table and the counter - the space had had become sacred to him.

"Another coffee? Please; on me?"

To Matt's side, the pink waitress stood notepad in hand, pencil poised. Chris felt momentarily outnumbered and strangely powerless.

"Thanks."

As he watched her walk away, his plans to be home by one o'clock retreated with her. Matt smiled.

"Good."

It was a simple enough word, yet at that precise moment it seemed to Chris as if it were bound up with meaning way beyond his comprehension. The sense of capitulation took him aback; after all, he had simply agreed to take a second cup of coffee with a pleasant and inoffensive stranger. For a moment he considered whether or not he might yet need to hatch an escape plan - a visit to the toilet perhaps, and then slip away through 'Peter's Pottery'. But then he would need to take his coat and thus give the game away.

"Where were we?"

As Matt spoke, the coffee and another lemon tea arrived. Matt handed the waitress a twenty-pound note which was sufficient to dismiss her.

"You were asking why I was here."

"Oh yes," Matt's relaxed smile returned, "and you were trying to decide whether or not to tell me."

Chris nodded, disarmed again by his companion's direct and perceptive affability.

"True."

"And have you? Decided, I mean. Or should I guess? I'm sorry," Matt hurried on to prevent offence, "it's just that I like playing these little games. I mean no harm I assure you."

"No, of course. That's ok; really." Chris paused. "It's no big secret. I mean, there's nothing I'm ashamed of or trying to conceal. Daft really."

"Your being here?"

"For the first time in eleven years? Yes. And chasing ghosts, too."

Matt rapped the table gently with his fingers, his smile suddenly broadening. There was a lilt of boyish excitement in his voice.

"You see! I *knew* you'd be interesting. Eleven years, and ghosts too!

The words worked their magic and Chris relaxed instantly.

"Eleven years. I don't know why I waited so long. I mean, it's crazy, isn't it? Almost as if I was scared of the place!" He looked around again. "It's funny; it's almost as I remember it - except for the new espresso machine!"

"Progress," Matt suggested.

"I'm not sure the waitress would agree with you." He took a sip of his coffee.

"And your ghosts? Have they moved on - or are they still here too?"

"The ghosts?" Chris smiled at the thought of 'The Bay Tree' being possessed by a range of tray-carrying poltergeists. "People have undoubtedly moved on - like me, really - but the ghosts are still here." He looked again at the void by the counter. "Just over there, in fact."

Chris realised, as Matt turned in his chair to follow his gaze, that it was the first time this man had removed his attention from him since his arrival.

"By the display there," Matt suggested, "just behind where the lady in the blue jacket is sitting?"

"Just there."

Matt turned back.

"Was she pretty?"

Chris wanted to be surprised, wanted to be affronted even; he wanted to demand what right the stranger now facing him had to pry into his history, to ask questions, to demand answers. But he couldn't. The question - speculative though it might have appeared - seemed the most logical thing in the world.

"At least pretty. I had been sitting here, like this. I'd just finished a walk and popped in for a coffee. It was a Sunday, around this time. The kind of regular thing I liked to do when 'I belonged'!" Both men laughed gently at this. "I don't know where she came from, but suddenly she was there. She obviously knew the people who ran the café because she was showing off a purple dress she was wearing. I got the impression that she was just trying it on - perhaps she was going to buy it and wanted a second opinion. Her hair. It was just on the blonde side of light brown. Straight, and so long. Almost to her waist. Against the purple of the dress it was marvellous. And when she laughed, her head moved in such a way as to create this kind of fantastic ripple down her back. Took my breath away."

Chris paused and allowed himself to relive that now-ghostly moment. He became conscious of the lull and was immediately embarrassed by it.

"I'm sorry."

"No need. Sounds like the most marvellous moment to have experienced. I could be quite jealous! Did she notice you?"

"Me?"

"In my experience, when someone has such a strong reaction, the other person cannot but sense it and react too."

"Another theory?"

An apologetic nod gave Chris the answer.

"She saw me, yes. That's all I can say."

"And afterwards?"

"Afterwards?"

"There must have been more. I suspect that one incident - powerful though it was - would not be quite enough to create the kind of ghost that resides in that corner. You spoke to her?"

"Not exactly. I came back to 'The Bay Tree' a little more regularly after that, of course."

"Hoping to see her."

"Yes."

"And did you?"

Chris shook his head, the tone of his voice changing slightly.

"No. And it was always profoundly disappointing. I used to arrive with such nervousness, just in case she was here; in case I saw her; in case she spoke to me."

"But you did see her again."

Chris looked at Matt, surprised by the degree of certainty of his assertion.

"I did. In and around town. In places like the supermarket, or in the library. I used to always be on the look-out. I guess I became a little obsessed."

"And she?"

"Sorry; I'm not with you?" Chris picked up his coffee.

"Did she see you? Those times in the supermarket or wherever; when you saw her, did she notice you?"

Chris nodded.

"And there was never contact? Never a word exchanged?"

"Never." Chris's voice fell. "Almost; but no."

He looked down at the table then felt Matt's hand on his arm.

"I'm really sorry. That must have been so hard for you; wanting and wishing, feeling that if you'd just managed to break the ice, if fate had given you a chance…" Chris looked at him. Matt's hand remained on his arm. "After all this time. Perhaps I can understand why it has taken you so long to come back - but I'm afraid I don't possess a theory which helps people handle 'what might have been'…"

Chris lifted his mug and downed the remaining coffee in a single gulp. He smiled as he replaced it on the table.

"And I was kind of hoping you might have had one of your theories to help me out!"

"Do you need one?!" Matt removed his hand from Chris's arm and allowed his voice to mirror the more upbeat note Chris was trying to sound. "After all, you've come back here and faced your ghost. You've moved on. Eleven years is a long time too. Perhaps you should distil the best things and keep hold of those."

"Another theory?"

"Not yet - but it does show promise, don't you think?"

They both laughed.

From beyond the counter, the coffee machine growled and spluttered at another cup. Outside it appeared as if the sun was beginning to win the battle against the clouds, defiantly bathing the courtyard in sunshine. Chris checked his watch then felt the back of the chair for his coat.

"Planning to get away?" Matt asked.

"I ought to, really."

"How about one more favour?"

"Another favour?" Chris feigned a puzzled look. "I wasn't aware that I'd actually done you any favours. Probably the other way around."

"I just wondered if - as someone who 'belongs' here - you wouldn't mind showing me round the old church."

"And then I'll be free to go?" Chris quizzed playfully.

"And then you'll be free," Matt echoed.

They rose together and pulled on their coats. Chris looked towards the counter and the waitress who appeared to be watching them closely. He realised that he had not yet paid for his first two coffees and began to dig in his pocket for some money.

"Don't worry about that," Matt said, his hand on Chris's arm again, "I've taken care of it." And then, with a slight wave, he gestured towards the waitress who smiled and waved back.

"I don't know about me, but it seems as if you're the one who belongs here!" Chris said, as he followed Matt towards the exit.

"I have found," Matt said, pausing to let Chris catch up with him, "that how people treat you and their attitude towards you is dependant on how you treat them. So I try and be pleasant, and I try to be generous."

"Your money! You gave the waitress twenty pounds and took no change. That must have been far too much."

Matt smiled.

"Perhaps; who is to say?"

Outside the weather had indeed moderated. There was late-summery blueness about a sky now punctuated by white clouds. Away on the horizon, the remnants of the dark grey mass that had borne the day's earlier unpleasantness had almost retreated out of sight.

They turned to the left and walked beyond the cottage-like shop fronts to the small road boasting both cul-de-sac and car park signs. A portion of the church came into view behind a low stone wall and its accompanying trees and hedges.

"If we cross here, there's a small path - just over there."

Matt followed Chris's instruction and traversed the road, reaching the path first. Without speaking, he turned down the path to a gate at the far end which opened into the church grounds proper.

It was a small, squat building with a low tower adorned with a predominantly wooden conical structure at its top. A few people milled in small groups around the church, reading the parish notices or examining the names and dates on the few tombstones that seemed haphazardly scattered in the far corner of the plot.

"Isn't that marvellous!" Matt said, enthusiastically. "I have read about this church, of course. There's a similar one a little further along the coast, not far from Hastings - but it's not a patch on this one."

"I've always found it peaceful," Chris offered defensively, immediately feeling that he was going to be out of his depth when it came to factual matters. He followed Matt to the entrance where they stopped.

"See here?" With his index finger, Matt drew a line on the wall where there seemed a change in the way the building had been constructed. "This bit - here, on the outside - is more recent. They must have added it a century or so after the original church was built. It's still very early of course, but not *as* early."

He moved toward the archway over the main door then stopped again.

"And this."

Matt pointed to a rough cross which had been gouged out of the stone portal. He traced his finger across it slowly, almost reverentially.

"Do you know what this is?"

"Apart from a cross?"

"The Knights of the Crusade, when they returned home to England, would find the nearest church to their point of landing and, with their battle-scarred swords, carve crosses into the stone. It was a ritual; their way of giving thanks to being home and saved." He ran his finger over the cross again. "Imagine that, Chris. Think how long this has been here and who must have carved it; what they must have seen and been through. Their relief and gratitude."

He turned and smiled, then taking Chris by the arm, led him out into the open air again.

"Didn't you want to go inside?" Chris asked, a little surprised at their about-turn.

Matt stopped and smiled.

"A notion - but couldn't we say that this is your return from your own crusade?'

"I'm not with you."

"Confronting your ghosts. Slaying the past. You've been away for years - probably longer than most of the Crusade Knights! - and now you're back, safe and sound."

"Where I belong?" Chris laughed gently, amused by his new friend's flight of fancy. "Is this another theory?"

"No, not a theory."

Suddenly the smile went from Matt's face and Chris had the sense that something as yet unseen had captured his attention, as if his concentration had been stolen by an incident elsewhere. Chris, unable to fathom the source of this diversion, glanced around but could see nothing out of the ordinary. When he turned back to his companion, the benign smile had returned.

"What did you say her name was?"

"Who?"

"Your ghost. Her name?"

"I never found out her name."

At that moment, a voice, clear and purposeful.

"Matthew?"

It was a questioning voice, and it was female.

In the split second before he moved, Chris caught something in Matt's smile that he had not seen before. It was a smile full of theory and proofs, of knowledge and wisdom, and somehow of certainty.

Taking a step back, Matt half turned, revealing as he did so, a woman now walking towards them. She took two further paces, then stopped.

"Katherine!" Matt said, greeting her, "I'd like you to meet Chris."

That recognition was instant and mutual was evidenced by a certain blush that rose in both their cheeks. Her hair was shorter than it had been, but the years had been kind; her face displayed tell-tale traces of having lived and grown older, but there could be no doubt. As Chris faced his ghost - in the flesh this time and not ten feet distant - he faltered. After all this time, and after all those days of longing and years of regret…

"Perhaps," said Matt, "now I'll go and take a proper look at the church."

They watched him walk away. Chris wanted to call him back, to demand an explanation - any kind of explanation - but found he could not. He turned back to Katherine who was staring hard at him.

"Is Matthew a friend of yours?" she asked.

"Matt? No. I've only just met him. Just now, in fact." Chris paused. "But you know him?"

Katherine turned momentarily to check Matt's progress.

"Not really."

There was an awkward silence. Chris struggled to know what he should do. He was certain that Matt would - as he seemed to know everything - and Chris found he wanted to be told; he needed guidance. The very thing he had spent countless moments wishing for and dreaming of had now happened - but it had happened eleven years after it should have and in doing so found him with a different life.

He perhaps struggled with this for a split second before Katherine moved towards him, her hand extended.

"Hello, Chris," she said. It seemed a new beginning.

He took her hand - perhaps for a moment too long, he could not be sure - then allowed it to fall.

"You've cut your hair."

As soon as he said it, he knew it had been a ridiculous statement to make; but under the pressure of needing to move on, to move forward and somehow progress, it was all he could think of. And he wasn't even certain where he wanted to move on to, or where his notion of progress should have been taking him. It was as if his life had come to a complete halt and he desperately needed something to re-start it. In this context, 'you've cut your hair' (as he instantly replayed it) seemed pathetic.

But she laughed - and Chris realised with a shiver an echo of that very first laugh.

"Once or twice!" Katherine confirmed, smiling.

"The first time I saw you it was almost to your waist."

"In 'The Bay Tree'."

"In 'The Bay Tree', yes."

There was a slight pause.

"I was much younger then," she said, "I don't think I really thought about it. Girls don't at that age."

Chris looked at the woman before him and wondered about her use of 'girl'. How much history did she have?

"Would you perhaps like a coffee?" he suggested.

"In 'The Bay Tree' - for old times' sake?"

She appeared relaxed at their sudden encounter - an image he was absolutely certain he did not convey himself.

As he followed her back along the path towards the road, he tried to make sense of where he was and what he was doing. He tried to break the situation down into neat little blocks of fact: he was walking towards a café to have a drink with a woman he had just met; a woman he had - in some oblique sense - 'known' for at least eleven years; a woman who (once upon a time) had filled his dreams and occupied his waking moments. There had been days, he was sure, when simply to have known her name would have been satisfying enough; but now there she was, just ahead of him. He could have reached out and placed his hand on her arm, or rested it against her back. He could have taken her marvellous hair - now a few inches below shoulder length but still wonderfully straight - and run his fingers through it.

He stopped. Katherine took two additional paces then stopped too.

"Is there something wrong?" she asked, turning to face him. They had reached the gate and her left hand now rested on it.

"Wrong?" He tried to smile. "No, there's nothing wrong. It's just…" It was impossible to elaborate.

She coloured slightly.

"Coffee; white without sugar. And possibly a warm scone?" It was his order from the time he had first set eyes on her. She tilted her head slightly to acknowledge how he must have been feeling. "I know."

The café was less than half full when they arrived, the distance between the gate and 'The Bay Tree' having been occupied by weather trivia.

"Shall we sit here?" Chris suggested the table he had recently vacated, but Katherine headed for the one nearest the counter.

"I used to know the people who ran 'The Bay Tree'," she said as she slipped off her coat and sat down. "I was at college with Sam, their daughter. We used to sit here sometimes in the evening just after the café closed, drinking hot chocolate and talking."

"That would have been a while ago," Chris suggested, trying to gain some temporal bearing.

"Yes. Sam lives in Cleveland, in the States; she moved away - oh, let me see - at least nine years ago it must be now."

"And you?"

"Me?"

The waitress arrived as Katherine spoke.

"Hello again," she said cheerfully, looking at Chris, "you must really like it in here!"

Katherine smiled.

"We're old hands," she said, offering a meaningless - and simultaneously meaningful - banality. "Two coffees, milk no sugar; one scone - warm; and an almond slice, if you have any left, please."

"I think we do." The waitress scribbled on her pad then walked the short distance across Chris's sacred ground to the counter.

"You were saying?" he prompted.

"Yes?"

"That Sam went away. And I asked about you. Did you move away?"

"Not really. I spent a few years in Portsmouth; and then some time in Winchester, Petersfield - places like that. I never went far. My parents still live in Chichester."

Her words reached him laden with uncommunicated history. The supermarket, the library, all those shared places; Chris sensed that they might have been relevant for her too.

"But you did, didn't you? Move away I mean. One minute I noticed you about the place, the next..." She tried to lighten the observation and make it seem less than it was. "Where did you go?"

"Birmingham first. I got a job working for Rover."

"Making cars?!" She feigned shock.

"Not really. 'Administration' is probably a safer description. After that I move to Manchester."

"Why Manchester?"

"I met someone. It was where they lived."

The clattering of mugs, plates and cutlery interrupted him. He was glad. Something inside him wanted to erase the last eleven years as if they had never happened; he wanted to close that book and throw it away - into the nearby sea would do! - and then reopen the volume that, all those years ago, he had never even had the courage to pull off the shelf.

"Are you still there - in Manchester?"

There were questions that he wanted to ask too, but which politeness, decorum, or a misplaced sense of reserve simply prevented him from uttering. Something in her manner - perhaps the way she now played with her spoon, or the way she was resting her hand on the table - suggested to him that Katherine was facing the same struggle. Or was he just fantasising again?

"No. We separated a couple of years ago." he paused; she chose not to fill the gap. "I mainly work in London now, but I live in Horsham. Well, between Horsham and Crawley."

"Under the aeroplanes?"

He smiled.

"Of course!"

She cut her almond slice into four pieces then picked up the first of these and bit it in two.

"Good?" He asked.

"Mmm." She replied, as she finished that morsel. "But then they always were."

"I've never been to Portsmouth." It was the only gambit he could think of to try and begin to fill in Katherine's history. After all, he knew nothing about her: the three places she had lived, and the name of an old college friend was very little to go on.

"It's ok, I guess. I grew to dislike it after a while. Especially the summers and the tourists. And the places the tourists weren't you didn't want to be! We moved back to the country when Peter became ill. The city wasn't very good for him as it turned out. So we tried smaller towns. We had to be relatively close to hospitals, you see. I liked Winchester at first too; but then I realised it suffered from the same problems as Portsmouth. Have you been there?"

"Winchester? Yes - but only as a tourist, I'm afraid!"

It was a joke and she laughed.

"See what I mean!"

"So you're in Petersfield now?"

"No. Actually I'm just in the process of moving back here. I'm staying with my parents while I look for somewhere of my own - now that Peter's confined to the hospice."

"I'm sorry."

"About Peter?"

Chris nodded.

"He's been very ill for a long time. Actually, I think he'll be glad when it's all over."

She paused. Chris wanted to sympathise, to ask about Peter, whether or not anything could be done for him. Yet he also wanted to know other things, things he could not possibly ask. At that precise moment, as she raised the mug of coffee to her lips, he noticed her wedding ring for the first time.

"I guess that's why I came here today," she continued, oblivious to his sudden discovery, "to remind myself of the place; to see if it is somewhere I could come back to; somewhere I belong."

Her last words shook him.

"Matt!" The name slipped involuntarily and a little too loudly from him. On an adjacent table, a conversation paused. Katherine put her free hand to her lips.

"Whoops!" she said, with a smile.

"What's funny?" Chris asked, a little confused by her apparent lack of concern. "We abandoned him in the churchyard. He could be looking for us?"

"I don't think so."

"Are you sure?"

"Of course. He'll just go home. And anyway, no-one is supposed to care about Estate Agents, are they?"

"About who?"

"Estate Agents. Matthew." She paused, expecting to see some kind of acknowledgement from Chris. "I'd come out here with him to see a couple of houses. He said he needed to go and make a quick phone call to check something about our first viewing. Asked me to wait by the church for him. He was gone ages! I nearly went home myself."

"He was in here - talking to me. He didn't say anything about being an Estate Agent. Said he'd come here to see the church. We talked about…"

The smile left Katherine's face.

"About what?"

"The past. He seemed interested. Genuine. Helpful."

Chris could tell that Katherine was replaying her own encounter with Matt; deciphering their conversations, his manner, his uniqueness.

"Not like an Estate Agent at all?" she suggested, her voice indicating that somewhere either a fog was clearing or a mist was descending.

"Absolutely not."

For the next couple of minutes they sat making small talk, finishing their pastries and coffee. Chris looked around the café again, trying to fit this latest encounter into the tapestry of his other 'Bay Tree' experiences. It was a small but seemingly intricately woven pattern.

"Do you?" They were walking towards the car park and Katherine's car. She had apologised but said she needed to make her afternoon visit to Peter in his Brighton home. Chris suddenly wanted to drag her back to their unfinished conversation, feeling a need to complete their encounter properly - and a need to understand what it really meant.

"Do I what?"

"Belong here?"

She looked around in a broad sweep, absorbing the scene as she did so.

"Possibly more here than anywhere else." Her tone lightened. "And you? Or is your heart in Birmingham or London or some other great metropolis?"

Chris smiled.

"Certainly not in any metropolis! And here? Matt seemed to think so - he had a theory about these things."

They had reached her car. She pulled the keys from her bag and allowed her fingers to play with them.

"I must go. Sorry." She paused. "Do you have a card or something? Most professional people seem to these days."

He laughed.

"I do - but I tend not to carry them around to hand out on Sundays!"

"It would be good to meet again," she suggested, a little hesitantly.

"For old times' sake?"

"Something like that."

"Perhaps soon - if you can find space in your schedule when you're not being stood up by somewhat dubious Estate Agents!"

"I think I can manage that," she smiled, then leant forward and brushed her cheek against his. "Eleven o'clock, on a Sunday?"

Chris nodded.

"Shall we make it next week? I don't think I have the stamina to wait another eleven years!"

She reddened slightly as she laughed, then opened her car door and got in. As Chris walked towards his own car he heard her engine start and then the tyres on the loose gravel. He stopped and waved, then she was gone.

By the distant church - under one of the trees near the path - he thought he caught a glimpse of a tall, elegant man looking his way. But it was probably a mirage of sorts - no doubt Matt would have a theory about that sort of thing too.

Welshman

"Told them it would win, but they wouldn't listen. 'Specially not Mickey. 'Welshman!', he said, 'Trust a bleedin' Taff to bet on an old nag like that!'

"Maybe I can't blame them; after all, my record's not been that great has it? Or I wouldn't always be sitting here surrounded by what's left of the day - crumpled slips, and fag ends spilling out of the ashtrays. And broken dreams. Small little dreams. Unimportant ones. But dreams that can be rebuilt after a night's sleep or a few pints of beer. Maybe both, though in my case beer doesn't do much for my sleeping.

"And the youngsters are no different. Pauly will have gone home, got changed and picked his girl up from work. Maybe they'll go to the pictures - something she'll probably pay for anyway, unless he's had a good day - and then off somewhere dark for a shag in the back of that clapped out Escort of his. Ha, ha! His stories about what he's done in the back of that car! Beer or no beer, doesn't seem to matter to Pauly; he's always full of himself the next day. The beer did me in that department too, not that I care so much nowadays. Neither me nor Joan either.

"But then today's a bit different, isn't it? Not for Pauly, I mean. Nor for Mickey neither. Down 'The Dragon' as soon as they open, blowing whatever he's got in his pocket. Back for more tomorrow. There'll be empty ashtrays and new papers on the walls. The pens will have been tidied away and the floor swept. It seems a bit futile really.

"I wonder what they'll say when, come the first race, I'm not here. 'Where's that dumb Welsh Bastard then?' someone will say, and they'll have a joke at my expense. They always do, so why should my absence make any difference? It won't. I'm sure it won't. But when I'm not here on Thursday either? Or Friday…?

"I asked Margaret not to say anything. After the third race, it was. She's a good kid, Margaret. Young, but knows her stuff. Bright as a button. I slipped over to the counter for a quiet word, just after Pat had got home in that photo-finish. Don't know why I did; maybe I just had a feeling. That was only three after all. There were still two more to go. And then Welshman. 'Just in case', I said to her, 'if I get lucky, don't let on, eh?' She'd smiled. She's over there now on the phone to Head Office. She said she'd leave it late, just to be on the safe side. Not wanting to spread it about. I looked at her after Welshman had come home and she'd smiled. That was nice.

"Of course I hammed it up a bit, for the others. Made like I'd had a quid on the old boy to win and was excited about picking up twelve. They'd had a good laugh, even Mickey who'd taken the piss. 'That old bag of bollocks can't run as fast as my old woman!' he'd said, and laughed like it was a new joke. It wasn't. It's Mickey's standard joke. His everyday joke. Cracks him up every time. Anyway, I laughed, 'cos I was supposed to laugh too. Mickey can be a nasty piece of work if you get on his wrong side, drunk or sober.

"I wanted to let on. After Prince Sundown went in I wanted to tell someone. There were only Toaster and Welshman to go, and 'cos I knew Welshman'd win it was getting to be difficult. Like I had to share it. Like I was afraid the excitement would be too much for me to take on my own and I needed someone to help me out. But I couldn't. Not his lot. Nice as pie within reason - as long as you're poorer than they are. All mates in the same boat, see? But get one step ahead… I didn't want to find out. Maybe I'll never be able to come back here again. Maybe I'll have to find somewhere else. Coral's at the top of the High Street, maybe. Or Hill's over the bridge. Maybe I won't be able to go into any of them again. There ain't no such thing as a secret - especially where money's concerned.

"I've worked it out on this little bit of paper. This one here. All afternoon I've been updating it in secret, then screwing it up as if it's a loser before sliding it back in my pocket. 'Cos I knew, see? When Toaster strolled home I knew there'd been some reason for me to put a fiver on too. Margaret had asked me if I knew what I was doing. Can't blame her. She was only looking out for me. A bloke who normally bets in twenty pence multiples suddenly hands over a roll-up ticket for a fiver... Either I'm nuts or... Maybe there ain't no either.

"And then there's Joan. I'll have to be careful how I tell her. She'll start on at me as soon as I get through the door; the same old routine about wasting money. About wasting everything. About how she never has anything 'cos I spend all my money in the Bookies. How she ain't forgiven me for letting the redundancy money slip away. What was I going to do for Christ's sake; open a bleedin' hairdressers or something?! There ain't much a guy of fifty seven can do after he's spent all his life in the Dockyard, is there? Not when all the ships have gone and taken the need for the only skill he's ever had with them. I could have died then - the day they told us - and been content enough. I'd seen the future. I'd watched old Arthur Moore turn from being a right sort of bloke into a dying old man in less than two years. Him and Elsie too. I didn't want that. I didn't want it, but I could see it coming. Maybe it's come already. I don't know.

"But I do know what Joan's like, and she won't be expecting anything good. She don't know what good is any more. Winning a tenner at Bingo's as good as her life gets. Guess when Pete left for Australia all those years ago, guess that's when she started to die inside. His new life; the end of hers. Maybe we're both that way. God knows I miss him too. But maybe this will help. This number I've got written down in front of me. I've checked it with Margaret. I wasn't far out; a couple of thousand maybe. She put me straight. 'Are you all right, Taff?' she'd said. 'Want a cup of tea? I'm just going to phone through now, OK?'

"Apparently they deal with this sort of thing with a cheque. Tomorrow morning. She said I'd probably have to get in early. They'd want to make a big deal of it. The publicity's good for business they say, but I don't want none of that. They'll get back ten times as much with other poor sods trying to do what I've done. But they won't of course. 'Cos they won't have Welshman to rely on. Maybe they'll study form a bit more. Maybe they'll listen when someone points out something telling - like a sparkling run from two years ago that no-one's even considered. Some'll talk rubbish about weights and distance and who's best around a left-handed track, but they'll have no idea.

"I'll have to break it gently. 'I've had a bit of luck, Love.' Once she's had her little rant and I've had the chance to make her a cup of tea. That'll be a sign in itself. 'How much luck?' she'll ask, all suspicious like. And then I'll have to be careful. Make sure she's sitting down. Maybe I'll say 'How would you like to go and visit our Peter?' That'd be good, 'cos then she'll know I'm not joking. That'll mean something. Maybe more than the numbers, these numbers here on this tatty piece of paper.

"When they called Welshman home - a storming late run, just like that sparkling piece of old form said he would - I was doing the calculation. Writing down numbers. One - nine - eight - three - three - seven. Just numbers. Not the right ones, but close enough. I'll have to tell Joan then. As soon as she hears me talking about Pete and knows I'm being serious. I won't be dragging it out. Wouldn't be fair; and its going to be hard enough for the old girl as it is. A lifetime's worth of Christmases.

"Ah, there goes the phone down. I'm staring at the wall and the runners from the five thirty - Welshman's race. There ain't a sound in the place 'cos Margaret's about to close up for the night. I'm staring at that one word - 'Welshman' - and I know Margaret's waiting to tell me what's going to happen in the morning. And now I'm scared. I'm scared 'cos I've got to move. I've got to slip off this little stool, the one I've had my bony old arse on for the last twenty five minutes, and I've got to walk somewhere. Just a few feet to the counter. I've got to find out if I can still walk. I've got to find out if I can handle what's going to be dished out to me. I've got to go home to find out if Joan still loves me; to see if money in the bank makes all the difference. I've got to go through losing my friends and starting again. I've got to catch an aeroplane and fly thousands of miles to find out if my son's forgiven me for whatever I did that made him go away.

"There's the latch from the counter. Good old Margaret's going to help me off the seat, I bet. The first hurdle. Suddenly I feel old and scared 'cos a second-rate eight-year-old racehorse has given me one last chance."

Evening Class

He opened the door and threw a javelin of light into the room. But it was not a darkened room he was looking for. In the half-light he could see the blackboard-trace of another's lesson, and against the wall, the outline of an overhead projector. Tools of the trade. He would have turned and closed the door - would have, but for a slight rustle that caught his attention, as if the light had awoken sound. His fingers found a switch and there was a buzz as the blackboard neon struggled to life. In one corner, a woman was sitting. She seemed suddenly upright, as if she had been leaning across the desk by which she sat. Asleep perhaps.

"I'm terribly sorry. I was looking for the Creative Writing people."

His automatic reaction was to turn, to cover up embarrassment and leave. But some other instinct prevailed. Did he not fancy the trace of a tear on the woman's cheek, the shadow of sorrow about her eyes? And why was she sitting in the dark anyway? Having half-turned away, he actually moved a little further into the room, one hand still holding the door.

"Are you all right?"

She nodded.

"Is there anything I can get you?"

Again a slight motion of the head, meant to satisfy him, meant for him to accept without question. He turned fully away this time, his hand going back to the light switch, then hesitating as if uncertain of the action it should take.

"Please. I don't suppose you have a cigarette?"

In her first word were the answers to most of the questions he could have asked, not in the word itself but in the manner in which it had been uttered. She was looking at him, watching his hand desert the light switch as he rummaged in his jacket pockets. Cigarettes, a lighter. As he handed her the packet - open, one cigarette showing itself beyond the others - he realised that he was right; she had indeed been crying. The hand that took the cigarette did so without confidence; the lips that held it, faintly trembling.

"Are you sure you're OK?" He watched her draw.

"I'm sorry." She blew out a little smoke. "There's a machine. Could I have some coffee?" She made a motion, taking her eyes off his face, as if she were looking for her bag, some money to give him.

"Of course."

As he stood in the corridor getting the coffee he thought it had been a stupid thing to say - "of course" - but what else could he have said? He waited for the second cup. If she didn't want to talk he could drink it elsewhere.

When he got back to the room, she seemed more relaxed. He thought maybe she had combed her hair, calmed down a little.

"Thank you." As she took her coffee he saw her notice the second cup.

"Would you like me to go?"

He had intercepted her look, an immediate defensive stiffening in her features. Mistrust. He tried to sound willing - yet unwilling - to leave her on her own.

✳

"I was looking for Room 27," he said, sitting now in the row in front, a couple of desks to her right, "but I've never been here before so I was just trying doors. You don't happen to know where 27 is?"

"No."

"I guess I'll find it." He paused and watched her stub out her cigarette. "I didn't mean to intrude. I was going straight out, but then I heard you move."

She picked up her coffee and looked away from him, volunteering nothing. He guessed she was reading the words scrawled on the blackboard. Involuntarily, he looked back over his shoulder. 'Tomorrow', 'Ever After', 'The Light of Day'.

✽

"Has anyone seen Tom?"

"Who's Tom?" A middle-aged woman, bespectacled in over-large glasses, looked up from her book at the small man who had spoken; a slight, dapper figure standing in the doorway.

"Tom. You know. The chap I told you was coming."

"Ah, your protege!"

"For Christ's sake, Beet!" The man was annoyed by the tone of her voice: she had said 'Who's Tom' with false enthusiasm; 'your protege' with sarcastic deference. He was tempted to be rude to her, to put her straight for once, but a figure appearing suddenly behind him saved him.

"Evening all."

"Ah, Tony. Seen Tom?"

"Who?"

"Arthur's protege."

Arthur ignored her. "Tallish chap, fairly young. New. Meant to be coming this evening."

"Sorry Arthur. Only people I've seen are the young lads from Car Mechanics and two Brazilian girls smoking cigars in the canteen."

Tony walked passed Arthur into the room.

"Hello Bee."

The woman gazed up from her book but said nothing. Provoked in turn, Tony mumbled something under his breath then lowered himself resignedly into a chair.

"Looks like another scintillating evening," he said.

"I hope Tom turns up."

"Who *is* this 'Tom'?"

Arthur turned back into the room, briefly relieving himself of his corridor vigil.

"New chap at work. We got talking the other day, you know. Asked what there was to do in town; that sort of thing."

"And you mentioned our clandestine clan."

"Said he scribbled a bit, so I asked him if he'd like to come along."

"He won't come." Beatrice spoke from the depths of her book.

"If someone's told him Beatrice is going to be here then I expect he'll stay away."

Beatrice shot Tony a brief look of hatred as he lifted himself out of his chair and made his way to the door.

"You're not going Tony?"

"Don't panic, Arthur. Coffee, that's all."

"I'll come with you. Maybe he's got lost."

✲

"I don't usually behave like this."

"I'm sorry?"

Her words had come suddenly from behind him. He turned his eyes back to her from their study of the blackboard.

"Silly reaction really. Typical woman!" She made an attempt to laugh, but it was stifled somewhere as if caught trying to escape. He smiled slightly, sympathetically, trying to convey understanding. "Funny I should end up here though."

"In the dark."

"Yes. She paused, experimenting with the slightest of smiles as if to test out the range of emotion available in her face. "He's not worth it anyway."

"Ah." Tom pulled the cigarettes from his pocket and offered her another. "We seldom are."

"Thanks." He lit it. "Another woman, you see. I guess I just needed somewhere quiet, on my own."

There was a brief pause.

"I hope you told him where to go." It was his offering, half-joke, half-serious, to cap the well, to set the limit on her divulgence - especially as it was none of his business.

"Something like that." She drew on her cigarette and looked for her bag again. Having located it at her feet, she looked at him. "What about you? It doesn't look as if you're in the middle of anything melodramatic."

"I'm lost, remember."

"Yes." She laughed a little now. "Room 27. What's in Room 27?"

"I hate to think actually - though I do have an idea what's *meant* to be there."

"I'm keeping you; I'm sorry."

"No, not at all." He paused then leant forwards as if to impart a secret and whispered, "To tell you the truth, I didn't really want to go at all."

She laughed at his play-acting, the air of conspiracy.

"Actually," she said, leaning forward in turn and glancing over her shoulder, "to tell *you* the truth, this was just a ploy to save you."

"To save *me*!" He laughed, amused by the novelty of her idea. "From who?"

She paused, then dramatically: "From *them*!"

Two figures went by in the corridor outside. She saw their shadows and pointed. They both laughed.

"See; they're after us!"

"Shall we make a run for it?"

He had said it within the nature of their game, unthinkingly, automatically, but already she had picked up her bag and was beginning to stand.

"There's a pub round the corner; they'll never find us there!"

Two figures - a man and a woman - walk past Room 27. Whether they registered it or not, the cry of "and what do *you* know about literature?!" which suddenly rang out from inside made no impression on their progress.

Hester

What Hester could see from her seat as the train picked up speed and began to rattle towards Ruislip was unsatisfactory. She had never found the suburbs particularly edifying; she wasn't even sure if she understood them that well. But today they seemed especially disappointing, and even the falling dusk and the oncoming orange hue cast by street lights failed to rouse the greyness she saw. At least the rain had held off.

She tried to remember the last time she had been out this way, knowingly embarked on a journey that saw her buffeted and jarred by the Metropolitan Line. Her bones were not what they used to be. She had vague recollections about a visit to Harrow, but that had been a long time ago - perhaps ten years, if not more? - and she was as sure as she could be that she had been conveyed there and back by car. Passing through Harrow-on-the-Hill station on her way west earlier in the day had felt like being transported through another world, or another time. Hester should have perhaps taken this as prescient; an indication as to how the day might pan out.

Looking down at her hands, she was suddenly surprised to see them bereft of gloves. Once upon a time she would never have left the house without her gloves, no matter the season or where she was going. It had been 'style' back then, and a style she had stubbornly clung to long after fashion had moved on more than once. As the train flew past another batch of semi-detached splendour, she tried to recall when that had been, when her style had been de rigueur. But increasingly Hester struggled with time; not in the small, everyday segments of time like hours and minutes, but in the great and vast expanses of it. The occasional flash of her reflection in the window as they rolled back towards the city served as a reminder of those now infertile chasms. Her only consolation was that it had not always been thus.

As the train began to slow down, a young man seated across from her stood up. He was wearing a dark top with the hood up, two white leads appearing from one of his pockets and disappearing into the hood. He looked as if he were plugged into something secret, the cowl a futile attempt to hide that connection from the prying eyes of the world. Instinctively she glanced outside to see if the rain had started or if there were tell-tale slants of water on the window, but there were none. It was something else Hester struggled to understand, these 'hoodies'. She had learned the word from one of her great nephews and it had lodged somewhere, even if the precise meaning was now lost to her. She looked back towards the young man now standing by the doors. Was that now 'style', she wondered; style in Ruislip?

She looked up at the map of the line fixed above the windows across from where she was sitting. Even though she had consulted it more than once in the last few minutes, she found herself constantly drawn back to it; the only guide she had, the only way she could know where she was, how from where she was going. And even though the names meant little to her, she clung to the promise of Finchley Road as if it were the pot of gold at the end of the rainbow, her particular heaven.

Finchley Road was a *real* place; it was her part of London. It was where she had lived ever since…but that was a long time ago now. Hester had met Tom Conti in Sainsbury's on Finchley Road; he had been very pleasant. That was how real Finchley Road was - and, by implication, how unreal all these other places were. She read their names to herself: Ruislip, Ruislip Manor, Eastcote, Rayners Lane, West Harrow, Harrow-on-the-

Hill, Northwick Park, Wembley Park. They seemed fictional, just as Ickenham had seemed fictional.

Martin and Ruth had not been in Ickenham that long, at least as measured by Hester's timeframe. It had, she recalled, been a 'big thing' when they had announced to the family their intention to decamp from Maida Vale. It was not so much the physical movement that caused her some confusion, but what the move represented. They were merging their separate existences into one; going from two small flats to one house; from being close to the city to being 'suburbanites'. That was how Martin used to phrase it; he used a tone which suggested a blend of adventure and maturity. In her own small way, Hester had regarded the shift as something of a defeat, measuring it in relation to her own situation and what such a move would mean for her. Martin and Ruth had married of course - though she struggled to recall whether that had happened before or after their move - and now they were contributing to Ickenham's economy and population with the arrivals of Sam, Ella and, most recently, Poppy.

Someone had told her - Ruth probably - that Ickenham had once been a small village miles from the big city, and whilst she had been there - especially when being driven to and from the station by Martin - Hester tried to imagine it thus. The rather obscure notion of them living in a 'village' disoriented her somewhat, though she knew that people were increasingly referring to pockets of London as 'villages'. "It's all marketing, of course," Martin had said once they were out of Ruth's hearing and heading back to the tube. She had always liked Martin, her favourite of her brother's two children; yet he seemed unfulfilled to her, as if he had been unable to grasp his true potential or to follow through on it. Ruth was normally a pleasant enough woman, but Hester couldn't help but feel that Martin could have done a little better; better than Ruth, and better than Ickenham. But there were children now and so everything was settled.

The train started to slow and they drew into a station. Hester checked the signage: Eastcote. The map said that Ruislip Manor should have followed Ruislip, so where was that? Hadn't the young man with the hoodie disembarked at Ruislip? Momentarily confused, she focussed on the tube map again, verified their current location. Definitely Eastcote. Only six more stops. She would need to concentrate.

They had both said how well she looked, and having handed her coat to Martin to hang up, Hester looked at herself in the hall mirror. "Tea?" Ruth had unnecessarily called over her shoulder as she retreated into the kitchen. The woman who stared back at her was not the same Hester she felt herself to be. It was not that she was unaware of her age. How could she not be when even simple things like walking and climbing stairs had started to become problematic? When cleaning was difficult and bending over was a challenge? Shoe horns had suddenly, after all these years, been proven to have a very real purpose! Neither was it her almost-white hair nor the myriad of wrinkles which caused Hester sadness, but rather that the physical picture she painted was becoming ever further removed from how she felt. The face that confronted her did not belong to the person she was inside.

They had been attentive, of course. She had been seen into a large green armchair that occupied the dominant position in the living room, her tea placed on the small side table which nestled beside it. Martin and Ruth had sat facing her on the sofa, behind a long coffee table boasting plates and knives and at least three different type of cake. There was an initial awkward silence during which she felt more like an important visitor, some kind of dignitary, rather than a member of the family, though both of these - the silence and the feeling - were almost immediately punctured by the sounds of children careering down the stairs.

When Sam and Ella appeared - their explosive entry instantly usurped by a sudden shyness - Hester was taken aback by how much they had grown. It was, of course, the way with children; she had seen enough of them in her lifetime to understand how fast they grew. Yet even so, their height and the way their features had developed took her by surprise. They could have been completely different children, ones she had never met before.

"How long has it been, aunt?" Ruth asked promptly, filling the now renewed silence which had previously been broken by the children's noise. It was also a question which allowed a bridge to be built between a six year old, a four year old, and their great aunt who was nearly fourteen times Sam's age. "Sam, Ella; say hello to aunt Hester."

The children came forward slowly. Sam offered his hand in faux formality, and Ella, after a brief pause, bravely leant into Hester to give her a gentle hug.

"Must be three years, if it's a day," said Martin, answering his wife's question.

"Surely not," said Hester somewhat disingenuously, knowing if that were the case then it was no wonder she didn't recognise them, Ella least of all.

"When we had that big family gathering at Kew Gardens, remember? For Dad's birthday." As Ruth cut into a large chocolate cake for the children, Martin endeavoured to fill in the gaps. "It wasn't long after Ella's first birthday. And Sam fell over in the Grand Pavilion and cut his head on one of the flower bed walls. Blood everywhere."

Hester tried to join the dots: Kew, birthday party, blood. The image of dark red and vibrant green came to her as if from a mist, yet it was too indistinct to materialise in any meaningful way.

"Yes please, Dear," she said instead to Ruth, who was looking her way inquisitively, knife poised above the chocolate cake, plate in hand. "Just a little."

They had talked amiably enough for a while. It was the kind of conversation that defines infrequent family gatherings; mainly enquiries about health and work and 'circumstances' that are usually met with a straight - if gentle - bat. If she had not noticed it before, she noticed it now: the silence-saving tendency to discuss those who were *not* present but who formed part of the linkage between those who were. And so Martin and Hester compared notes about Martin's father. To Hester it felt like a natural validation of what she knew of her brother, rather than any kind of 'checking up' on him. She also knew that people tended to slant depictions of their status or well-being depending on their audience, and so 'triangulation' of what William had told her with her nephew was useful.

"That's fine then," she had said, as if - in his absence - William had passed some kind of test, and that both she and Martin could now relax.

Ruth asked about Finchley.

"Do you miss Maida Vale?" was Hester's immediate response, deflecting Ruth's question away from what she regarded as irrelevant into more meaningful interrogation, suddenly wondering how she herself might have responded if she had been transplanted from her beloved home.

"Us?"

Hester had smiled, trying to convey an understanding as to how difficult and complex it could it be to uproot oneself and move into a different environment - even though it was something about which she'd had no personal experience in a very long time.

"Well, it's been quite a while now," Ruth bristled slightly. Martin fidgeted. "But we're happy here. Settled. And it's great for the kids, what with the park down the road; the open spaces."

"And the schools are good," Martin offered in support.

"But it's been nearly seven years," Ruth clarified. "I think if we had been missing it at all we wouldn't still be here now." She stood. "More tea?"

Hester turned to the two children whose attentiveness had begun to wane as soon as they had finished their cake.

"And do you like school?"

"Sam's at school; Ella starts properly this September," Martin interjected, to help Hester with context. He looked at Sam, and after his look prompted nothing said, "Sam; aunt Hester wants to know if you like school."

"It's fun. We read and draw. I'm doing spellings and painting pictures of Vikings."

Sam's words came out in a rush, almost unpunctuated. His pitch and immature pronunciation defeated Hester who continued to smile but turned to Martin.

"Where's Poppy?"

"She's upstairs, asleep. Still has her routine. She's very good like that." He turned to Sam and Ella. "Go on and play then."

Released from the clutches of the grown-ups, the two children bounced up and headed for the door.

"Quietly!" said Ruth as she met them coming the other way, refreshed tea pot in hand.

Hester didn't want any more tea. She hadn't managed to eat the over-large piece of cake Ruth had given her just a short while ago, so - not wishing to be rude - hoped no more would be offered.

"Martin, dear, can you fetch my bag please?"

❋

"What was that all about?!" said Ruth, an unmistakeable note of frustration in her tone. Restored to her favourite armchair, she was cradling a glass of red wine in her cupped hands. It was getting dark outside, and with the curtains still open and the lights off, the sitting room had taken on a calmer if not more sombre air. Focussed on her drink and resolutely ignoring the detritus of tea and cakes that remained on the low table in front of the sofa, she declined to look at Martin; she knew he had to respond - after all, Hester was his family.

"It's tradition, that's all," he said, picking at a morsel of cake.

"Whose?" she said, then not waiting for a reply, "It was 'tradition' last time with Ella, and then Sam before that."

"Don't ask me where it started; I've no idea. But as long as I can remember it's something my family have always done." He paused. This was not the first time they'd had this conversation - but he did expect it to be the last. "You can't blame Hester; it's just her way."

"I don't have a problem with the present, Martin. Don't look a gift horse, and all of that. In fact, it's very generous, and we'd be daft not to be grateful given how tight things are."

"It's not uncommon for people to give gifts for new babies," he offered, seeing a chink.

"As you say. And I don't object to that, I really don't."

She paused, deliberately leaving a gap for Martin to fill. It was one he had no possibility of avoiding - like a huge pothole in the middle of the road.

"So what do you object to?" he said, as his wheels bounced and his suspension crunched. "Hester's harmless enough. She means well."

Ruth knew that was all he could offer - and that it was the extent to which his loyalty reached.

"But she's so superior about everything. As if it's a gift with ties. As if it gives her the right to dictate, or lecture, or whatever word you'd like to choose."

"Contribute?" he suggested weakly.

"What does she think we're going to do?" she carried on, ignoring him. "Cash the cheque and then blow the lot on weed or coke or something?!"

"I hadn't thought of that," he said lightly. Ruth looked up at him and smiled for the first time in what seemed like a long while. "Do you know where we can get some?"

"Probably in the middle of town, near that pub where all the fights are. After all, given that this isn't the Godly borough of Finchley, I suspect there are drugs and prostitutes and all sorts just about everywhere!"

Martin had always been a little surprised by Hester's mild denouncement of Ickenham. It was as if where they were living was not just not-Finchley, but suddenly it was not-Maida Vale either. Her advice - or 'monologue' as Ruth had subsequently dubbed it - on what to do with the money, on parenting, on the children's education, was pretty much on a par with their experience of her after Ella had been born, yet this time there was something about it that seemed less tolerant, less great aunt-like. Having discussed her visit in advance, they had prepared themselves for her inevitable instruction, but the boundaries they had anticipated she would honour had been undoubtedly crossed as Martin's aunt shared her views on multiple topics.

"Maybe she was having a bad day," he offered after a pause. "She said something about the tube when we were heading over from the station."

"Maybe. But she seemed different somehow. Harder almost. If she were a youth I might have described her as having an 'edge' - but Hester being 'edgy' just doesn't fit, does it!"

Ruth laughed at her own joke and Martin knew the crisis was over. He watched her drain her wine and then stand up and move over to the curtains.

"How did you say she was on the way over to the station?"

*

Inevitably, Martin's interpretation varied from Hester's own. Indeed, she had started her own private assessment almost as soon as she had finished her second cup of tea. She was still sensitive and sentient enough to observe a certain tenseness in the air as she sat in the armchair, her bag on her lap, especially when Ruth returned from the kitchen with the replenished teapot. It was not a mood borne of excitement or anticipation, which, considering what she was about to bestow, surprised her a little. Martin knew, of course, why she was there. She couldn't recall the episodes after Sam and Ella's birth, though she felt certain they couldn't possibly have taken place in Ickenham.

Both he and Ruth were undoubtedly prepared for the moment when she handed over the small envelope bearing the word 'Poppy' perfectly formed in a calligraphic hand. On that basis, Hester knew there could be no surprise involved, but had she been wrong as to expect a little frisson of something approaching gratitude?

It was Ruth's manner that had unbalanced her the most; a manner that almost suggested that she wanted to refuse the gift. More than anything else, it engendered a feeling in Hester that she was not actually welcome, that they wished she were gone.

They took the envelope graciously enough, and when she insisted Martin open it to examine the contents, both he and Ruth expressed an appropriate degree of thanks at her munificence. On that basis, Hester could only find such behaviour commensurate and acceptable, yet the tension she had noted and the underlying desire for her to be elsewhere had done the damage. In consequence, she had swiftly determined to have her say. She had opinions too, and suddenly felt that her donation had earned her the right to share them - especially in the face of betrayal.

Whether that had anything to do with Ruth's subsequent refusal to let her see Poppy - "She's only just gone off to sleep, and I really don't want to risk disturbing her" - it was impossible for Hester to say. The other children seemed to be making enough noise to ensure that no-one in the house would be able to sleep, but as Martin reminded her, babies were a law unto themselves. He tried to compensate by showing her around the rest of the house and the unusually long garden they enjoyed.

"It's ideal for the kids to run around in when it's a bit drier," he had explained as they reached the small shed set to one side.

"And we're thinking of putting a trampoline in for them. One of Sam's friends has got one and he seems to love it."

Hester imagined at least part of the money she had just given them being diverted for the purchase. Was that an acceptable use for it? She wasn't sure, but part of her objected to even having to think about such things. Shouldn't she be free of any responsibility in the matter? It was not a question Martin had posed, of course, but a link she had made by herself, and one which now distracted her from the herbaceous borders to which she was now being directed.

Pulling on her coat and taking a final look in the hall mirror, Hester wondered just how much had been changed by the passage of time. It was not simply that the face in the glass lay bare the difference between what she saw and how she felt, but it suddenly seemed to represent the moving on of the world. She felt stuck in the slightly younger Hester that she still imagined herself to be, not having recognised that things had shifted around her. If she had felt like the older Hester, the one who stared back at her and with everything that implied, would she be more in-tune with how things really were now? Would she be better equipped to deal with the way families - her family! - had metamorphosed? Or the experience of going through Harrow on the underground? Or the fact that not everywhere was like Finchley?

Following Martin out through the front door, she wondered whether she shouldn't be aspiring to be older; to 'be' as old as she looked. If that were the case, then wouldn't she enjoy the greater wisdom that came with that?

But this was something of a specious argument, of course. As she fumbled a little with her seatbelt, conscious all the while of Martin waiting more or less patiently for her to deliver the appropriate click from clasp and buckle, she knew such musings were academic at best. She could not be something that she was not, and if people saw one thing and she felt something else, then everyone would just have to learn to deal with it.

As they pulled out of the drive and made their way towards the station, she had said "This still doesn't look like a village to me".

The Glove

And it was only then I noticed the glove on her left hand.

It was the colour first. A light grey; gun-metal perhaps, reminiscent of a battleship or a cruiser. But it was soft. I could tell from the way it was moulded to her hand that it was soft, flexible. And did I say hand? I should have said arm, because it was a long glove, almost to the elbow. The stitching was fine, I could see that. Not fine in the sense of it being delicate, but fine in the sense of the quality, the thoroughness of it. Double stitched; triple stitched. Almost as if the glove's job was protection on a completely different level to the norm. To protect her, or to protect us somehow?

So clearly not a fashion statement. And even if she had been wearing the other half of the pair on her right hand and arm, 'fashion' would still have been a stretch too far. The grey; the stitching; somehow the material too.

If she noticed me looking - staring - at her left arm she gave no hint of it. She continued to talk in her measured, even way without breaking stride as it were. I had already noted that when her speech demanded animation, she resisted; when it needed passion, she refrained. Control appeared to be everything to her; somehow she epitomised and embodied it. Even the glove was an extension of that control. The protection - if that's what it was - was entirely managed and thought through.

She paused to take a sip of her wine and I was suddenly conscious that she had left a question in the air. What had we been talking about? Holidays? Travel? I recalled a fragment. She had been talking about rail travel.

"Have you ever tried one of those double decker trains you get in Europe?" I hoped that responding with a question of my own would be enough to cover up my misplaced attention.

She displayed no sign of irritation.

"In Switzerland, for example?"

I nodded. It seemed safe to do so.

"I've no idea how they manage without having hugely tall tunnels."

For other people it was a remark which would have prompted a laugh; meant as a joke, it was designed to elicit a particular response. In her case, even with the slight smile she offered me, it was clear she only intended to convey that she too had no idea how such twin-level trains fitted onto a conventional railway line - especially in a country where tunnels were so plentiful.

"On some services I think they reserve the upper deck for first class passengers," she continued. "Once I took a train from Basel and wanted to go upstairs but couldn't. Had I known, I might have paid the extra."

When was that? When did she take a train from Basel? And how old had she been then? Indeed, how old was she now?

We had met just fifteen minutes ago. Although there had been the usual pleasantries as we ordered drinks, there had been none of the embarrassed difficulty such new meetings often engender. She had been perfectly balanced from the start. Wine, no crisps or nibbles ("maybe later"), a seat by the window would be fine. My complimenting the colour of her jacket - a standard ploy, but it was a shade of peach which really suited her - had been taken at face value; she had smiled at my first joke. If slightly unusual, it had not been a difficult beginning. And then what?

That was it. She had leaned forward to remove the peach jacket, and that was when I first noticed the glove.

"Aren't trains cheap in Switzerland? Somehow I have always imagined that they would be."

She smiled at my naïvety.

"Not in Switzerland, no."

The bar was filling up. It had been a safe place to meet. Her suggestion. Attached to a gallery of modern art in the rejuvenated docks area, it was popular and slightly trendy without being too much of a place to pose. Having said that, many people who drank there had probably never set foot in the gallery itself, and even though I had done so only two or three times myself, I felt certain I could identify those who would only ever focus on the bar.

I glanced towards the table to my left. The couple there were clearly looked like art lovers, so they were a 'yes'. And the table beyond them? A definite 'no'. Then more: no, yes, yes, maybe.

Toni was finishing her short story about Swiss rail travel. Would she be an art lover? Possibly - but in an antiseptic, calculating way.

Did I tell you her name was Toni? Sorry. Short for Antonia, obviously. I knew that before I met her, of course. The brief phone call to test the water; to see if there was any kind of vibe. And then, on the basis of, what, just a few minutes' chat, the question as to whether to meet or not. It had felt an easy decision from my perspective. No, that's not quite right. A comfortable decision. Or maybe a safe one.

I had made some bad calls in the past, but this time it felt just fine. Don't get me wrong, I wasn't deluding myself. I had enough experience - had seen too many false dawns! - not to expect anything significant. These days I was happy to settle for a pleasant evening and a quiet chat. Perhaps that wasn't very ambitious, I don't know.

❊

She rang me two days later, exactly as she had promised. When we'd left the bar I had the impression that she was being cautious, non-committal; almost as if she were tying a bow in the end of a piece of string to make it look nice… though I've no idea why I should think that given how she'd been that evening. Honest. No, honest was the wrong word. She had been accurate, precise. She said she would ring because she was going to ring. When I heard her voice I felt guilty that I had doubted her.

"I want you to meet someone", she said without any build-up or lead-in.

This was a new one on me. For an instant I panicked slightly. Our encounter had been unspectacular. I'd left with my modest ambitions for a pleasant evening completely fulfilled - but now she wanted me to meet someone… I remembered her speaking fondly of her mother. Surely we had not got our wires crossed? Toni seemed like the last individual in the world who would be capable of such a thing - or of allowing it to happen in the first place.

"My sister."

"Your sister?"

From her slight pause I could tell she had instantly registered the surprise in my voice. Or was it relief?

"My sister, yes. Fran."

Not knowing what to say, I said nothing.

"I enjoyed our evening. I hope you did too. At least I thought you did..."

"I did," I said, perhaps interrupting too quickly - but not quickly enough to knock her out of that even flow of hers.

"So I would like to meet you again. And I want to bring my sister along too. Is that all right?" She paused. It was clearly my turn.

"To see you again, or to meet you sister?"

"Both."

*

It wasn't until later I realised this embryonic relationship wasn't about Toni at all. It was to all be about Fran. Toni was there in the picture, and our first meeting proved to be more of a fact finding mission for her, to sound me out, to validate if I was somehow 'suitable'. Make no mistake though, it never felt as if I was being tested. Not surprisingly I had assumed my meeting Fran was in order to gain her approval of me on Toni's behalf, as if a 'second opinion' were needed. But that assumption wasn't to last long.

There was also something in that follow-up phone call which made me realise any attraction I had felt - or indeed manufactured - for Toni at the gallery bar was based more on intrigue than chemistry. Not that she was an unattractive woman. However, I soon arrived at the notion that primarily she was interesting in a quirky, off-the-wall kind of way, rather than a sexual one; this second introduction - the prospect of meeting her sister - only served to enhance that hypothesis. I moved quickly from the all-too-familiar state of naive anticipation to the kind of excitement an anthropologist or archaeologist might feel when they are on the verge of making a new discovery.

I found myself creating advance mental pictures of Fran. Because I had nothing else to go on, inevitably these sketches were based on using Toni as a template, and every variation I came up with looked and felt like her with various minor adjustments. Toni was slightly shorter than average and, if one were being harsh, far from physically outstanding. That was not the same as saying her plainness was unattractive. Beneath that peach jacket she had worn a relatively short skirt; one short enough, at least, to promote legs that were well-toned if not that long. These, allied to her slimness, gave the impression of someone who looked after themselves physically, but not obsessively so. I couldn't see her in the gym; there was no way her demeanour could possibly countenance such frivolity. And there was the unanswered question about the glove. So I concocted a picture of a girl who had probably been good at hockey at school and now rode horses regularly. Was this accurate? If I intended to find out, I never really got the chance.

Perhaps inevitably, my expectations for Fran were upbeat. Isn't the way that men are generally made? Hence, slightly taller, slightly longer legs; her dark hair would be longer than Toni's - certainly below shoulder length. Whatever identikit image I created, I was sure there would be no long grey glove.

*

And there wasn't. But neither was there dark hair of any length. Fran was without doubt strawberry blonde and indisputably natural. As it happened she *was* taller than Toni, but given she looked nothing at all like her sister, that ended up being the only one of my predictions that came anywhere close.

We met in the same gallery bar. As usual I had been a little early and, having furnished myself with a drink, managed to secure the same table Toni and I had used the previous week. I sat facing the door so immediately noticed Toni when she walked in behind another woman. I looked beyond them, expecting to see Fran following Toni in, but there was no-one else there. Then I noticed Toni tap the arm of the woman who had entered in front of her and point in my direction. The penny had just about dropped by the time Fran reached the table, Toni diverting to the bar to get their drinks.

"Adrian, hi," said Fran, extending an un-gloved hand.

With what was, I was certain, astonishing clumsiness, I had managed to stand up just in time to greet her, my mind trying to assess this suddenly revised scenario and failing miserably.

"Fran," I stumbled, managing quite unsuccessfully to take the question out of my phrasing.

"You were expecting someone else?" She laughed easily. It was another divergence from her sister, as if they occupied opposite sides of a negative image, one black, one white. She slipped effortlessly into the seat opposite me. "If Toni hadn't just pointed you out I would still have recognised you."

"Really? How so?"

"Her description. It was very accurate."

"That doesn't surprise me," I said, trying hard not to redden. Fran's laugh made that even harder. "I hope it was complimentary, at least."

She laughed again.

"Toni doesn't do complimentary - not in the sense you mean, anyway. But you can relax; you've nothing to worry about!"

I wanted to decipher that, but Toni's arrival with two glasses of wine prevented it. She placed the glasses on the table then leant forward and kissed me on the cheek.

If I had been unbalanced before, I was now completely knocked sideways. As little as I knew her, that brief kiss - no more than the brush of skin - seemed the most out-of-character thing she could have done. Convinced that I was, by now, the colour of beetroot, I glanced at Fran who was smiling as if nothing at all unnatural had happened. I felt I had been treated to a display of some sort, though for whose benefit I had no idea.

"How are you?" she asked. It was a marginally softer tone than she had adopted in our previous meeting, and one I could not fail to notice.

"I am," I hesitated, acutely conscious of how flummoxed I must have appeared at that precise moment, "pretty much as you left me. I'm sure you'll make your own deductions…"

It wasn't intended as a joke, but Fran clearly thought it hilarious.

Toni put her gloved hand on my arm briefly.

"Poor Adrian," she said, glancing at Fran.

One way or another, it proved the perfect start to the evening. Within moments we were all suitably relaxed and Toni demonstrated herself to be the perfect conduit between Fran and I. After less than an hour I felt as if I had known both of them for years. It was a degree of comfort, misplaced or not, which allowed me to pose the question whose answer would resolve at least one thing that had been bothering me since I had been introduced to Fran.

"You don't look like sisters," I ventured, pausing fractionally in case there was any immediate interjection. None came. "I mean, to be honest you don't really look alike. At all. And you're both…"

"Very different?" suggested Toni, taking advantage of my hesitation. I nodded.

"We get that a lot," Fran confirmed, seemingly completely unfazed by my articulating what was, after all, quite an obvious observation. "Blonde, dark. Taller, less so."

"Out-going, less so," Toni suggested with a wry smile.

It felt like a well-rehearsed routine; but at least I hadn't offended them.

"Sorry to be so predictable," I said.

"It depends," Toni said, her face returning to the considered seriousness of our first meeting, "on your definition of 'sisters' really. Are we from exactly the same genetic gene pool? Obviously not. But is there a relationship? A close, familial relationship - blood-tied or not?"

She let the question hang for a second.

"There is," Fran answered. "And it is partly genetic - just in case you think we're weird hippies or something. But it's complicated."

"Complicated?" I echoed.

"Very," Toni confirmed. "Maybe we'll explain it to you one day - but not now. Is that OK? Just humour us. Just assume that we are sisters, because that's how we'll behave; regular sisters. And in any event, that's not the most important thing right now is it?"

They both looked at me. It was clear that they expected confirmation. The conversation had taken a turn I had been unable to foresee.

"If you say so. I mean, I guess not."

"Really?" checked Fran, concerned my unanswered question would get in the way. "Does it make a difference to you?"

"To me? How?"

"If Toni and I weren't sisters - or were sisters. Does that matter in any material way to you?"

I could have taken time to consider my answer, but it was there on the tip of my tongue before I could check it.

"Not in the slightest."

I felt the pressure in the room ease a little and they both raised their glasses in perfect synchronisation.

Of course the follow-on question now begged was that if their being sisters did not make any material difference, then no 'material difference' to what exactly? And more specifically, in relation to me? Although we carried on making small-talk as if nothing had interrupted that initial, innocent flow, we knew it *had* been interrupted. It was a sensation, a wispy cloud, that could almost have been seen hanging over our table as we sat there.

And it was a cloud which succeeded in making me increasingly less comfortable. I found myself forcing responses, forcing laughs in order to keep the flow going. Toni and Fran seemed unchanged, carrying on as if I had never even asked that original question - or perhaps as if they had never answered it - but I could tell, from Toni at least, that she sensed the disturbance in my equilibrium.

I offered to buy another round of drinks.

"I don't think so, do you?" she said, as if she were correcting an errant child. Almost as if it were a prompt, Fran stood up. I didn't know what to do. Toni put her hand on my arm again. "One of us will call you. Is that OK?"

The confusion that had opened my evening returned in spades.

"Sure," I said. "I mean, I guess so."

"We like you, Adrian. Really. We would like to see you again if that's OK with you. If you could put up with us."

Fran leant forward and kissed my cheek. The opposite one to that Toni had christened a couple of hours ago. There they were again, different sides of the same coin.

"Please?" she said.

I smiled and waved my arms to take in the general scene.

"You know where to find me!"

✻

Afterwards, as we lay there in the pregnant silence, slowly restoring equilibrium - which in my case had been shifted to God knows where! - I was determined not to be the first to fall asleep; determined not to conform to the stereotypical male reaction to love-making, even though it was my natural response, even though I was overcome with a need for slumber.

I turned my head to check the clock on my bedside table. The last hour or so had flown by, with time seeming to travel at wildly variable velocities rather than remain constant. At least that was how it had felt.

She had, I confess, taken me by surprise. Not her turning up unannounced, though that did come somewhat out of the blue, but by the way she initiated and then accelerated through the preliminaries, leaving me metaphorically hanging onto her coat tails as we sped physically through the rooms of my flat and mentally across the groundwork of our relationship. It was as if she had no time for convention, for niceties, for subtlety.

Our initial coupling had been animalistic, rough - violent almost. I had taken my lead from her, there was no other option. She seemed to have arrived already aroused, her mind made up. That first time it was as if I could have been anyone, just the other party in some kind of contract; as if the obligation I were fulfilling was based on mercantile rather than emotional foundations. It had taken, it seemed, almost no time at all. As we lay there, panting hard, my mind racing, trying to catch up with the reality of this bizarre, wonderful, confusing, extraordinary situation in which I found myself, the slowing of her breath seemed to correspond with a release. I felt tension leave her, as if our love-making had freed her from some terrible obligation. It was as if she had achieved something, succeeded in overcoming a challenge she had set herself, untied a knot.

I had been unsure what would happen next. My inability to foresee what might be about to transpire when she walked through the door was now compounded many times over. My role thus far had been more functional than anything else. Although we lay holding hands, I had no idea what my next move was supposed to be, or indeed if I was supposed to do anything at all. Nor could I predict what she might do. I had a sudden image of Glenn Close, and hoped I wasn't trapped in 'Fatal Attraction'. I hadn't seen her arrive with a large knife sticking out of her handbag, so that was something at least.

I must have tensed a little with the thought because she squeezed my hand and turned a little towards me. Her gaze was slightly strange, as if she was examining me for the first time; as if I were a stranger. And in a way I suppose I was, given how little we had seen of each other. Yet here we were, lying naked together, hands clasped, the rise-and-fall of our chests still betraying the traces of frantic activity.

It seems strange to say it, but she looked different too. How much my perspective had been changed by our physical proximity - or by the gloss the sudden shift in our relationship had overlaid upon it - I was unable to say. It was almost like meeting her again, as if the initial encounter in the Gallery bar had been with another person or had happened to someone else other than me.

"Are you ok?" she asked.

It was a simple enough question but with no immediate or adequate answer available. What could I say?

"Yes, no, and maybe," I ventured, "all at once."

She laughed and turned a little further towards me, allowing her free hand to rest on my chest.

"I hope more 'yes' than the other two."

I tried a smile that was meant to convey that how could it be otherwise? A smile designed to lay bare my underlying confusion; a plea, wordlessly, for some clarification.

She moved her right leg a little, allowing her foot to rest against my own, gently rubbing my calf as she did so. My physical reaction to this subtle gesture was immediate and involuntary - and all too evident. She glanced down toward my thighs, to where my penis was stiffening visibly.

"Something tells me that the 'yes' is getting a little stronger."

I moved my head towards hers, turning a little myself, and cupping the back of her head in my left hand. She was ready for my kiss; a slow, delicate and intimate affair this time, still full of passion but devoid of our earlier roughness. I eased my head away a little, trying to concentrate on her eyes; watching them as my fingers as they played through her blond hair. I let my hand travel to her shoulder and then down to her right breast and the perfect nipple that was also beginning to harden.

"Yes," I echoed, and then rolled over on top of her, my mouth finding hers once more as she freed her hands to put them behind my back and pull me closer, as if there might still be a gap between our bodies that needed to be filled.

That second time she had alternated between impatience and indifference. Although I strived for control - as if I needed to re-establish myself somehow - it was a goal I never quite managed to achieve. Thinking back now, I can only try to unpack her ability to achieve superiority, something I had never experienced before. It was as if, during the encore, she had been trying desperately *not* to complete our love-making - and this to as great a degree as she had been previously keen to get to it over and done with as quickly as possible. Eventually, when she had finally resolved to seal our second contract, she did so with an abandonment that was astonishing. It felt as if she were giving everything she had to me - rather than taking away everything I had.

As I lay there, I was struck by the extremes to which we had ventured; the opposing poles of action and emotion I had just experienced. It felt as if she had taken me, in a single evening, to every place I could ever expect to go with a woman; as if she had gifted me with the sexual bookends between which all my future experiences would be contained. And even though I was able to regard our love-making in the context of what she had given me, I could not dispel the notion that it had all been for her; none of it was for me, as if I happened to be a subsidiary or irrelevant partner, the accidental beneficiary.

Because of that, I had suddenly been certain that she would not start a third cycle for the simple reason that there was nothing else she could offer me - or nothing else she needed from me.

And I was struck with a sense of sadness, of loss almost; a profound notion that we would never make love again; that all too quickly we had reached a point which represented an end rather than a beginning - though the end of exactly what I was unable to say.

*

We arranged to meet the following evening, but of course she failed to show. Desperately hoping to see Fran walk into the bar, I felt a crushing defeat when Toni entered. Yet I found myself unable to manifest any kind of surprise. There was an inevitability about it.

"Adrian," she said coming straight over to me.

"She's not coming, is she?"

"May I?" Toni looked at the open bottle of wine in front of me and the spare glass on the table; the one I had intended for Fran.

"Help yourself; better than me having to drink it all."

"Are you ok?"

Pausing mid-pour, Toni must have noticed the way I reacted to her question, stunned by the echo from the previous evening, an echo hardened by the way she said it, the tone of her voice suddenly seeming so close to Fran's.

"How can I be 'ok'?" I asked, trying to remain as calm as possible. "How can I be 'ok' when I've no idea what's going on? As if I've ever had any real idea what was going on…"

She finished pouring her wine, saying nothing.

"First you. Then you introduce me to Fran. There's that whole, slightly weird sisters thing going on, which I couldn't quite come to terms with - which you say is 'complicated'. And then the other evening. Fran..."

"We're not," she said, interrupting.

"Not what?"

"Not sisters, of course. At least not in the biological sense. I thought we'd covered that."

"So friends then. And then, almost like a mercenary, you go around scouting for a man for your 'friend'." I was conscious of a bitterness in my voice and refrained from trying to hide it. "Why's that? To check them out? To test them, validate them somehow? As if Fran couldn't do that for herself."

"Partly, yes."

"Which part?"

Toni took a sip of her wine, her eyes never leaving mine. I had to look away for a moment, to compose myself; her stare was unnerving.

"Most of it really. I am a kind of filter, yes. I provide some kind of protection for Fran, if you want to choose to see it that way. Could she find a man for herself? Logically she could, but she's abysmal at it. She can't recognise the good from the not so good..."

"Neither, apparently, can I..."

She ignored my barb.

"She's been hurt - badly - more than once. Physically too. I'm sure you wouldn't want to see that happen to her again."

"But it's all right if I get hurt, is it? How I feel is of no importance?"

She took another sip of wine. I could tell this wasn't easy for her in spite of the calm exterior she was trying to display: that no-nonsense, antiseptic honesty from our first meeting was beginning to come to the fore again.

"Fran and I are partners. Lovers. Choose whatever word suits you best. We like 'sisters' because it's actually the least controversial description. If we were married, I guess you'd say that I was the 'husband' in the relationship - though it's not a term I'd choose to use."

"I can see that."

"See what, exactly?"

"That you'd be the 'husband'. It fits you better."

She nodded, apparently taking my comment at face value.

"And Fran is, of course, much more feminine."

"As I have discovered to my cost."

"We have wanted, for some time now, to have a family. To have a baby. Which, thanks to illness and the unforeseen side-effects of some powerful medication, actually turns out to be an option for just one of us. Fran, of course. Please." She raised her hand slightly to prevent my interrupting. "We discussed how we should try and achieve our goal. Not unnaturally, I was in favour of artificial methods; the anonymous, more antiseptic approach. But Fran was adamant that she wanted the conception of our baby to be as 'natural' as possible."

"Natural?!" Toni was unable to stop me getting that one out, but raised her hand again.

"Although I wasn't happy about it, she started seeing men. One-night-stands. At first she did so behind my back - until she came home one day badly beaten... I tried to persuade her to take the safer route, but she refused. Totally. She defined a line that I simply couldn't risk crossing. So we made a deal, a pact. We hatched a plan. Cold-hearted, manipulative - use all the derogatory words you like. I arrange the first date. I filter out the risky ones - 'test' and 'validate', to use your words. If I like them - and I *do* like you Adrian - then Fran meets them. If she likes them… Well…"

From somewhere I felt things begin to fall into place, those random jigsaw pieces I had picked up were beginning to form into a picture. Toni's narrative explained a number of the sensations garnered from my evening with Fran, primarily the feelings I'd had about her. I could see the reason behind her drive, that initial impatience, the mechanistic nature of it. And I understood the sense of an ending that had been manifested all too soon.

If I had wanted to, I could have taken comfort that I'd made it through the trials to 'qualify' - but that minor satisfaction would have to wait.

"But that's still not right," I offered. It was a hollow, meaningless and weak phrase I regretted immediately.

"What's 'right', Adrian, these days?" I had given Toni the opportunity to make the conversation philosophical, to try and take me out of it in a way.

"And it's risky."

"The physical abuse, you mean? We've not had any problems since I got involved."

I couldn't miss the fact that Toni assigned the physical pain to both of them.

"No, not that. I mean it's risky for you personally, isn't it?"

"How so?"

"Emotionally." My observation was, I sensed, ultimately petty; a cheap shot in a fight I had already comprehensively lost. But I felt the need to leave a mark, a bruise of my own, however minor. And on Toni too. I guessed that was the area where she was most vulnerable. "What happens if there's a man Fran falls for? What happens then?"

"It hasn't happened yet," Toni looked momentarily defensive.

"What if it had been me? Things got pretty intense there for a while." It was my turn to play my best card, even if Toni held all the aces. "Different, I would imagine, between a man and a woman. How it should be, perhaps." I rushed on, sensing Toni was about to object. "What if Fran had suddenly felt that *I* was the one, that it was my child *and me* she wanted? What if she was so determined that a pre-planned one-night-stand wasn't enough? What if she wanted the guarantee that the child - assuming we could make one - would be mine too? What if she came back again and again? What if that - changed things?"

I let the implication rest there in full view. I could tell it was something Toni had considered; and I could also tell that perhaps - just perhaps - I may have come closer to turning that possibility that anyone else before me. Even if that was only my ego talking, it was worth hanging on to.

When Toni replied, her voice was a shade quieter, less confident, the tone almost vulnerable. Almost.

"You're right. Of course. There is a risk - to me. I run the risk of losing her. Don't you think I don't recognise that? It's what makes the whole thing so painful - painful in more ways that you can imagine. How do you think I felt when I knew she was coming to see you, knowing what was about to happen? That's why my job is so important. It's important to Fran, but it's important to me too. Important personally. I have to trust you, not just for Fran but for me too."

She stood up and placed her glass back on the table. It was only then, as she retrieved her handbag with her other hand, that I noticed the glove on her left hand. It was like the one I had seen her wear before, but this time it was jet black.

"And you might be right, Adrian. Maybe you did get closer to her than some others have done. She never says; I have to guess, to judge based on how she is, how she seems. It's no consolation - for either of us I suspect - but I know she liked you. Very much."

Then she simply turned and walked away.

I never did uncover the reason for her wearing that glove.

My Dear Polly

So one must protest. As he sits by the Sailing Club jetty, pungent smoke from his freshly lit cigarette rising in a brief cloud about him, he knows that one must protest. Yet how? In front of him, a little girl, blond and pretty in her short Sunday-dress, lifts up dried slabs of seaweed. And a little boy watching, encouraging, talking to her in their own private language, a language excluding all adults. One day perhaps she will grow up to be like Polly, her innocence replaced by a more studied exterior, by cunning and calculation. No, that is too harsh. Inscrutable is better; or unfathomable. Is it for them, those two children picking up seaweed, that one must protest, to protect them now - and in the future - from what they might become? Smoke inhaled, filling lungs. Another thin blue cloud momentarily fogs the view of the bay. In the distance, beyond a forest of irregular masts erect like pins in a blue-grey pincushion sea, the hills. The blue fog made by the cigarette, the smoke breathed out, clears despite the chatter of children. Perhaps he should write again to Polly. Surely she knows that one should protest; knows it in her own way, after her own fashion. Yet she has never understood him, the way he might look at things - like now as he watches a yachtsman come from the jetty and go past him, middle-aged and middle-class. His shoes are red, over-dressy, attempting image. Not at all like the riding boots of the woman who took him by surprise on that great steed of hers in the park. Riding boots, purely functional. And he has never told Polly he had seen her because it would have meant explaining so much; trying to explain the unexplainable. She never accepted what he saw; that was the problem. No, it was not with Polly he wanted to protest; there was a need for reconciliation there, to be again like children picking up seaweed on the shore. And now the little girl has found a stone and runs after the man in the red shoes crying "Daddy Daddy; look what I've found!". A vision blurred by cigarette haze. He used to run after his own parents with discoveries, wanting to share, wanting to be praised. But now it is different. Now it is a struggle to be home again, even for a short while. A walk to the Sailing Club on a Sunday afternoon for no reason other than to get out. How could they understand his complaints? He has not told them about Polly, about the problems they had. And how could he tell them about the woman on the horse, or the little girl he is watching now, again at her friend's side, rummaging through the debris of the tide? What would they say except "So you saw a little girl among the seaweed; where is the need for protest there?" - for if he told them anything, then he must mention the need to speak. And he must speak to Polly for there is much to be said. He feels the warmth of the cigarette against his fingers. And what of the things he might have said to the Equestrian, the things he could still say now? She would understand him if he said "we must protest". He bends forward to stub out his cigarette on a slipway littered with fag ends. Has the little girl picked up a cigarette butt yet? "Daddy, Daddy; look what I've found!" Polly used to be like that in the days when they shared their discoveries. But then she started finding things of her own, things she would not share. The man in the red shoes goes by. Perhaps that is why he has started making his own discoveries; jealousy, retaliation. He could not share with her the woman on the horse, the woman in the riding boots to whom he had said "Good Morning" all those weeks ago. She had smiled at him. No, that is not for Polly. The sound of oars splashing through the water. Feel in the pocket for another cigarette. All he might tell her would be the facts of the visit: that he had gone home; that it had not been terribly successful. He could not say that he had seen a little girl picking up dried seaweed, and thought of her - Polly - and how he knew he must protest. The oars he had heard were being put up; a boat bumping against the jetty. No, it was reconciliation with Polly. "What have we lost?" he wants to say. "What have you found that I am excluded from?" A flare of a match, a puff of blue and the warm inhalation. Throw the match down, out of harm's way where the little girl won't pick it up. If he went back to the park perhaps the Equestrian would ride to his side again and they could talk. To tell about Polly, and the little girl now trying to lift a rusty mooring chain; "Daddy, Daddy…". Had Polly been a precocious child, picking up things, finding things? Undoubtedly she would have shared some of them; but even in those early days he knew she would probably want to have her own things, her own secrets. The men from the rowing boat walk past carrying fishing rods. The shoes: not footwear of Fishermen, but strictly Sailing Club gear. Once he had made a joke of yellow wellingtons and Polly had laughed. Creeping down to his fingers the warmth of the cigarette; inhale, out the blue plume of smoke elongated like a feather. Polly would turn his argument against him and say French cigarettes were a way of conforming. He saw them as part of his protest. The woman on horseback would not smoke ordinarily, but perhaps small cigars in the right company to make her own statement. The little girl trots off, past him - "Daddy, Daddy!" - to one day wear riding boots herself perhaps. Even so, something must be said, something done. The yachts' masts sway, crossing each other. The sun comes out again. Perhaps he should tell his parents about Polly; how they really were. "She has found something I am excluded from." "I am excluded" - would they understand? The woman on the horse. He had found things too of course; they must make their own discoveries, inevitably. The little boy runs off to find his friend. Perhaps they are brother and sister, gone in search of dressy red shoes. No, the red shoes go by again; not Daddy, he must have made a mistake. A good time to go. The sun shining on the water; standing up, its angle changes. Looking around, for what? The little girl? Polly? The woman on horseback? Polly he could write to, but the Equestrian who had smiled at him when he said "Good Morning", she must be encountered again. He wonders what status she now holds for him. A first step away from the shore, towards home. "Where did you go, Dear?" To say what? That one walked and thought of Polly, and of a woman on horseback? That he saw a little girl picking up seaweed and mistook a pair of red shoes for her father? One must protest at having to say any of this, at having to think about not saying it. Turning his back on the shore and the sound of the children returning. Often it was more important what one did not say, what one left out. All those things he had not said to Polly; saying them - if he knew what they were indeed - would that have made any difference? And "Good Morning" may have been all that was necessary for meeting a woman on a horse in the park. "I went to the Sailing Club" he would say and try to leave it at that, knowing all the important things would be left out. Perhaps that could be part of the protest, for if one must do so then there has to be a way. Now a road; a terraced street, each frontage hiding its own secrets. His reflection in a window as he passes. And to think that the woman on the horse had smiled at him when he said "Good Morning" in spite of all the things she did not know. An advert in a window for cheap fresh fish. He came this way once with Polly. Then he had seen no need to cry out against vague injustice when there was none. Two young boys come towards him, going to the water. Will they see the little girl or the red shoes? Only with their own eyes. While he, as they pass him, is on his way home: "I went to the Sailing Club". He would spend the afternoon in front of the television no doubt, to keep them company, to think "I must write to Polly", and to let his mind wander perhaps to a chance encounter. And he knows he has still to face his father's question - "How's Polly?" - which had not yet come. "I am excluded…" "She's fine" he would say, for that was all he could say. Riding past him on an ancient bike, an Old Boy who looks as if he would never have worn fancy red shoes to please anyone. Buy him a drink. A lemonade for the girl who cried "Daddy, Daddy". Turning the corner. Nod to an old lady who looks vaguely familiar. Out walking her dog. And how will Polly look in thirty or forty years when it is her turn to walk the dog? And where will he be? Or the woman on the horse? The little girl with the seaweed will be elsewhere, grown up, her place taken by another as his place shall be taken, someone sitting thinking "one must protest". But at least they won't think of Polly and say "I am excluded". Fingering the cigarette packet to find keys buried in his pocket. Perhaps next weekend to walk in the park; to wander thinking of what to write to Polly, yet longing above all to say "Good Morning" to a smiling woman on horseback. The silver front door key; different keys to different lives. The familiarity of the yellow door. Key in the lock. Remember all one's history as the familiar smell greets. Sound of the television set. Into the lounge. "You weren't gone long." And here is the moment: "We must protest"; "I am excluded"; "I saw a little girl picking up seaweed". All left out. He must escape. To escape from Polly too; finally. To gallop across the park and meet strangers fleetingly, fully. To see young children by the sea. "Coffee?" Retreat to the kitchen to think of her, blond hair, tall, slim, smiling eyes, full lips, sensual in tight rousers. The woman on the horse. Fill up the kettle with water. Three cups for three coffees. Maybe it is all to do with not knowing; there was the interest, the fascination. And the Sunday Film soundtrack coming from the television. "One must protest", in the end even against the Sunday Film. The impatient wait for the kettle. And where was Polly now, what was she discovering without him? "I am excluded." Perhaps the little girl has found her Daddy. He should tell Polly about her when he wrote. And the girl on horseback? The boiling kettle sends steam into the air, a cloud, a mist. No, not her; how could Polly understand? Three brown coffees. Perhaps he should take his upstairs. Coffee into the lounge. "I'm having mine upstairs" - "in my room so I can escape and think of what I have seen, what I know." "How's Polly?" Another question; the same question. "She's fine." Hot cup in hand, mounting the stairs. 'My Dear Polly'; the beginning was easy. Out of the window, in the distance, the row of terraced houses that led to the sea. The old lady with her dog perhaps going past the sign for cheap fresh fish. Would she see the children, the red shoes of the Sailing Club? A sip of hot coffee. And where is she now, the lithe one? Across what fields does she gallop, and into whose heart? 'My Dear Polly … So one must protest …' And he wants to cry "I am excluded!" but because he is, he cannot. Looking out of the window, sipping coffee; below the soundtrack of the Sunday Film.

Westminster

The door opens and two figures enter, dragging in their slipstream some of the chill fog from outside. They pause for a moment as the heater above the door blasts the mist away, refusing to allow anything to blur the crisp uniformity of the coffee shop's branding. Outside the air might be clouded in such a way as to render the edifice opposite indistinct, yet the patrons inside - all of them - know it is there. They also know what it represents too, even though seen from their soft sofas, the faux cosiness of the Cafe Nero experience, and through the damp lens outside, it could be a building that housed anyone or anything and not necessarily the Mother of Parliaments.

The men pause and look around, ostensibly to seek out a suitable and vacant table; yet there is, in the theatrical way one of them removes his heavy overcoat and shakes it lightly, something of a performance in their movements, as if they want to be seen, as if their arrival should be an event of note. Indicating two seats in the far corner, the now un-coated man points authoritatively towards them, then heads to the counter where, as luck would have it, there is no-one waiting. In her tight brown "barista" t-shirt, the young woman behind a display of blueberry muffins and panettone, smiles.

"The usual, Sir?" she asks, her professional tone edging toward a line of familiarity it manages not to cross.

"Absolutely," he beams equally professionally, and then in a practiced sonorous voice adds, "Laura".

She smiles a different smile then, more secret and knowing, certain that - contrary to the appearance he was trying to give - her name had only come to him thanks to her lapel badge and in spite of his having frequently used it over the past few weeks.

"And two almond croissants," he adds, as if the addition to their order delivered in an ostentatious French accent might succeed in interrupting her train of thought. "Let's push the boat out, shall we?"

Two minutes pass, and following the exchange of folding money and a loyalty card for a dark circular tray laden with food and drink, he joins his companion at their corner table.

"Ah, provisions!" the seated man says, moving a small leather Filofax from in front of him and placing it on a nearby chair which houses his own coat - even though that chair belongs to the next table. "You spoil me, Toby."

"Making notes already?" asks Toby, noticing that the Filofax is already open.

"Nothing quite so prosaic!"

"Or a diary? A commentary on the weather, perhaps? We'll make a weatherman of you yet, Ian!"

Toby laughs at his own joke. It is a full, well-rounded - if well-rehearsed - laugh that goes with his voice. Two people now waiting at the counter look over.

"Too late for that, Old Fruit. I'm afraid my ship sailed long ago."

"Which is why you're stuck with an old landlubber like me and where drinking plastic coffee is our only means of escape from 'you know where'…"

Removing his coffee and croissant from the tray, Ian retrieves his Filofax and finds just enough space to lay it open it on the table in front of him.

"Notes of a sort," he confesses, looking down at the exposed page.

"Aha!" says Toby, still cradling his coat, "straight to the point! I like your style." He hesitates for a moment as he searches out somewhere to deposit his own recently discarded garment, eventually settling - with an apologetic shrug - to rest it on top of Ian's. "So, where are we?"

"Cut of your jib," Ian suggests.

"Come again?"

"Cut of your jib. If you were going to persist with your landlubber theme, you should have said that you liked the cut of my jib."

"A step too far for me, that Old Boy. Never could join up more than a few dots."

Ian looks at Toby knowing that to be a bare-faced lie.

"As if," he suggests.

"So, where are we?" Toby repeats, turning his attention to his croissant.

"Essentially just about where we were a week or so ago." Ian flicks a page in his Filofax.

"No movement?"

"Nothing of any note."

"Why am I not surprised?"

"Did you talk to His Lordship?" Ian turns the page back and looks up. There is something derogatory in the appellation which is clearly noted and accepted. Toby, having just put some croissant in his mouth, points to his chewing and begs a moment to respond.

"I did," he says finally, cutting another piece of pastry before returning Ian's gaze. "His line is still the same."

"What he wants?" Ian prompts.

"And when he wants it. Even though," Toby slips more croissant into his mouth, though this time not begging a pause and talking through his eating, "even though I told him it might be impossible. That we couldn't possibly get things lined up in time."

"Does he understand the difficulty?"

"He says he does."

Ian lets a small laugh slip.

"But what he says and the truth of the matter are probably vastly different things!" When Toby fails to respond, Ian senses that he may have trespassed towards - but not over - a boundary. "I'm not saying it's just your man, obviously. They're all like that. Maybe mine is one of the worst. They have no grasp on reality."

"Indeed," Toby concurs, accepting restoration of equilibrium. "And it's always the same, isn't it? At the beginning of a session."

"Or the beginning of an administration."

Toby accepts Ian's offer.

"Absolutely. So put the two together..." He allows his voice to trail away and then scoops up the remainder of the croissant.

Ian pulls a pen from his jacket pocket then lays it on the Filofax but without writing anything.

"I suspect this term it could be much worse."

"Oh don't worry," Toby's voice rises again as he tries to be upbeat, "we'll bring them round. We always do, don't we?

When was the last time we had someone who didn't get it? Who didn't march to the inevitable drum?"

"And where are they now?" Ian asks, adding a layer to Toby's question, knowing the implicit meaning will be immediately understood.

For a moment that seems decisive enough for both men to lift their respective coffees and take a sip.

Toby recoils slightly.

"Too damned hot - as usual! I don't know why we come here."

"But you do," Ian suggests, smiling slightly. "As we always say - and usually at some point within the first five or ten minutes - because it offers us a means of escape."

"I know." Toby scans the rest of the clientele briefly. "But what about the rest? What about all these people?"

Ian follows his gaze, settling for a moment on a small group of orientals sitting near the entrance.

"Food. Drink. To rest their sore feet having walked all the way here."

"From where?" asks Toby, engaged again. "From where do you think they might have walked? Waterloo? Piccadilly?"

"At least, I would imagine. Who knows?" Ian sips his coffee again, then, more wistfully: "If only they knew."

"Knew what, exactly?"

"I don't know. Who we were, perhaps; or what we did."

"Aha!" says Toby, puffing himself up slightly. "Well, there you have it, Old Boy. There you have it! To them I suspect we're just a couple of suits having a break; freed from the chains of the office."

"Or chains of office," Ian suggests at which Toby offers one of his short resonant bellows. Two of the Orientals look round.

"I think," continues Ian, looking down into his coffee before lifting the cup towards his lips again, "you do the Great British Public a disservice. Or the populous at large, perhaps I should have said."

Toby replaces his cup on the table, his actions the mirror opposite of his colleague. "What do you mean?"

From his tone, Ian is suddenly unsure as to which element of his statement Toby is questioning. "About what: us or the Great British Public?"

"Us."

"Of course." Ian nods, unsurprised. As he lowers his coffee, Toby raises his own once more. Ian notes the choreography. "Well, look at us, Toby. Hardly your average 'suit', wouldn't you say? Yours, for example. Saville Row?"

"*And* the overcoat," Toby affirms between sips.

"Well, then. And it shows. Not like some Johnny Come Lately from the City, eh?" Ian watches his friend nod in a satisfied manner. "And if we're not from the City… Where might house two mature and experienced operators such as ourselves? And right near Westminster Bridge too."

Toby had marked Ian's pause as he described them. He found the sobriquet acceptable enough. For a moment he feels vaguely expansive and thinks about offering a second coffee.

"You're right, of course. Devoted to Her Majesty in some way shape or form. Obviously. Home Office, perhaps? Or the Treasury?"

Ian smiles at the in-joke. It is clearly familiar ground.

"As if. We're hardly - what shall we say - 'under-dressed' for the part!"

The notion brings another loud roar from Toby, appreciative of Ian's new aphorism. "Or the Foreign Office, perhaps?"

Ian smiles dutifully.

"Of course, we're not that far away from you know where... We might be two of those fit types who like walking. You know, brisk stroll past the Cenotaph; freed from the *highest* office..."

"Now you're talking, Old Boy!" Toby drains his cup with an air of satisfaction. "If people are going to mistake us for anyone, why not there? Are we not dressed for the part?"

"Better than many of the incumbents I would suggest. Or aspirational incumbents," says Ian, playing on his companion's vanity.

"Never a truer word, my dear sir; never a truer word."

Having had a sense that a second coffee might have been in the offing, Ian pauses and retrieves some croissant crumbs from his plate. He looks up to see Toby staring at a poster just over his left shoulder. But it is not a stare driven by study or the need to interpret, but rather something more vacant and wistful; a look spilling from history, the missed opportunity that might indeed have seen Toby ensconced in the immediate vicinity of Number 10. Ian has heard the story before - and more than once.

"Well," he tries to sound upbeat and decisive, "this won't get our problems solved, will it?" Toby looks back towards him, mid-recollection. Ian needs to haul him back. "We need to bend our minds..."

"Our considerable minds!" Toby affirms, unwilling to let an opportunity for self-flattery go by, thereby taking the bait Ian had set out in the minutest of pauses.

"Of course. Our 'considerable minds' to the matter at hand, and how we align the stars as it were and get our men seeing eye-to-eye."

Near the door, in a sudden flurry of activity and noise, the Asians rise en masse and prepare to leave.

"Where did we get to?" Ian asks, now forcing himself back to reality.

"Our last formal meeting?" Toby checks, seeing Ian beginning to scan his notes again.

"Indeed."

"Indecisive. Over two hours, if you recall, of going nowhere very, very slowly." Toby makes a gesture Ian finds difficult to decipher but assumes it to be resignation.

"Well," Ian's finger pauses half way down a Filofax page, "at least there's only one major sticking point."

"Only one?!" says Toby incredulous. "That's what you think? I know it appears that way, but believe me, even were we to find a way of resolving that particular impasse, then I'm sure other things would arise. I suspect there are issues waiting in the wings…"

Toby allows the phrase to drift off, perhaps out into the murk with the departing Chinese. Ian watches them go then hauls Toby's phrase back.

"'Issues'? On our side, you mean?"

"All I'm saying is," says Toby, dodging the question, "that even if we could bring our men together, they would find other aspects about which they were suddenly un-settled."

In spite of the balance of the response, Toby's inference is plain - as always. Ian notes it mentally, fails to smile, and tries to push on.

"That may or may not be the case, but for now what have we got to go on?"

"You tell me," Toby says, sighing slightly and deliberately sounding weary.

"I don't believe we have an issue in principal," Ian looks up for a reaction, but there is none; Toby appears to be listening, his eyes are once again focussed on the poster. "We have a difference over the dates and cost, and what a successful outcome looks like."

"Not much then."

"If we can engineer some movement on the dates - perhaps a quarter on either side - we can tie that one up. Allowing for our superior skills, that should be easy."

Toby nods in recognition of the flattery, but Ian can see he lacks commitment. He tries to fight the disinterest.

"Cost is actually the primary concern. My man will not accept such an astronomical figure -"

"Astronomical!" Toby rises to the challenge.

Ian knows very well that the numbers, the cost of the project, would have initially come from Toby's department, and his observation represents a more direct assault that he would normally countenance. But he too is under pressure.

"And so needs to be reviewed."

"But we spent weeks coming up with those numbers," Toby protests, allowing an edge of professional bluster to creep into his reply. He wants to sound hurt too; to give Ian the unmistakeable sense that he is feeling suddenly let down, betrayed.

"That's what my man thinks," Ian says carefully, edging back a little. "I told him that you had spent a great deal of effort crafting them. And that I was confident they represented the best set of numbers your man could put forward." Toby nods his thank you. "And so I think it is not actually about the costs, per se, but about the phasing of them."

"The phasing?"

"If we were able to package them up in such a way that my man could regard them as discrete steps, each associated with some kind of tangible outcome - how we sell the successes of the project if you like - then, provided he had some kind of influence at each stage, I think he might come round."

Ian pauses to allow the idea to sink in. He flicks back through his Filofax to find the entry from three weeks previously where this same notion was actually discussed in the committee meeting. He wonders why it should be any different now, and feels a little deflated that any chance of success partially rests on getting Toby on side.

"That might work," suggests Toby, slowly, "especially if we could persuade my man that the goal was still to deliver the whole thing, unhindered."

"Using your 'considerable mind'..." Ian offers an echo from a few minutes earlier.

"But you're not saying your man wants a veto of some kind?"

"It's not something we have spoken about. Indeed, that word has never entered the conversation. He's just nervous, that's all I can put it down to. A 'nervous newbie' who doesn't want to cock-up his first big project - especially such a high profile one allied with your own department. "

"Now that," says Toby, looking down at the table and allowing himself to contemplate another coffee for the second time, "is perfectly understandable. And very sensible, if I may say so."

"Noted," Ian accepts the gesture.

"But it won't be easy. I know how set my man is on this one, and His Lordship moves positions on such things very rarely."

"Yet if we can shift him a few months or so, and offer the parcel bundled in an alternative way."

"But I won't put a fancy bow on it," Toby protests obliquely.

"No-one's asking you to, Toby. Let's just see if we can edge him towards our position."

"Our position?"

"Sorry. No, not *our* position - obviously. Bad choice of words. If we can allow him to present *his* position in such a way that makes it palatable for my man… Well then."

Deciding against further caffeine, Toby rises suddenly.

"I can't," he says, picking up his overcoat and beginning to don it, "promise anything, of course. Let me have a think. We may yet be able to turn this around." Toby offers his hand which Ian, still seated, takes, rising only slightly. "Forgive me, I have to get back to prepare for Wednesday's session with 'You Know Who'."

"Of course, of course. You'll let me know how you get on?"

"Indubitably. Why don't we meet here on Thursday, same time?"

Ian nods and smiles, and then in an instant Toby turns and is gone, his large, dark blue frame absorbed into the mist outside. As he turns his attention back to his Filofax, Laura appears at the table to collect the cups and plates.

"Another coffee, sir?"

"Why not?" Ian smiles, then returns to his notes.

From two weeks previously he sees a brief entry:

'Cost and timing. Suggested a phased approach to try and make the pill easier to swallow and spread the cost. Under consideration.'

For a moment he wonders how he should frame today's entry, loathed as he is to say the same thing again. After all, progress is expected and he needs to be able to depict some kind of movement. With a sigh, he lifts his pen from the table and allows it to hover over the page.

Recommended Books

Which books? That was the question. As he sat at a library desk, encased in an individual brown shell like a bee in a wooden hive, he wondered which books he needed. They faced him, honeyed rows of them, side-by-side, ordered, numbered, catalogued, cross-referenced. Where should one begin? He looked down. He had placed the reading list in front of him: "Recommended Books". At least that was a start, he thought. He had come to the library with a sense of purpose, an air of determination in his quiet vaulting up the steps; he had even chosen this particular desk so he could see all these books, as if preparing to receive some invisibly transferred message. Sitting in this specific enclosure also allowed him a view of the stairs, the entire floor. When I get bored, he thought (as he knew he would), I can just let my mind wander. Then there was the Librarian; the young one he had seen the day before, the one who had looked appealing in her red dress. Had he come here for her too? His thoughts returned to the interior of his honeycomb. Which books? He had found only three of those on the list. Not especially promising: hardcovers, plain, yellow, blue. Uninspiring. Who would want to take such unattractive volumes from the shelf? But then it wasn't the cover that counted. He thought of the girl. Maybe she looked nice in her red dress, but what did that mean? He couldn't judge her on that alone. An old lady climbed up to his floor, her breathing pained, laboured. The lift was broken and she had struggled up here in search of what? He would watch her to see where she went, to gain some insight into her motivation. One book lay open in front of him and absentmindedly he tried to read. The words passed anonymously before him, meaning nothing. Why did he always find it so difficult to read in public libraries?

Other thoughts perhaps. The girl. Or being surrounded by so many shelves, all asking the same question - "which books?" - each volume begging to be read. No sign of the Librarian, but the old lady had progressed to his section, to the literature. An old school teacher perhaps, or merely a lonely old woman trying to make a new discovery at this late stage in her life. Surely discoveries were always possible. He looked down at his book prepared to make his own, to divine something new, something important; he was ready but nothing came. Today the words might just as well have not been there. He pushed the first volume aside and looked at the second. Only three from the list. A white clock by the stairwell. He had not been here long and already he wondered why he was bothering, what he was trying to achieve. The old lady took down a book and made her way to a chair. He might ask her a question, following a vague sensation that she might be able to offer insight. What is she reading anyway? In the corner of his eye he saw the Librarian. Not in red today, but otherwise as he recalled her. Perhaps more attractive. "Isn't she lovely, the Mistress?" Where did that come from? He glanced at the old lady; for a moment he almost felt as if she had whispered the words to him from her chair. "Isn't she lovely, the Mistress?" He looked at the Librarian arranging books on a trolley. And those words; where did they come from? On his desk the second book was still closed; they had not come from there. He searched his memory for the origin of this fugitive phrase. "Isn't she lovely…" The Librarian bending down, oblivious, unconcerned, absorbed in her work. Suddenly he thought of Betjeman. "Isn't she lovely…" He stood up and walked toward the shelves. The old lady looked up from her book. So, he thought, it's your turn to watch. And all the while conscious of the presence of the young Librarian, the attractive girl, the Mistress. B. He looked along shelves. Blake, not him; Browning, a fine Romance there. The old lady turned again to her book; he thought of the three on his desk, the ones he should be working from. Ah, Betjeman. Returning to his seat he noticed the Librarian gone. Where? The trolley was still there. Downstairs no doubt, out of his view. Back to the honeycomb with another book, collecting like a bee. What honey was he trying to make then? "Isn't she lovely..." His eye ran down the index; he would not be happy until he had discovered the poem. As he scanned, his mind was aware of the old lady, the shelves, the clock on the wall. Were they there even when he was no longer looking at them? The eye of the beholder perhaps; but that was all philosophy anyway. "Isn't..." The phrase returned in his mind but he was unable to find it. He checked again. There was a sound: the old lady stood up and walked towards the shelves with her book. Almost involuntarily he watched her replace the book and totter to the stairs. So, she was not taking it out with her. He checked his watch. He expected the Librarian to appear; where was she when she should be here, attending the trolley? Back to the index; perhaps he expected the phrase to have appeared, miraculously implanted by the old lady's departure. "Isn't she lovely, the Mistress..." He could not find it. Perhaps it was not Betjeman after . all; perhaps it was someone else. He began flicking through, studying the poems: could the index have been that much at fault? Then the sight of his other books - the second one still unopened - arrested his search. He rose again and began walking to the shelves. At the top of the stairs the Librarian suddenly appeared. "Excuse me Miss, but I'm looking for poem!" How could he ask her for assistance? B. Blake, Browning. There, suddenly, another Betjeman volume. He looked at the one in his hand: a different edition. Was this the book the old lady had been looking at? He took it down. "Isn't..." The Librarian was back at trolley, now taking armfuls of books for re-shelving. "Isn't she lovely, the Mistress, with her wide apart grey green eyes..." Then suddenly, as he read, she was there at his side. B. Blake, Browning. What should he do?

He read on conscious of both her and the poem. One by one, her books went back. To say something: "This poem..." But she was gone. He finished reading. He had found his poem, the poem he had wanted to read. The books on the desk: if only it were that easy. And to the old lady he would have said: "Isn't she lovely, the Mistress." Perhaps the woman had been reading the poem aloud; that was why heard it. He put the book back; I shall read it again, he thought. The Librarian was gone and he went back to his seat. What had she thought, he wondered as he opened his second book, standing so close to him, re-shelving like that. Probably her mind had been far away; surely there could be no place in there for him, not in the same way as he thought of her. The second uninspiring volume lay open, uninvitingly. "Isn't she lovely..." Perhaps the old lady knew, that was why he had had the vague desire to speak to her. Or this book, here in front of him; if only he were prepared to read, to try. Was this real involvement after all? The white clock; time and restlessness. He looked up. Those shelves - "which book?" All was quiet, no one moved. As a child, libraries had been a magic place of discovery. He thought of the old lady and wondered if there were a difference in age after all. Perhaps not. "Isn't she lovely, the Mistress..." There he had found something. He looked at his watch. The third book would have to stay unopened, he could not attempt it now. As he gathered up this things, he wondered where all his enthusiasm had gone; lost somewhere between the desk and the shelves, between the Librarian and the old lady. He stood. Should he leave those books there, those plain volumes? "Isn't she lovely..." He didn't feel like reading that again and cursed vaguely the green carpet, the shelving, the absence of a lift which made old ladies attack the stairs. He walked past the shelves all asking "which books?" B: Betjeman, Blake, Browning...

Vinno

Vinno killed his first person when he was only thirteen. It wasn't a cold-blooded killing of course; at least not in the sense of premeditation. His mother was seeing an unsavoury type from another block on the estate - her only diversion since his father had walked out on them and left her, Vinno and his kid sister to fend for themselves. Brad - the guy from the Parker block - used to drink too much. It was, Vinno knew, a common enough problem on the estate (especially since they closed down the car plant) and not one he considered unusual; after all, his mother liked the sauce a little bit herself. But Brad, an ignorant brute of a man, became violent when he was drunk - or, more accurately, when he was on his way to being drunk - and if Vinno were around the chances were that he'd feel the back of Brad's hand at some point. Tracy - Vinno's sister - was usually spared; more often than not because Vinno got in the way. He grew to hate Brad pretty quickly. It wasn't difficult. If his mother also suffered at his hands she hid it well. Vinno couldn't be sure. Maybe he hurt her where the kids wouldn't see.

Brad drove a small Ford van. He worked occasionally as a builder's mate, doing odd jobs on building sites in the town when he was sober enough to realise he was hard up. Brad had a reputation. He'd put a foreman into hospital one time for refusing to give him work, and the word spread. There was a routine where he'd turn up on site, demand work, collect money, get pissed, and then head back to Montacute Tower to beat-up Vinno's family. Brad drove the van like a maniac, even when sober. Vinno's mum once joked that Brad had probably never passed his test. She didn't joke often.

Vinno couldn't say whether or not the manner of Brad's driving had given him the idea. It probably hadn't, although later he allowed himself to be less than definitive on the subject. In any event, Vinno only admitted to wanted to scare Brad. On that day he knew he'd been out working, and he knew that sooner or later the dirty white van would career back onto the estate. Vinno waited near the much-vandalised lock-up garages, hiding behind a parked car. A little before eleven (he knew he should have been home and that his mother would be a little worried, but it wasn't as if it was the first time he'd stayed out late) Vinno heard the tell-tale squeal of Brad's attempt to navigate the narrow entrance to Montacute. He waited until the van was within thirty yards then feinted to dash out into the road. Brad, already the worse for wear, instinctively swerved to miss the boy. That there was no control in what he did led to the van slamming straight into the lock-ups. There was a scream from the engine along with the crunch of metal and splintering of glass. Vinno froze. He wanted to run, but almost instantly there was was someone there; someone who knew him. He had to think quickly and screamed "Brad!" He made sure the neighbour stopped him before he could get to the van.

The police were there soon enough - as was a fire crew to cut Brad's lifeless body from the wreck. The Coppers listened to his story - he was only running to get home, after all - then took him back to his mother. She was relieved to have her son back. Vinno watched as the Coppers told her what had happened. She was shocked, sure; but her son could see there was relief mixed in too. After the police left, she hugged Vinno for a while, rocking him gently. He knew he'd done her a big favour - and he knew she knew it too.

She'd christened him Vincent; he didn't know why, but guessed it was after some guy she'd known or a Hollywood movie star. For years she'd managed to stop herself shortening his name, even though his father referred to him as Vinny from the day he was born. As he grew up, Vinno began to detest the common abbreviation: he didn't like 'Vincent' either and he didn't want to be known as Vinny. He wanted something different. He derided his sister for submitting to 'Trace', and for a while attempted to find other derivatives of Tracy to see if he could conjure up something a little more enlightened. She told him to stop being silly; she liked being called 'Trace'. When he was ten, Vinno saw his first real bottle of wine. The Manzoni's - an Italian family from across the way - invited them over for a party to celebrate their daughter's new baby, and Vinno saw bottle after bottle labelled 'Vino'. Manzoni told him what it meant, and to Vinno it seemed somehow exotic and exciting. He stuck another 'n' in the word for effect and announced to the world that he was now to be known as 'Vinno'. For two weeks he beat up any kid at school who called him anything else.

By the time of Brad's demise, Vinno had already established a reputation for himself. He was tough, sure; but all the kids on the estate had to be tough to survive. He could look after himself pretty much, and though he didn't belong to any gang, other kids knew they were far better off in Vinno's good books than not. A kid from Parker once spat at his sister and Vinno knocked out two of his teeth with one punch. That summed up the kind of kid he was. Mr Manzoni - who'd taken a shine to the boy - would wave away objections to Vinno's behaviour with a cry of "but he's good to his mother!" At school the day after Brad's accident, a hush fell over the classroom as Vinno entered - last, as usual. Even Mrs Simpson noticed the change.

"Are you all right, Vincent?" she asked as he sat down.

"Miss?"

"After the...accident. If you need to be home for a day or so..."

Vinno looked her straight in the eye.

"No, Miss. But thanks."

His mother had always told him there was never any excuse for rudeness. It was one of the few things Vinno believed - at least most of the time.

In spite of the trouble he occasionally caused her, Mrs Simpson liked Vinno. He was a bright boy who, in her view, chose not to apply himself. Sometimes he would surprise her with the speed he could assimilate things - but most of the time he was lazy and frustrating. She had tried talking to him, persuading him of the virtues of a good education, and though he had steadfastly declined to take school seriously, she made a pact with herself to get him something from the exams he would be taking when he was sixteen.

The next two years after Brad's death passed quickly enough. Vinno was moved into my class when he started in year ten: no-one told him why, and he didn't care much anyway. I'd heard about him, of course - I knew the boy who'd had his teeth punched in - but I'd never spoken to him. Maybe it was luck that I had the only spare space in class next to me; if you can call it luck, that is.

Vinno didn't mix at break like the rest of the kids. Sometimes he'd go off, then suddenly reappear just as the bell was going. That was odd. And something else. The rest of us used to cheat like shit - especially in maths - but he didn't. Ever. Once, just as I was going to lean over to Fatty Pete and get an answer to a sum I couldn't do, I felt Vinno hold my arm. You didn't ignore that.

"What you doin'?" he asked.

"Jus' gettin' the ans'er from Fatty."

"Why?"

I couldn't answer that one either.

He pulled me back and started to show me how to work it out. By the time he got shouted at for talking in class he'd done enough so that I could do it for myself. Don't think I ever got another answer from Fatty Pete after that. I started to try for myself, and if I needed help I'd ask Vinno.

Later that year some of the kids managed to get hold of some blow. We'd been smoking fags for ages now, but we'd assumed dope was some ultimate adult sensation. Vinno didn't smoke - or at least I'd never seen him at it. When he saw what we were doing in the park after school one day, he came over.

"What's that?" he asked, knowing the answer.

"Dope," said Fatty Pete, proudly.

"You said it."

If Vinno didn't smoke, we knew he drank; sometimes he'd arrive back at school after lunch with the faint small of his mother's whisky on him. He was only drunk once. Mrs Simpson (who was teaching us all by then, old man Harvey having had his nervous breakdown) called for the Head, and Vinno was marched off to Butler's office. We didn't see him the rest of the day, but he was there - late again - when we sat down in the morning.

"You ok?" I knew it was none of my business, and that he was just as likely to kick my head in as answer me - but I had to know.

"Got a lesson for you, Marty. You can do what you like in life, OK? - but just don't get caught."

We were getting closer to the exams and our escape from school forever. Most of us seemed to rip roughly through puberty, determined to get it over with as quickly as possible, all wanting to be men. All except Vinno. He kind of glided through it, like growing up was something to be savoured; almost like he'd been there before and knew what was coming. I even wondered once if he might not already be a man, and puberty existed just to show him how he'd got there - or what he'd missed. It fitted, kind of. No fags, but drank booze; that seemed pretty grown-up. Didn't play football or indulge in any of the juvenile stuff that got the rest of us into trouble. It seemed that Vinno's trouble was of an entirely different order.

In late March there was a robbery at the local Post Office. A couple of days later two coppers came into class to speak with Mrs Simpson. She called Vinno forward and he left with the Bill. Came back a little while later - and acted like nothing had happened. I don't know when the rumours started - before or after that visit - but it was whispered that Vinno had been involved somehow in the Post Office job. He was known to hang about with some older types from Montacute - and there was always the legend of Brad. We knew he hadn't suddenly turned goody-goody or kept his nose clean; the odd scuff on his face or bandage round his hand was enough to fuel the speculation.

When we could find time between the blow and the football, the rest of us would-be men were trying hard to discover girls. They wanted pretty much the same as we did, and, by and large, were already best part of their way there. Breasts and short skirts had stirred us for a while of course, with the exception of the odd one or two, but the fact that they weren't interested in boys our age didn't help. The lads from Parker who'd already quit school were prime targets for the girls in our year. All we could do was to look on and wish time would pass a little more quickly. Very occasionally there was a story of manly heroism almost being rewarded, but none of us could seem to boast more than a quick grope - often paid for with a few fags or a lump of black. The exception was probably Vinno, of course. Yet even though all the girls seemed interested in him, he treated them with the same cool detachment he showed the rest of us. Dumb Mike once suggested he was gay. Luckily for him it was out of Vinno's hearing. For the rest of us, we took it for granted that Vinno was already an accomplished sexual athlete - he just chose to keep it private, like everything else.

Tracy, only a year Vinno's junior, was catching up fast. She was a good-looking kid; slim like her brother, with long dark hair and flashing eyes. She wasn't as wild as him, but liked to pretend she was. Guess she figured that Vinno's celebrity allowed her to be a little precocious, and her brother's classmates - by being that little bit older than her - were obvious targets. She used to hang around with a couple of other girls from her class, Lisa and Pammy. They used to try and out-do each other in the amount of make-up they could get away with, or in the shortness of the skirts they wore. Sometimes, when we played football in the park after school, they'd hang around, sitting on the benches, teasing us something chronic. It bugged most of us, I guess; I mean, it had to, didn't it? They were both good looking kids too - and they already seemed to know what sex was all about. That was part of their allure. Most of us seemed to be able to handle the taunting okay. We'd josh each other about it; tell rude jokes; gee each other on to see if we could get close enough to get a feel for free. Pammy had a reputation for being easy meat - all you had to do was ask her nicely.

For Fatty Pete though, the teasing was difficult to handle. He'd got it into his tiny skull that he was in love with Tracy, and seeing her flaunt herself made him angry. More than that, it made him want her more. She knew it, of course, and so the girls used to pick him out - and boy, when they got the bit between their teeth, were they something! I guess Tracy also felt a little bit sorry for Fatty; he was shite at everything and we all gave him a hard time because of it. Vinno didn't like Fatty Pete. Maybe there was nothing in him for Vinno to respect. It was clear when he respected someone for who they were or what they were trying to do; he even stepped in on Mrs Simpson's side more than once. He knew Fatty had the bug-eye for Tracy and he despised him for it. One morning a rumour started that Fatty and Tracy had been seen together in the park the previous evening. After break, Fatty returned to class with a split lip. Said he'd fallen over. Vinno didn't look at him and we all knew what had happened.

Then things went pretty quiet for a few weeks. Somehow Mrs Simpson had managed to drum the importance of exams into a few of us. It even seemed like Vinno was making more of an effort, especially in maths where he seemed to have the knack. He wouldn't admit it, mind. We started doing test papers in preparation, and for those of us who - despite our public bravado to the contrary - were actually hoping for a good result or two, the significance of early June began to establish itself. It was a quiet kind of time. There weren't so many fights; there was less football, less leering after girls. We were't angels, don't get me wrong, but it was different.

From what I knew, Vinno's home life had become a little more stable too. His mother had found herself another man; he had something of both Brad and her former husband in him but seemed, in the main, to be a little bit better than both. Things weren't perfect; maybe they never would be as far as she was concerned, but at least she and the kids weren't getting beaten up. Vinno didn't talk about Chas - that was the guy's name - but perhaps that was enough; that and the fact that he didn't pull any darting-from-behind-cars kind of stunts.

It was the Saturday before our first exam when all hell broke loose. A few of us were hanging around the park. We'd gone there to play football but as hardly anyone had turned up, we were just sitting around smoking. We saw Lisa and Pammy, and as usual Dumb Mike whistled at them - something which at first seemed to have pulled them in our direction. It hadn't, of course.

"Guess what?" Pammy said, intent on proving that she was as loose with her tongue as she was with every other part of her anatomy. She didn't wait for us to guess. "Trace's pregnant!"

"What?!"

As Dumb Mike spoke, I instinctively looked around.

"Where's Fatty?"

"Fatty? Why Fatty?" Pammy missed the connection.

"'Cos Vinno's goin' to be lookin' for 'im."

Lisa laughed.

"It ain't Fatty's baby!"

"Who's put her up the duff, then?" asked Mike.

"She won't say."

"That don't matter," I said, "'cos Vinno's going to think it's Fatty's and he's goin' to go lookin' for 'im."

It was a perfunctory council of war, but it didn't take us long to decide that there two people we needed to find - Vinno and Fatty Pete. Dumb Mike and I opted for Vinno, the rest split up to go searching for Fatty.

We left the others scouring the park and made our way towards the centre of town. There was a small arcade of shops not far from the school where I'd seen Vinno hanging about with some of his older friends. The Post Office that got done was there. Not seeing him, we nipped into a couple of shops in the unlikely event that he might have been inside. There was nothing doing.

"What now?" said Dumb Mike as we stood outside the newsagents.

Not only did I have no idea 'what now', but it hadn't occurred to me what we would do if we *did* find Vinno. The prospect of having to somehow deal with him made me shiver.

"Dunno. Let's go back to Montacute."

As chance would have it, we arrived on the estate at the same time as the others, who, having drawn a blank in the park, had swung by the school on their way to Parker. Fatty Pete lived in Parker.

Others had beaten us to the estate. Three Cop cars were parked by Montacute and another flashed by us, lights and horns going like the clappers. A small group of people had gathered there too, all looking upwards. From the edge of the estate it was impossible to see what they were looking at, but when we got closer - or as close as the Fuzz would let us - everything became clear. On the walkway on the fourth floor - Vinno's floor - a figure was standing precariously on the railing. He was screaming. It was Fatty Pete. Invisible at first, once I realised what was going on I could just about see the hands holding the back of his trousers; and then the figure doing the holding. It was Vinno. I could see he was shouting, but it was difficult to hear what he was saying above Fatty Pete's screams. At either end of the walkway, two Coppers waited.

"Get back!" I heard Vinno shout. "Get fuckin' back!"

The Coppers didn't move.

Fatty was screaming for help, but there was no-one who could; he was at Vinno's mercy. I found myself wanting to try.

"Vinno, don't!" I shouted. "Vinno, don't!"

Vinno couldn't hear. Or he didn't want to hear. Keeping one eye on the Coppers, it appeared as if he had begun to talk to Fatty Pete. The screams subsided a little, replaced by sobs. He appeared to be answering Vinno's questions. For a brief moment it seemed as if sanity was returning.

And then Vinno let go.

All around there were screams. Fatty Pete's scream of terror was multiplied a hundred-fold by the echo from the tower blocks and the cries of the onlookers. He fell in slow motion, screaming all the way. Just a couple of seconds, then none of us looked. The screaming stopped.

Hidden by cars, we couldn't see where Fatty had fallen, which was probably just as well. I looked up. The Coppers had their hands on Vinno. He wasn't struggling. Behind me I could hear Pammy and Lisa crying, and from somewhere else another cry I recognised but couldn't locate: Tracy. The figures moved from the walkway and a few moments later reappeared at the entrance to Montacute: two Coppers followed by Vinno, another Copper on each arm. He didn't look at us; just stared straight ahead, straight at the car that he was to be bundled into - like he was staring at his future.

They locked him up of course. After all, they had no choice. There was no mistaking his intention with regard to Fatty Pete. Rumour had it that he admitted wanting to kill Brad. And someone said that he coughed for the Post Office job and a load of other stuff too. His mum was heart-broken. They didn't send him to prison like we expected, but decided to lock him up in one of those secure hospitals. A couple of weeks after the trial, Tracy and her mum left Montacute and went away.

I still think about Vinno sometimes. Obvious I guess. He was important to a lot of us in a strange kind of way. He gave me the best piece of advice I'd ever had: 'Do what you like, but don't get caught'. Guess I'm glad I followed it too - though that doesn't stop the nightmares where it's me and not Fatty Pete being pushed off the walkway at Montacute. Yep, that's right; Vinno's sister was having my kid.

Anne

She did not like the London underground at the best of times. Many years previously - and before her own lifetime, when they still ran steam engines below ground - it had been, she supposed, a revolutionary mode of transport, new enough and fresh enough to possess an air of excitement and adventure. But that romance was now long since gone and it had become part of the fabric, like arteries pumping the city's lifeblood around. At least that was how she felt about it.

For the most part however, her reaction was one of general indifference; yet here, descending the escalators of Tottenham Court Road station, such indifference moved beyond a somewhat detached emotional response. To her mind, this particular cog in the machine represented all that was bad about the outdated London system: it was cramped, always busy with too many people; it was dingy and dirty; and there was an unpleasant smell about the place that seemed, to her at least, unique to this location. Evidence of renovation or remodelling (or whatever they were calling it this week!) was growing, and Anne assumed, with surprisingly little satisfaction on her part, that once the work was completed at least some components of her distaste - the darkness, the filth, the odour - might be compromised away.

She moved closer to the handrail as a stream of people walked down past her. Someone bumped her shoulder; a bag rapped the side of her leg. A typical journey then.

On the tiled side-walls, posters were promoting West End shows. Depictions of the joyous cast of "Cats!" were interspersed with images of the slightly less joyous cast of "Les Miserables", all of which could only combine to darken her mood further. She could see no point in musicals. Many years previously, when she had lived in Central London, she had been persuaded to try one or two. It was not, she had told herself, such a big leap from opera - which she could just about cope with - only to discover that it was indeed a jump, and one far beyond the range her sensibilities were able to reasonably accommodate. The idea of "Les Miserables" made her hackles rise particularly, and she could imagine Victor Hugo grave-bound spinning. In her most severe and puritanical mood, to translate the original from French into another language seemed sacrilegious enough, so the 'dumbing down' of the classic story another few notches into musical theatre was beyond the pale. Being an intelligent woman, she was of course aware of the arguments about making great art 'accessible', but for her such modern incarnations were actually stripping that same art of its core greatness, creating something 'other'. As she stepped off the escalator she found herself wondering - not for the first time - whether people might wish to glue arms back on the Venus de Milo in order to make that more accessible too.

The overhead sign read "Ealing Broadway, 3 minutes". She would take the train one stop to Oxford Circus (another station she ordinarily avoided like the plague), and then down to Victoria from there. When she came up to town, her usual route from Victoria was to Russell Square via Green Park, a journey that had the distinct advantage of missing out the Central Line altogether. If someone had wished to challenge her, they might well have argued that her present routing would get her to and from the British Museum slightly quicker than going via Russell Square. But she preferred that station, the ensuing walk by the gardens; it had become her journey of choice, primarily because it allowed her to arrive at the museum in as neutral a frame of mind as possible, having avoided being undermined not only by Tottenham Court Road station itself, but by the hoards of tourists who trod the path from there to the British Museum's doors.

Today she had been compromised by her offer to run an errand for a friend back in Sussex, a good deed framed explicitly enough to force her into the large 'Paperchase' on Tottenham Court Road itself, and then, in consequence, encumber her with a large carrier bag that seemed to be growing heavier by the moment.

"Ealing Broadway, 2 minutes".

All this was a far cry from Horsham, of course. Indeed, the soul-destroying repetition of an inner London commuter's daily routine had been a significant factor in her decision to move out of the city. That and the opportunity to take up a relatively senior position at the Horsham Museum. She had been aware that moving into a provincial role represented something of a risk. The British Museum had been her home for years. It was where she had first embarked on her chosen profession, and though her progress had been relatively modest and her breadth of responsibility at any one time never particularly wide, it was an institution which had quickly come to mean more to her than just a job - and leaving it after nearly twenty years was, for some of her colleagues at least, breathtaking folly.

Neither her new job nor living in Sussex had proven particularly easy at first, and it took her well over a year to acclimatise to both. Now, a further twelve years on, she knew her original decision had been vindicated; it only took a brief journey on the Central Line to confirm as much! In her work she had also moved on professionally. What was locally regarded as her 'classical training' in Bloomsbury made her stand out from her workmates further south, and opportunities arose from time-to-time which allowed her to spread her influence in the county; at first in smaller, local institutions at

Henfield, Steyning and Storrington, and then, more recently, as Consultant Curator at Parham House.

If she had been reflecting on her career at that moment, the telltale breeze from the approaching train would have roused her from that reverie. Once again shifting the carrier bag from one hand to the other, she inched towards the edge of the platform. It was early afternoon; hopefully the train would not be too much of a crush. Yet even if it were, it was a brief discomfort which, although reminiscent of her past commute, needed to be endured.

During those first few difficult months in Horsham, she had made a point of returning to the British Museum once a month. It was, she judged, both a safe way of medicating her removal from daily life there as well as providing her with the opportunity to keep at least part of herself attached to the familiar and well-loved. Initially her return visits were spent as much behind the scenes catching up with old friends as anything else, drinking tea and gossiping. But as time passed and those friends moved on too - retiring, mostly - she found herself less and less an ex-member of staff and more and more a visitor. Unsettling at first, it was an experience which offered her a freedom she had not felt for two decades. Over time, this 'invisibility' allowed her to explore with a new passion, to uncover that which enthralled and fascinated her rather than be preoccupied by that for which she held some kind of responsibility. And so it was - and this very much to her own surprise - that she found herself recurrently drawn to the Assyrian collection, a civilisation and epoch which had held almost no interest for her all the while she had been resident there. Today had been no different. An hour in her favourite galleries, an hour or so general meandering, and then lunch. It was a battery recharge that was sufficient to allow shopping, Tottenham Court Road and the Central Line; the whole, a private umbilical cord which, in confirming an ongoing attachment, permitted her life in Sussex. She was also able to justify it professionally, to others as much as to herself. It was, she argued, an opportunity to keep her finger on the pulse, to see how the biggest museum in the land was operating, to see what changes and innovations were in train - however minor - and to steal those she could adapt and adopt in her provincial world. And if this argument was indeed valid, it was one which needed to bear fruit now more than ever.

Although there were some free seats, she remained standing for the short jump to Oxford Circus, indulging - as did all Londoners pretty much - in the Underground's unique pastime of looking without seeing, of managing to avoid any meaningful contact, and to remain safe within the security such lack of engagement offered. It was, of course, a somewhat contrary pursuit given the very real and intimate physical contact a rush hour crush could often enforce. The rise of the mobile phone had been a massive boon to the City's travellers, providing them with an even better excuse for keeping their heads down for the entirety of their journey, and thereby not only maintain privacy but mitigate the risk of actually seeing anything at all.

Hurrying through Oxford Circus station - and seemingly always against the tide of bodies going in each and every other direction - she gained the southbound Victoria platform to find her next train already approaching. She knew she would arrive at the mainline terminus at an 'in-between' kind of time, most likely having just missed one Horsham train and thus facing the maximum wait for the next one. But it was of little consequence. Sitting down this time (even though it was just two stops) she managed to catch her reflection in the opposite carriage window just as they were on the move. It was a split second of recognition, a breaking of the major unwritten rule of tube travel, that of not making eye contact - even if it was with yourself.

Considering her age and her rather sedentary profession, Anne was many things she had no right to be: older than she looked, slimmer than she should have been, and - if you were prepared to truly look into them - with eyes that were clear, deep and blemish free, her age betrayed only by the soft wrinkles in the skin around them. Given the dryness of her passions - for facts, history, the absoluteness of things - she should not have been as spiky, forthright and emotional as she sometimes could be. Perhaps once upon a time she had been charming (and charm-able!), warm, smiling, personable and engaging; but that would be to describe a person she would have failed to recognise had such an individual looked back at her from the reflection across the carriage. Yet although she dealt in the black-and-whiteness of 'exhibits', she still liked to think that she did so with the temperament of an artist rather than that of the museum curator. If this were fanciful, it was probably her only self-indulgence - other than a weakness for the British Museum in general, and sculpture in particular.

It was this weakness - allied with an almost reverential love of the sculptor - that was now in danger of causing her considerable trouble. Whilst much of what she had grown up with during her burgeoning career was cast or hewn or chipped and chiseled into remarkable and venerated artefacts, and whilst much of what she had become responsible for were those very same physical objects, she found herself inexorably drawn to the individuals who had executed those castings, made the moulds, poured-in their molten contents, and to those who had wielded the mallet, the chisel, and who had sat, hour upon hour, covered in dust and fragments of marble. These were her true gods, and the protection of their creations was really about their persistence as heroes. It was her job to ensure they were never forgotten.

Even if this notion was romantic - and there were those who had divined it in her, analysed it, and challenged her accordingly - and she privately acknowledged and accepted the charge, publicly she would assert the logic of her position, of her responsibility, almost as if she had taken a sacred oath that only death could see her break. And whilst she had, thus far in her career, skilfully managed to navigate the waters between artist and artefact in such a way as to ensure a harmony of purpose, her present challenge threatened to puncture that perfect record.

Emerging from the underground at Victoria and onto the platform concourse represented, geographically at least, the return to battle. Checking the departure boards for her next train she found she had twenty-seven minutes to kill, exactly as she had suspected.

"Look Anne, no-one doubts your knowledge, professionalism, and integrity in all of this - and no-one can possibly question your contribution over the past few years - but we must move on..."

His use of the word 'integrity' had riled her somewhat, though she was unsure exactly why. It had been a compliment of sorts. But Terence - "Terry, to my friends!" - had quickly settled on such a negative appreciation of her that, no matter what he said, there was always bound to be something she could find to rouse her to the fight.

It wasn't as if - at a basic level - she had any real objections to what he was trying to achieve, this Johnny-come-lately fresh from a multi-award-winning industrial museum somewhere in the Midlands. His brief - at least as he had explained it - was to work alongside the current Sussex staff (and Anne in particular, given her seniority and influence) with the goal of 'modernising' their 'offering' to the public.

"We need to find ways of getting more people through the doors. It's all about footfall. We have to engage our customers, delight and challenge them in equal measure. We have to find ways to sell to them."

As she walked towards platform four, the sight of a man reading the paper, his pose marginally too studied and his pinstripe suit just a little too showy, brought back that first meeting. Her goodwill and the persona of a modest, collaborative colleague had lasted less than fifteen minutes, invisibly expelled from the meeting room by his use of business jargon and words like 'footfall', 'customers', 'engage' and 'sell'. Perhaps 'modernise' most of all. Her transition into combat mode had been evident to everyone else in the meeting other than Terence for the simple reason (if one were being generous) that he didn't know her well enough to be able to recognise the material shift. Thirty minutes later, Chris, the most junior member of her team took what, on reflection, was something of a brave step by praising Anne to her face (as they waited for the kettle to boil) and denouncing Terence's "bullshit bingo". Anne had been forced to rebuke Chris of course, but secretly she was appreciative of the support and hoped he had a good future ahead of him. It was pleasing to know she had allies. She hadn't lost her touch entirely.

Pulling out the new pamphlets and leaflets she had recently liberated from the British Museum, Anne settled into her seat hoping, as ever, that the one next to her would remain empty for the entirety of the journey to Horsham. Terence's grand plan for modernisation, to be executed throughout West Sussex where it made sense to do so, was to try and replace the static with the mobile and digital. He envisaged a museum-world with more screens, and more 'collateral' for people to touch and interact with. It was, he asserted, a strategy that worked. "But only at large industrial museums in the Black Country" was what she had wanted to say. Given a second chance, she was certain she would say it now. With the battle lines drawn and it being clear to Terence where she stood, he would no longer be surprised to encounter such a statement.

"I understand what is required of us" - this was exactly what she *had* said - "and it was something we did at the BM for a number of years, continuously trying to improve things, making a visit more stimulating, especially for children."

"Well then." He had smiled one of his pin-stripe smiles.

"But we aren't the BM. We don't have the resources, the funds. And what we 'sell', as you put it, is something completely different; a smaller scale, let's be honest. And nowhere near as tactile and physical as many other museums."

If he had noted the subtle barb about his recent past, he chose to ignore it. He had come back with counter arguments of his own; that there was a fund for making changes, and that no-one expected local museums to suddenly feel like the Science or Natural History Museums.

"We aren't South Kensington!" he had said with a flourish, and glanced around the room almost as if he were expecting applause for a gem of a statement intended to encapsulate everything.

The one concession Anne had made during their first meeting was that, while he continued to hone his proposals, she would utilise her next visit to London - today's visit - to see what the British Museum was up to and whether there were any ideas they could use. She knew from experience there would always be changes, but most were subtle: improving signage and labelling, switching to different colours or fonts; changing the layouts in cabinets and galleries where exhibits were small enough to be easily moved around. And yes, there were one or two more kiosk-type displays that used computers and touch screens.

She knew that if this kind of thing was the extent of Terence's ambition then it should be possible to find common ground, but for her the sticking point was that he also wanted to simplify what was on display, to move things out and into storage. He wanted to 'declutter'. Given his recent background it was only natural that his perspective was coloured by scale, the practical and the pragmatic. He did not - as least as far as Anne could see - allow a single artistic molecule to influence his approach to their work. The embodiment of this was his stated desire to retire around seventy percent of the sculpture they currently had on display.

It was difficult for her to keep a sense of perspective given that Terence's views occupied one end of a curatorial spectrum were forcing her to take an increasingly extreme opposite view. The collection of sculpture under her aegis was limited, she knew that; in many ways it could be argued as being minor - even considering some of the pieces at Parham House - but from one perspective this actually made the collection more important. If they had lost a Degas or a Giacometti to storage, would that have been such a big deal? Personally she would be distraught, but comforted by the fact that there were so many other places in the world where one could see their work. But in West Sussex? In her museums? The majority of such artefacts were from local sculptors' limited outputs and the *only* places in the world where they could be seen. If these were relegated to the back room or a crate in storage somewhere, then for Anne that would be equivalent to the sculptor never having existed at all. They would have killed them.

As it was, their continued existence was already tenuous. Little-known and reliant on their continued and mainly posthumous presence, these sculptors were dependant upon Anne's modest endorsement of their worth - a piece on a plinth here or in a cabinet there - and a limited but loyal audience. Visitor numbers were slim at best and falling at worst. As she flicked through the British Museum leaflets promoting the kind of major scale special exhibitions she used to know so well (even if they were not her favourite events) Anne momentarily longed for the boost such shows could provide; an injection of interest, enthusiasm, support and funding that could stand a museum in good stead. In Steyning or Henfield any event on an even remotely relative scale would be revolutionary! Recognising this was in danger of giving weight to Terence's proposals of course; or at least the motivations behind them. What if he was right? What if taking up his suggestions *did* lead to a sufficient boost in visitor numbers, the fabled 'footfall'? It might breathe new life into her charges, perhaps leading to more people becoming aware of those she was championing and trying to protect. But what if the innovations failed? What if the artists were forgotten in the interim when the museums were closed for refurbishment - another contentious point! - or if the sculptures never made it back from storage in spite of record visitors, the increased income, the publicity?

If there was a balance to be struck - and part of her could not deny the feeling that a compromise existed somewhere - as she sat waiting on the train any further thoughts on the subject were interrupted. At first there were the sounds of voices, then the sense of presence, a flicker in her peripheral vision, and then immediately in front of her a boy and his mother.

"Here will do," the woman said, indicating the seats opposite Anne.

The boy more or less threw himself into the seat by the window, simultaneously managing to remove his jacket. He handed it to his mother as she prepared to remove her own.

Anne watched the scene play out in front of her, the woman putting coats in the rack overhead then removing a paper bag from its much larger canvas companion before hoisting that upwards too. Anne recognised the bold, geometric shapes of the Science Museum logo adorning the paper bag from which, now seated, the woman removed a book and passed it wordlessly to the boy.

"He loves the Science Museum," she said, almost apologetically.

Anne realised she had been staring. She tried a smile.

"And so he should," she concurred. "Science and a boy his age, match made in heaven."

She had never been good at guessing children's ages, so an approximation was all she could manage. He could have been anything between eight and thirteen as far as she was concerned; probably around eleven. She glanced down at the leaflets in her left hand and tried to squirrel them away before the woman noticed - but it was too late, a connection had been made.

"We come up at least once every holiday and half-term," she ventured, her tone suggesting a need to justify where they had been. "More in the summer holidays, of course."

Anne nodded, hoping to close down the exchange - not because she wanted to be rude, but because she felt she had more important things to consider. She glanced at her watch wishing the train would move.

The woman had evidently not finished.

"We have this arrangement. We take turns to decide where to go, which museum to visit."

Anne looked back to the woman at this point, unable to stop herself. She was probably in her early forties, a little care-worn perhaps, but smartly enough dressed and clearly educated. Her voice was calm, her tone even, her accent precise enough.

"It was Toby's choice this time - hence the Science Museum. Then it will be mine. And then we discuss and agree on the one after that. Then it's back to Toby's choice again." She paused, expecting a response.

"That sounds like a good plan," Anne said, encouragingly, glancing at the boy who was too absorbed in his book to contribute. "I expect he always chooses the Science Museum?"

The woman smiled, pleased that her new travelling companion had taken up the baton. Anne wondered how many adult conversations the mother had been engaged in recently.

"Oh, he would love to! But we have a rule: you can't choose the same museum for consecutive visits. So, the next time it's Toby's choice he'll probably go for the Natural History. That and Science. Isn't that what all kids want to see? Big animals and somewhere with lots of buttons to press!"

"What about you? Doesn't that get a little dull?"

"Sometimes, I suppose. But as long as he's happy... My favourite is the V&A actually. I love it there. When it's my turn I tend to choose the big galleries; the Tate, the National. And the British Museum, of course." She nodded towards the pamphlets that had not yet made it to Anne's bag. "Our joint choices can be anything. We went to Greenwich last holidays.

That way he gets to see a broad range of things - even if he doesn't really like them yet. I think it's important, don't you?"

Anne nodded and smiled. She knew it would have been possible to answer the question, but doing so would have taken too long, committed her too much. Undoubtedly she would have found herself compelled to divulge her own theories and prejudices, and the last thing she wanted to do was to influence - or be influenced. Not here, not now. What this woman was doing for her son was laudable, to be celebrated; there should be more people with the drive, conscience, ambition to do as much for their children. She wanted to ask the woman what worked for her, how those establishments succeeded or failed in engaging them? How did they fight off boredom in a young person only really interested in pushing buttons, computer keyboards, and life-like reconstructions of dinosaurs? But now was not the right time.

From somewhere outside a whistle blew, and then there was a jolt. The train was moving.

Hobart

It started with his name. It always did. Hobart. "Dear Hobart"; that was how the letter opened. A friendly beginning not only from someone he didn't know (in spite of the christian-name-only signature at the bottom), but also the representative of a committee of invisible, largely faceless individuals. He was aware of one or two of them by reputation of course, renowned throughout their mutual profession and fit to be acting as judges on that score alone. However, unlike his own, their names were largely unremarkable, even if their work was not. What, he wondered, did they make of his: a hand-me-down appellation, the result of his one-generation-removed pseudo-Australian artistic parents who somehow never forgave themselves for having deserted the motherland well before the boys had been born.

He glanced up from the letter and across the kitchen table at which he sat, facing the window and garden beyond. He reminded himself that he had had the best of it, recalling conversations with his brother who had insisted - incontestably - that his own antipodean inheritance was far worse.

"Who the fuck in their right minds calls their son Sydney?!"

It had been a long-standing complaint, though the adoption of an increasingly aggressive tone during his post-teenage years - allied to a liberal sprinkling of swear-words - was a trend which levelled out once he had reached his mid-twenties. In their most recent past, if the subject had come up at all (which it rarely had), Sydney greeted it with silence and a resigned shrug of the shoulders as if everything that could be said had been said long ago. He still managed - in Hobart's eyes at least - to invest a "fuck them!" in the pose his shoulders would adopt.

"At least yours is interesting. I mean, who the hell has ever heard of anyone called 'Hobart'?!"

At the time Hobart knew of none other - though he hadn't searched that hard - and more recently had looked tentatively and briefly, and found no-one with that name on LinkedIn. It was a cursory and inconclusive search; he knew that.

"I mean" - this was his brother, still ranting on his in memory in spite of the current view out into the garden where Hobart could see the flowering tops of the foxgloves he had planted a few years ago - "most people don't even recognise Sydney as a bloke's name. I get some real disappointed looks sometimes, mainly from guys who think that Sydney's going to be some shit-hot hippy chick with tits the size of fry-pans! And Syd's such a crap shortening, I can't even use that..."

These were issues Hobart had not faced. He had never needed to shorten his name (why would he?), and people naturally assumed it was a man's. At school, an older boy had teased him once with the shortened 'Hobo', but Sydney had soon sorted the offender out and the trend died away before it had even begun. Bart was the obvious reduction, but he had never encouraged it and for reasons he couldn't divine, it had never really been tried. Overall, 'Hobart' was a name that conferred a degree of intrigue in advance, before people met him in the flesh, even before he had needed to generate any himself.

"'Hobart'; that's an interesting name..."

He would have settled for a few dollars every time he had heard derivations of that one.

After those first two words, the letter sought to maintain an air of familiarity, as if it had been dictated by someone with their arm around your shoulder. Although the raw content of it was material and ostensibly significant, it strove to retain something of a relaxed tone. It had, Hobart perceived, the air of a special handshake about it; it seemed to have been written by people who belonged to a very exclusive club, and addressed to someone who either inhabited - or might wish to inhabit - that same sphere. There was an undercurrent of invitation about it. It felt like a nod and a wink, somehow. Or at least a nod.

There had been, the letter outlined, a competition. It was an admission verging on the apologetic; a sense magnified when the letter admitted that - without his even knowing - he had been entered into that self same competition. It was not, of course, like the Olympics themselves the letter said. There was no sense of 'higher, faster, stronger' about this event - though Hobart could see how the higher part might apply under certain circumstances.

And why not? the letter asked rhetorically, countering its own apologetic opening. After all, the Olympics represented the best of humankind, so why should that not be extended - in the spirit of celebration! - and embrace *all* that could be achieved? It would be, it suggested, a victory of the mind. The Olympics could only be a triumph if it was given a platform upon which to be successful, and thus - by a thread of argument which was clearly self-promoting - why should there not be a prize to recognise one of those very foundations?

Hobart paused in his more studied re-reading. The premise, he knew, was specious at best, and yet there was some kind of thin logic beneath the surface; a logic that was easy to accept if one had a reason for doing so. Having already read the letter once, he was fully aware of its message, and on that basis - unless he chose to be supremely principled - he could only nod and at least partially agree with them.

It was not a logic that Sydney would have accepted, of course. In fulfilling his role as the family rebel, the self-styled firebrand would most likely have pronounced the whole thing "complete bollocks!" (that cussing again!) and barred his younger brother from having anything to do with the letter or those from whom it had come. Hobart knew Sydney's lack of political correctness would have allowed him to make the latter point with an unfair and probably inaccurate slander on the basis of sexual orientation.

Irrespective of interpretation, the facts were undeniable. There had been - under the auspices of an off-shoot of the British Council and with the tacit if not particularly visible endorsement of the IOC - a decision to create a series of prizes awarded to those Architects whose contributions to the Olympics had been deemed worthy of further recognition. The panel responsible for the shortlisting, as well as the final judgements, had deliberately restricted themselves to projects of a certain size and scale on the basis, they argued, that the designers of the Aquatics Centre, the Velodrome, or the Olympic Stadium itself were highly likely to already have a visible public profile - as well as being in a position to reap the inevitable rewards of the praise and name-dropping that would occur in the media coverage over the duration of The Games. Their desire - said the panel - was to seek out and recognise the sublime, the functional, and the aesthetically pleasing from the myriad of smaller but no less vital contributions.

Hobart wondered just how wide the shortlist had been. When he had been on-site during construction there was building work everywhere. It sometimes felt as if they were building a whole new city rather than an athletics park. Yet even so, as the heavy work finished and the big machinery gave way to dressing the site, it seemed to Hobart as if the entire enterprise had shrunk somewhat; as if it had become focused on just a few key buildings. Wasn't it all about the main stadium and the aquatics centre? If you took those and two or three other things away, what was left, really?

The answer was, of course, quite a lot. And the panel had been at pains to assert that many of the structures which fell into their stated category were somehow unobtrusive - even if some of them were quite large. A new or revamped tube station was hardly modest or invisible, yet because people took it for granted it was somehow made anonymous. Hobart's own offering was a subtle, discrete building that served as an information hub of sorts during the games, and which now had been scaled back with nearly two thirds of it given over to small retail outlets. If you emerged from Pudding Mill Lane station and walked for two minutes in the general direction of anything 'Olympic' it was 'just there'. He had been informed that it had served upwards of half a million people one way or another during the games, and on that front it was already functionally successful.

Strangely, even on this second read through (and perhaps the third or fourth perusal of the key paragraphs), Hobart struggled to identify exactly what he had 'won', if anything. The recognition was evident enough: the letter, his name, references to his building and its multi-faceted 'contribution', all spoke to that. Yet defining the extent of that recognition and any sense of the prize which might be attached to such achievement was much harder to discern. If not impossible.

What *was* clear was that he had - as a result of all this praise heaped on a surprised and unexpecting recipient - been invited to some kind of ceremony at which there would be public recognition of the glories of modern architecture. His place had been reserved, he was told, even to the extent that he would be seated at one of the 'top tables' - the implication clearly being that a prominent location near the stage (assuming there was one) would facilitate a shorter journey for award winners to go up and receive their gongs. Assuming there were any. Yet even all this detail (including, surprisingly, a sample menu!) still provided no indication as to whether he was one of the lucky ones who would be called upon to make that short journey.

The dinner would attract prominent members of the press, he was assured, along with the most bankable contributors in his own profession including those who were always scouting for new and promising talent. It was a carrot without doubt, as if those lucky enough to be stretching their legs under spotlights and general applause might also be strutting a professional catwalk to their next opportunity or perhaps that perfect career move. There was a stick too of course. In addition to the implication that not attending would be verging on professional suicide, there was a 'small fee' relating to participation in the pageant.

"Swindlers!" That's what Sydney would undoubtedly have said (with or without the 'f-word') if he were to have read the letter. "Just a money-making scam to take advantage of the poor saps who are naive enough to believe all their bullshit!"

And Hobart knew his brother would have been at least partially correct. But he also knew that part of *him* - and quite a large part of him at that - believed the baloney; that *he* was naive enough and flattered enough to accept the accolade (whatever it was and almost at whatever price he had to pay); that if he had the chance, however remote and even for the shortest of moments, to bask in some kind of pubic approbation then it was an opportunity he could not turn down. Such an admission, even a private one, stimulated a little guilt - though if his guilt was as an apologetic reaction, then for a moment he struggled to identify the party towards whom he should feel such an emotion.

It was, of course, entirely possible that he was both the guilty party and the one who had been betrayed. For a few seconds he juggled with the notion that his being potentially duped and endorsing the facade (if that was indeed what it proved to be), was nothing more than self-deception. The possibility that he might, simultaneously, be both sinner and the one being sinned against struck him as being the most obvious conclusion. He imagined the window through which he looked into the garden suddenly turn from a frame for the garden and into a large, highly polished mirror in which he might be reflected - the face of the hurt, let down, sacrificial Hobart into whose eyes stared the victorious, publicity-seeking, award-winning other.

Yet this was a vision which disappeared almost in the instant it arose. The lawn, the hedge, the digitalis still there as they had been before, but the echo - if there was one - was not of his face but Sydney's.

He tried to shake the intruding image and returned to the letter, skipping to the bottom of the second page where a tear-off slip was awaiting some personal details to accompany his acceptance of the invitation. If he had glanced to his left - which he did not - he knew he would find the pen and cheque book he had recently used to pay his annual gym subscription. It seemed portentous somehow, even if he could make no immediate link between sweating on a treadmill and a black-tie dinner.

Inevitably perhaps, something made him pause rather than immediately reach for his pen - the logical next move given that he had already made up his mind to attend. The hesitation was not caused by the event itself, but rather a compound buried within him; an episode from his past which fused both Sydney and his profession. It was only natural that, at the very moment he was being praised for his achievements, he should reflect on his past. Never far from his consciousness, one specific reflection had been activated by everything contained within the letter - and especially the invitation, where in bold print on the acceptance slip, it stated he was welcome to take someone with him to the ceremony. This was no surprise. In his limited experience, such functions were often attended by couples to bolster the numbers - and the organisers' income! - and make the evening more appealing for the professional participants.

Once he had attended a dinner where he shared a table with no-one other than architects. It had been monumentally dull and the entire thing a flop. Yet at events where the mix was more representative of everyday existence, there was a natural firebreak in place which prevented single subject monotonous conversation to dominate the evening. Some of his colleagues thrived on the former - especially the more experienced and renowned of them. Under such circumstances they had a perfect platform to show-off their expertise, quickly delving into shallow pontification and empty opinion. Hobart knew this must be true of many professions, not just his own. He guessed that in this present case perhaps forty percent of the attendees might end up being 'outsiders', which would make the whole thing much more palatable.

His own struggle - and that which caused him to pause - was that he would have wanted to take Sydney with him. Yet he could not. Because Sydney was dead. And because he had killed him.

It had been four years ago - before he came to England. There had been no fight, no argument. There was no wielding of knives or pulling of triggers. Everyone agreed - including the papers that had carried the story - that it had been a tragic accident. Perhaps. But given the nature of that accident, how could Hobart do anything other than assume responsibility?

They had been living in Singapore. The city was booming, eating up every acre of land it could find or create, every metre of space above the ground, throwing up ever more elaborate, expansive - expensive! - buildings. His career was still a relatively fledgling one, but it had been a great city in which to practice one's profession especially when architects were in significant demand. He had followed Sydney there from the UK almost as soon as he had graduated, lured by his brother's stories of wealth and riches, of the promise of a lifestyle beyond belief, and of the opportunities available to young men like them. Hobart had not hesitated, and within two years found himself already responsible for half a dozen small but innovative constructions. His was a name that was beginning to be noticed.

If the commission for the mall extension had come as a surprise to him, it was not one he was going to turn down - even if it represented a divergence from the environment of the office complex on which he had initially found himself concentrating. He had been charged with designing something unique - a challenge in a city where it seems as if there is a mall on every street corner. Given he was working within an existing footprint, and given that a shop was a shop was a shop, Hobart decided the real potential for delivering something different would be in the open atrium he was planning to include and in how people moved between between floors.

In addition to the bulk standard escalators needed - though these he would burnish in a mix of copper and deep purple high-gloss plastic - he had alighted on an idea for a spiral staircase that would appear to be 'floating' in the atrium. It had taken a significant degree of design time, sketching, and calculation to arrive at a method where novel use of hidden supports, pillars and disguised stanchions would enable his stairs to be built. He had used Sydney as his sounding board during the design process. His brother grew increasing enthusiastic about the idea, and proved himself an invaluable sounding-board as an educated layman and potential mall user.

When it came to fitting together the multi-part kit in situ, the builders took nearly a week to finalise the assembly, during which time they worked from scaffolding and cherry pickers. Not a single step was taken on the treads themselves.

Sydney had pleaded with Hobart to allow him to 'christen' the stairs by being the first person to climb them from bottom to top, and then back down. Hobart had been surprised how much the project had come to mean to his brother, and allowing his to christen the stairs was a simple enough gift to bestow on him as reward for his unofficial contribution to the project.

It was two days before the official opening of the mall extension when the atrium was finally cleared of machinery and Sydney and Hobart stood at the foot of the stairs looking up, surrounded by workmen and mall executives.

"They've put a ribbon across the top tread," Hobart explained as he handed Sydney and over-large pair of scissors, "when you get to the top, pause and cut the ribbon. Make sure you smile for the photographers; you don't want to cement your place in history looking like an ugly fucker!"

After the first forty steps or so, Sydney paused and waved down to him.

"Looks just great, Bro!" He said, and then resumed his ascent.

It was sometime later - perhaps a month or so after the incident - that the cause of the collapse was finally made public. Hobart had under-estimated some of the forces that would be generated in his complex helix design, even under the lightest of loads. And minor miscalculations in the angles of the stanchions, the strength of the cables used, the thickness of the supporting pillars - and their number - all contributed to an inherent weakness in the structure. He had no idea how he'd missed all of that; nor how the small army of engineers he had used had missed it too. Perhaps they had become blinded by the potential magnificence of their achievement: a large, shining, sweeping staircase that did indeed appear to simply hover in mid-air.

Sydney was a little over halfway when Hobart saw him stop and grab the handrail. From where he stood, nothing seemed amiss; he even managed to shout up a joke about his brother being afraid of heights. And then came a strange singing sound from somewhere; a high-pitched complaint initially grew almost imperceptibly, and then so rapidly that it took them all by surprise. Hobart suddenly saw Sydney swaying - and yet he was standing motionless some seventy feet above him.

The official report suggested that failure of the stanchions to ensure sufficient rigidity caused a harmonic motion which, once started, was unstoppable. Unbeknownst to Hobart, the first hidden pillar had started to fracture just after Sydney had paused to wave. By the time he had frozen many feet further up, a second had started to splinter too, and when this one shattered - with a crack that made the floor on which they were all standing, shake - it was too late. Simultaneously, two of the supporting cables snapped, causing those around Hobart to drive for cover. Then another pillar gave way. Above him Sydney's movements were becoming increasingly violent, not merely with the swaying of the structure but in his attempt to run to the top of the stairs to safety.

The images of the catastrophe - taken by those same photographers who had been engaged to record the triumph - showed Sydney less than twenty steps from the top at the moment the entire structure buckled and broke apart. When they managed to extract him from the ruble, a twisted mess of concrete, wood, plastic and cable, he was already dead. The coroner found that it was not the fall that had killed him, but being hit repeatedly by falling staircase parts, in particular the top section of six treads.

The weeks between the accident and the inquest - and the few weeks through the enquiry and beyond - were something of a blur for Hobart. Even now - or perhaps, especially now - sitting in his kitchen, holding his letter, they seemed as unreal as ever. He had been acquitted of negligence, though at the time he suspected it had been a close call. Of necessity becoming something of a hermit in his forty-third floor Marina Bay apartment, it was more blessing than hardship when his phone eventually stopped ringing, the tangible consequence of the accident being the loss of his job and consequent fall of his professional stock. No-one wanted Hobart to design for them.

After three months, he woke up one morning and decided to leave. Thanks to friends in London and the power of the internet, four days later he arrived from Singapore destined for an obscure out-of-town bolt hole where he intended to eke out his anonymity until it was time to go back to work. The contacts he retained in the Far East offered one or two introductions in the City, and slowly and without any kind of plan, he began working again. His somewhat vague and redacted cv meant the early work was all small scale, small budget. There was nothing challenging. But it allowed him to earn, to normalise. He felt as if he had been given a second chance - and one that was only bearable because he had discovered that Sydney had somehow never left him.

He moved - to a house with a kitchen table from which you could look out onto a garden where you could plant foxgloves - and began to work more. He had one small development earn two column inches in an industry rag. And as he expanded his UK portfolio - with Sydney constantly urging him on and still swearing in his ear - he became fearful that someone would make a connection, recall the Singapore staircase.

But no-one ever did. It was as if a loss of memory became corporate, shared by everyone. And then the phone rang and it was someone from the office of the Olympic Organising Committee...

He looked down at his letter.

"Sign the fucking thing," Sydney ordered, and Hobart picked up his pen.

Fourteen

At least the bus station was where I had left it. Foregoing the old route into town, we had taken a right down Spring Lane and swung around the edge of a car park belonging to a pristine supermarket. At first I'd assumed that the bus had been forced on a detour, but when we pulled up at a bona fide stop and almost all my fellow passengers got up to get off, I knew it wasn't so.

They'd closed the High Street too. Instead of rumbling past the old cinema we took another right, out-flanking the main shopping drag on a road that used to be little more than a back alley but had now been transformed into a small well-tarmac'd mini-bypass. There was another stop - this time for a bright, over-large pelican crossing - before we eventually came in sight of the terminus.

I wasn't now surprised to find the draughty old building I'd once spent so much time in had been replaced - though only by a draughty new one. The buses were still green, though no longer the subtle dark and under-stated green to which I had once been accustomed. Now the livery was lurid. At night you could have probably left the street lights off and still seen one coming a hundred yards away. Heard it too. Progress seemed to have contributed little in the area of noise abatement here, and even less in terms of air pollution.

Strange how the changes had seemed to manifest themselves all of a sudden. For the previous three miles - those miles between towns - the journey through little suburbia was pretty much as it always had been. Of course some things had changed - like the name on the big factory down by the river, or the colour of the Bingo Hall's brickwork - but it was still my old town. Not that there's anything in that. Had I been given the option then it certainly wouldn't have been "my town" at all. I'd have chosen somewhere with more character, some history; a place of interest. But I didn't get the choice. Maybe none of us ever do. I suppose I shouldn't have been so surprised at the metamorphosis, certain that my naïveté didn't endorse the absurd assumption that it was only in big towns that things happened. Of course there would be supermarkets, car parks, pedestrianisation. I knew that. But even as I descended from the bottom step of the bus, I also knew that I had't expected it here. Not really.

I took a few paces forward - to the middle of nowhere really - then dropped my bag. I checked my watch. It was still only twelve or so. From my top pocket I pulled a packet of Marlboro and lit one. One of *my* changes. I found myself taking the first puff almost over-publicly, as if I were displaying my own brand of defiance: "Hey, I can change too!"

I had time to kill. I'd said I'd be there around one or so and still found myself not wanting to be early. There was change and then there was *change* - and I hadn't got used to this first dose just yet. I decided to walk up the High Street, the newly pedestrianised High Street. I'd have time to go at least as far as the cinema (almost to where the last bus stop had been) before needing to track back.

The pub on the corner opposite the Bus Station had lost the image I naturally associated with it. Instead of the rather peculiar fifties character it had once boasted, it was now bathed in bright purple neon lights and vibrant signage presumably intended to entice people in. I walked up to one of the windows. They had been blacked out from the inside with the kind of material that turns glass into mirror so that you simply end up looking at yourself. If historically I used to think twice about going in there, I'd certainly not have trespassed now. Sure, as I paused there for a second staring at myself, I could see that I'd changed too; but with me it was just age, not a full character make-over.

A couple of doors away, the old paper shop I'd frequented as a child was now a mobile phone shop. High tech out-pacing the low I guess. And it seemed the same story over and over. There'd been a large camping and outdoor clothes shop that was now a brash and bold MacDonald's. Like the newsagent's, this transition seemed strangely apposite. The old wool shop that had supplied my mother with endless balls of double knitting and 'chunky', had become a second-hand shop, its windows home to at least two or three hand-knitted garments whose source material may well have once been purchased from those very same premises. "What goes around, comes around", I found myself noting in a flight of mental obscurity.

In what felt like the ultimate attempt at meeting past and present head-on, I decided to go into the Bookmakers near the cinema. I'd worked there for a while after leaving school, trying simultaneously to forecast what I'd do with the rest of my life alongside the 11:07 dog race from Hackney. Don't think I ever managed to get that dog forecast right - which seemed pretty much in keeping with the rest of it really.

I'd progressed about half-way, with both cinema and Bookies now in sight, when there was a tug on my arm. I stopped and turned. Facing me was a man, about my age; he was slightly shorter than me, with pale, thinning hair, and a strange smile on his lips. Just beyond him, a woman also stood looking at me. I looked back at the man. His smile spread a little further.

"Mike!"

There was a degree of recognition in his voice as undeniable as it was forceful. The fact that he'd got my name right led me to the instant conclusion that I was probably expected to respond in a similar manner.

"Hi!" I heard myself saying, offering my hand as I did so. As it was taken, I tried to imagine my assailant with a little more hair and a little less weight; tried to take a few years off him to see how he would look.

"It's been a long time!" he said, his voice carrying a slight nasal twang. That twang did it.

"Sure has, Pete. Must be ten years."

"More like fourteen!" Pete said, pleased to be closer to the truth. He'd been a prat and I'd hated him, but now I found myself offering him the chance to be right about something. As I recalled it, when we were younger he'd seldom been right about anything. Pete motioned the woman forward. "This is my wife", he said proudly, introducing her as if she were some kind of possession. "Meet Rusty, our Doberman" he might have said with equal effect. She smiled weakly. "This is Thelma" other men would have said, or "Thelma, meet my old pal, Mike". But not Pete.

"What are you doing now?" he asked, relegating Thelma (or whatever her name was) into the background again.

"Me?" I paused. "Oh, I'm between things at the moment, What about you?"

Pete, it turned out, had become an Accountant - well, he was never going to be a professional footballer or astro-physicist, was he? - and was working for a small firm on the industrial estate just outside of town. I wanted to ask him how far he'd travelled in his life; to discover the length of the invisible cord that tethered him to this one-horse town. Maybe he'd left it once and had met Thelma. If that had been my experience, I'd certainly not have wanted to take the chance of leaving the place again. Yeah, I know that's unfair. Maybe Thelma was the chord and he'd never left the place.

After a couple of painful minutes, I made my excuses. Pete offered me his hand and Thelma smiled. I walked away grateful that I'd managed to escape without the fatal exchange of addresses and phone numbers.

The external facade of the Bookies was one of the few things that hadn't changed much, except they'd put a new pictures in the windows and had the old doors replaced. As soon as I walked inside this stability proved to be illusory. The counter had been moved and re-shaped, and where I'd once walked up and down on a Saturday, marking up the whiteboard with prices and results, there was now a huge wall of television screens, each displaying pictures and numbers and information in bold, bright letters. It was all there, and all at the same time. Screens changed by the second. A price fluctuation was there instantly; a result immediately known. Marking those up had been my job, and now look at it.

I had planned to stay a while - even try a bet at Hackney - but I found I couldn't. I scanned the rest of the place quickly. This wasn't what I remembered - nor what I wanted to remember. Behind the counter, a woman looked up. It was Margaret. She had been my old Manageress, and she was still there. Suddenly she looked my way, and I caught in her eye a flicker of recognition. I turned and left.

Walking round behind the cinema, I crossed the same road the bus had driven along and made my way into the park. It was a strange hybrid between that and a common. Parks usually have railings or hedges that define them, and gates you go through for access; but this one didn't. It was immediately open, all of it, stretching the length of the road - and open to the roads on two of its other sides, as if it was common land. But it was compact, too park-like to be a common. Fitting, somehow, that it failed to be either.

In the middle of the park (I'll call it that; after all, I had for years) was an kidney-shaped expanse of water. It was too small for rowing boats and canoes, but on Sunday mornings would be populated by brightly coloured model yachts being raced around tight little courses by their remote control wielding owners. As a kid I'd always wanted one of the big yachts, wanted to race on the lake (though 'lake' was a misnomer too!). My dream didn't come true. Walking alongside the water, I discovered that it was so dirty that - even though it was just a few inches deep - I couldn't see the bottom like I'd once been able to. And there were hundreds of small jellyfish floating near the surface; small, live, transparent jellyfish. They must have come through the inlet from the creek.

I walked up the bank at the far end of the park and on towards the church. My bag was getting heavy so I stopped, put it down, and lit another cigarette. As I paused, I took in the squat, red-brick church that faced me. It seemed a strange kind of a place, more like a hall than a church; an impression made even stronger by the fact that the clock tower stood alone to the side, not quite joined to the main building. Once, in the narrow gap between the two, a girl called Angela had let me feel her breasts. It felt an industrial construction rather than a holy one. I'd never been inside of course, and had always found myself trying - and failing - to imagine it as a place of worship and celebration. The confetti that sometimes lay outside I used to think had been planted there just to prolong the illusion.

Leaving the pavement, I cut across the grass in front of the church and headed for what had once been the Vicarage. Like the church, this was a squat, square building, but at least it bore the hallmarks of being a place someone might have lived in - rather than the considerably more dubious claim of being the temple in which one was supposed to worship. No-one had lived there for a while, at least not in the context of the church. Now it was a hospice.

I waited at the foot of the six stone steps that led up to the front door and dragged slowly on my cigarette. From somewhere I heard the sound of a bird, and glanced back to the three lime trees that stood at the rear of the church. It was an instinctive, almost defensive movement. The cigarette felt warm in my fingers and I looked at it before letting it fall to the ground. I pushed my shoe hard against it, picked up my bag, and walked up the steps.

There was a small desk in the hallway with a little brass bell and a large brown book on it. The desk was unattended so I rang the bell. From a nearby doorway a woman in a dark blue uniform appeared. She smiled professionally.

"Can I help you?"

"I'm here to see David Wilshire."

"And you are?"

"His brother."

Taking a pen from the pocket of her uniform, she opened the book and offered me the pen. As she did so, I showed her my driving licence; I had been told to bring ID.

"If you could just sign in please, Mr. Wilshire."

There were carefully ruled columns for the visitor's name, the patient's name, the date, and time of entry and exit. I filled in all of them except the last. She put out her hand and I returned the pen.

"If you'd like to follow me."

She led me through the hall and up a broad staircase to the second floor. As we moved along a corridor I caught a glimpse of the church through a window; it looked no less industrial from here.

"If you could just wait a moment."

We had stopped outside a room - there was the number '14' in brass on it - and I watched her open the door, walk through, then close it behind her. A few seconds later she emerged.

"I'm afraid your brother's asleep. Would you like to wait downstairs, or come back later?"

I found myself glancing at my watch.

"I don't really have the time," I lied, "if I could just see him. I've come a long way."

"Very well. But please don't disturb him."

She pushed open the door and I went in.

"Remember," she whispered as she was about to shut it behind me, "no noise."

I nodded, and there came the soft 'click' of the door catch as it shut. I placed my bag against the wall. The curtains were drawn and without a light on, the room had a nocturnal feel to it. I could make out the bed and the fact that there was someone in it, but that was all. I went to the window and eased back the curtain a little. Outside, the clock tower stood straight and erect against the sky, proud in its geometric accuracy. As I stood there the clock suddenly chimed. My watch was on the hand that held the curtain back; I could see it was half twelve.

From the bed there came a sound, the rustle of someone moving. I froze, half-expecting to hear David's voice call my name; but there was nothing, just the movement. Pulling the curtain closed a little, I allowed enough light in the room for me to be able to see. By the bed was a single chair. I walked to it and sat down.

David was laying on his side, the covers of the bed pulled up towards his face. I could see the top of his pyjamas, their dark blue a violent contrast to the pale of his face. He was thin and drawn. He had always been a striking individual, but now his cheek bones and strong jaw line offered nothing other than to give him a haunted look. They had cut his hair close, and for a second I imagined I might have been looking at a survivor from the Holocaust.

He had been through his own holocaust in a way, though I didn't really understand much of it myself. Older and brighter than me, he had left school as I started my last year; went off to college, and off to a bright future and a brighter life. Where I had struggled, he had flourished. Those things I had found difficult, he found easy. As I rebelled, he climbed ever upwards. I had idolised him, envied all the things that he could do. I had wanted to be like him; wanted to be top of the class; wanted to be the best cross-country runner in the school. I had watched him training - sometimes doing lap after lap around the park, the lake and the church - and I had hated him for it too. When I failed in the things I tried, I had wanted him dead. And now he very nearly was.

When I moved away - pursuing my first failed career - we began to lose touch. It was an easy enough thing to happen, especially after mum died. He used to write, but then stopped. I blamed myself and tried harder to keep up my end of the deal, but there was no response. There were rumours - mainly from unreliable third parties and distant relatives - that David had come off the rails. Some blamed a woman, some blamed drink.

Drugs were never mentioned. And then there was the letter from Simon, "a friend". He had promised David that he wouldn't tell me, but he just thought I ought to know. I don't think I got all the story, but I got enough - for me, at any rate.

I didn't know what to expect. I had come with a bag full of clothes - in case I needed to stay - and a head full of memories. Perhaps I had thought I might have needed those too. By now though the town had wiped most of them away for me, and here we were, just me and my big brother. And though he was no more than a shell of his former self, even lying there he was still capable of kicking the shit out of whatever memories I had left. Even dying, he was more than a match for me.

I thought about waking him, but didn't. The nurse had spoken. And if he had woken he might have wanted to know about me, about my life; and when I told him how I had failed it would have been like old times and I would hate him for it as if it was still his fault. I didn't want that. Part of me *did* want to hear what had happened to him; wanted to understand, to know the story. I knew how towns changed, how roads became pedestrianised, how progress marched; I could see that. But I didn't know how people changed, how my big brother had come to be back here, in our home town, dying in this bed. I caught a glimpse of my face in the mirror that stood on the cabinet by the bed.

I went back to the window and looked out. A little boy was walking with his father towards the lake; the boy was carrying a small, white boat. I closed the curtain.

Back in the hallway I looked for my entry in the book. The nurse appeared again.

"He's still asleep," I said as she handed me her pen.

I checked my watch and filled in the last column. She followed my hand. Fourteen minutes. Fourteen; like the number on the door; like the number of years since I'd seen David. I offered her a smile as I returned her pen. She didn't respond. I picked up my bag and left.

Back at the bus station I checked the timetable for the bus back. It would be another thirty minutes or so. There was a concrete bench nearby. I dropped my bag on it and lit a cigarette. Then feeling a sudden gust of wind, I pulled the collar of my jacket high against my neck.

Twins

He sits in his professional leather chair making notes, waiting for me. He is relaxed, cross-legged; his pen - gold, no doubt - writing words that cannot be seen from my couch, even straining my neck in an attempt to use the reflection in the large mirror behind him. He glances up from his pad, sensing my interest. He offers a smile - one is supposed to be reassured - then goes back to his note-taking.

A backdrop of dark wood, books. Everything his visitors would expect to see - from his bow tie to the volumes of Freud. As he looks up again. Even the heavy silence seems manufactured from mahogany.

"Where were we?"

He adopts an over-friendly, patronising tone, meaningfully laying down his pen as he does so.

- 'We' were nowhere.

Not that he hears my reply, shielded as it is within my head, private. There is dialogue, but he only gets his half of the story. That makes me feel good.

"You were going to tell me about the accident."

- Like hell!

"When you lost your brother."

He must doubt my sanity, using an undisguised trick like that. "Lost my brother", as if he were a child who had wandered off in the Fun Fair never to be seen again.

And, the accident! Oh, how he would *love* to hear about that; about my reaction to it - then or now. He would listen, then layer my words with meanings never intended; not by me at any rate. But then that would justify his fee, his work. Him, really.

On the mantle, over what should be a roaring fire, in the silence a large clock ticks. The second-hand sweeps ponderously yet methodically in its confinement; counting down my visit, counting up his bank balance.

"It must have been difficult; especially as you were so close."

- Close? Like this far apart?

He fails to see my mental picture of two fingers measuring some minute distance, yet still studies me with those benevolent dog-like eyes, begging for some morsel to satisfy - what? His curiosity? His professionalism?

"Michael"

Suddenly his eyes seem to harden. His eyes, not mine. The tick of the clock is amplified, pitched a little higher, a little more intrusive. He picks up his pen, writes another note.

- Stephen

My name. My brother's name. Our names. The names of the two of us; one here, one not here.

- Michael, Stephen. Friends, brothers. An accident.

The room darkens with the memory of it, as if it were taking on the characteristics of that day. And it now seems cold - cold from his trickery! From his magic! The books on the shelves lose definition; their spines begin to mingle in my blinking; the clock grows larger, its face ever brightening above the black hole of the grate. Look away!

It had been a foul day; all rain, sheeting rain. The motorway was dark, wet; lorries spraying water everywhere. We had talked about who would drive, who'd had the least to drink.

One of us had driven, one had not. There had been, all of a sudden, too many lights, too much water. Suddenly there was no more road.

- One lived, one died. Twins separated, severed.

One died. One lived. Michael. Stephen. Now which name to answer to? Which name was mine? Both. Both.

Old-Age Travellers

Bob's partner was a tall slim man. His blonde hair, long and unkempt, gave the impression of having not been combed for a century. It also made it difficult to define his age: thirty-five? fifty-five? His donkey jacket and leather boots - well-worn by love rather than over-use - seemed so much part of him that he might have been welded into them at birth.

We talked as he and Bob made their way down Thackley Field Locks towards Leeds, his weather-beaten smile and self-rolled cigarette suggesting - paradoxically perhaps - a man who had found that elusive and indefinable thing for which we all search. I'll call him Dave, partly because he looked like a 'Dave' - and partly because 'Bob' was a woman.

Dave and Bob had spent the winter in Skipton and were now making the downhill journey through Leeds and on to Lincoln. Why Lincoln? I didn't ask; it didn't seem relevant - and it probably wasn't a question a true traveller would deign to answer. He declined to commit to the duration of their journey too, as if that wasn't important either. The River Trent would, he acknowledged with a mix of anticipation and chagrin, be "faster"; such was the nature of rivers.

Dave liked Leeds. He liked the Leeds and Liverpool canal too - except where it and Leeds met, demanding the navigation of more than enough swing bridges. You could instantly tell swing bridges were not Dave's favourites. Still, after six years on the canals I guess he'd learned to live with them. To try and impress, I mentioned the largest flight of locks I'd ever encountered, at Foxton. "On the Grand Union," Dave said pleasantly, his voice lacking superiority or the sense of being a man who'd 'been there, done that'.

Another boat was travelling with them through Thackley. A jaded blue sixty-footer crewed by a solitary man who, Dave told me, had been on the canals "half a lifetime". What was that, I wondered: twenty years? thirty? Enough at any rate for him to be able to express concern about the "amateurs" they had just encountered, though his adjective - "dangerous" - seemed strangely out of place in this quiet and slow world.

The Field Locks at Thackley are not the most watertight on the network, with Bob - on Dave's suggestion - removing her long woolly jumper and resorting to a waterproof as she tillered their boat, "Constance", through. On one of the leaking gates (just below where a wagtail now bobbed looking for leftovers from the lock's draining) a small plaque displayed the date it was commissioned by the British Waterways Board: 1986. Perhaps it is not too surprising that in our age of modern technology some of the more traditional manufacturing skills may now be a little wanting.

I left the boats as they dropped through the middle lock of the flight and made my way back to my car. Driving home via the ring road, through the heavy Bank Holiday traffic, it seemed a little bizarre that based on some trite public image, nine out of ten of us would have all too readily labelled Dave and Bob "new age travellers" - which is exactly what most of *us* are, and plainly what *they* were not.

When I wished them well as I turned to go, it seemed fitting that they failed to hear me, my voice drowned out by the torrent of water plunging through the lock gates.

When It Happened

No-one could say when it happened. Or, more exactly, when it started. Even now, after all this time and with the luxury of much hindsight, origins are still unclear. And in simply asking the question - "When did it start?" - you also have to ask when they first started to arrive. Another imponderable.

We know now - or at least we think we do - that they are much like us; perhaps just a little taller, that's all. They would have blended-in right away, without causing any stir or alarm; modest, quiet, softly spoken, polite. Thinking about it, there are probably some places, some cultures, where they most certainly *would* have stood out; remarkable for being unobtrusive, passive, demanding no attention.

After 'the Crash' in 2008, a recovery was always inevitable. And while at the time it seemed as if things would never get better and would always be desperate, deep down everyone believed in 'recovery' - the word at least, even if we didn't truly know what it meant.

Of course the politicians and the economists took all the credit. Things had improved because of their actions, their prudence. There had been prolonged debates about Growth versus Austerity until the meanings of those two words faded into nothingness. And actually no-one really cared what it was called - or, in spite of what they may have said, how we got there - we just wanted things to *be* better, to *feel* better. And soon enough they did. In spite of economic close calls in countries like Greece, Ireland and Portugal, eventually a new equilibrium prevailed, and people began to get used to low interest rates, higher levels of employment, optimism, stability.

We still do not know how they helped, or how many of them helped, or what they did, but we are certain - a few of us in the global band of brothers - that they did. How else could we have dug ourselves out of the mire?

And then their influence grew. Or perhaps it all happened in parallel. There are various theories. Other, smaller things started to change. Bizarre things. For example, the trains started to run on time - just about everywhere. The excuses of 'leaves on the line' or 'the wrong kind of snow' were relegated to an ancient lexicon, as much in the present as "Beowulf". And when this started happening, more people started using them, more trains were provided, some old lines were reinstated, prices fell. When the number of cars on the road began to level out and then fall, the politicians took centre stage again to claim victory, lauding their own skill and expertise, pointing to agreements at climate change summits, decisive action. And then, one year, the ice caps started growing again.

It was probably convenient that there was someone willing to take the credit; it stopped difficult questions being asked, impossible theories being posited. There are some who believe that governments were infiltrated in order to affect policy and to get things done, but there is no evidence either way. Some of those in power seemed on occasion too good to be true, too lucky; and their proposals suddenly radical, simple, full of common sense. Changes were given labels, and labels mantra, and the world became obsessed with nebulous notions and an undefinable sense of 'doing what was right'. Not everyone subscribed of course, and not everyone benefitted from all the changes. When the Internet started to become somehow self-policing with a gradual reduction in the 'less desirable', some commercial interests were impacted but no-one seemed to suffer in any meaningful sense.

But it was with war where the most important metamorphosis occurred.

At first it seemed like failure; a plague of gremlins. On bombing raids in the Middle East, rockets would jam or, if fired, miss their intended target and explode harmlessly in the desert; bombs would fail to detonate and simply embed themselves in the earth. Then planes started to malfunction. Not disastrously so - no-one died - but they developed faults, had to return to base early, even failed to take-off. There were calls for more spares to be sent to the Theatres of War, commitments were made to greater build-quality. But things simply got worse.

Long-range missiles ceased to be long-range, and then ceased to have any range at all. Waging war became difficult for governments; it was something that was getting harder and harder to do from a distance. All protagonists were affected. Suicide bombers found themselves with vests packed with inert material, or - if the explosive was still viable - with timers and triggers that proved faulty and unreliable. Bullets became blanks. To fight on any scale became difficult. And with remote attack options off the table, the only way to engage in combat reverted to the medieval and intensely personal. For a few, it was a massive step backwards. Even in the age of the Internet, sophisticated computers, and vast investment budgets, if you wanted to fight with someone you had to do so face-to-face, mano-a-mano. To threaten someone many hundreds of miles away, you now had to go to where they were in order to do so - and when military transport started to misbehave too...

Everyone was confused. The politicians could not explain the faults, the defects. After a while the aborted bombing run or failed mission ceased to be newsworthy. Stories of suicide bombings dissolved. Gradually people simply stopped fighting; war became like an old photographic negative losing its image.

At one point a Cardinal from South America suggested that the very atoms of war, the building blocks of explosives and metals, had been granted a sense of morality, a code by which to work - or not. How else could you explain why commercial flights flew without any trouble and yet war planes could not? Gods were invoked.

Unable to contest boundaries or ideologies through trials of strength, and unwilling to best your neighbour by physically killing him yourself - by *really* spilling his blood - people were forced to talk, to negotiate, to arrive at practicable and workable solutions. And as the wars stopped, the rebuilding started, and people began to go home. Borders became meaningless. This time the politicians were joined by the clergy in claiming victory, and even as they did so the notion of supremacy, of any supremacy - political or religious - was starting to fade as well.

I met one of them once - or at least I think I did. She had an aura about her; calm, precise, quiet, likeable. But above all, profoundly wise. She wasn't in a position of power, and simply went about her day-to-day business in much the same way as the rest of us; how else could you avoid attention whilst doing great things? I wanted to challenge her, but refrained from doing so. After all, what could I have said that would have made any sense?! And she just seemed to *know*.

In truth though, I couldn't say for certain if any of us has actually met one of them. So we can't say exactly what they look like, or where they are from. We can't know how long they have been with us, nor how long they are staying. But we believe in them totally. Economic stability, the end of global warming, no more wars. How could we not?

And the fact that the trains now run on time...

Candles

There is something magical and enchanting about the way a candle flickers. Like a mischievous sprite, or something that cannot be contained; a lively, leaping thing that defies description as it pirouettes in the small cone of air that embraces it. Perhaps it is inevitable that candles are used for celebration, to illuminate an event.

When someone - usually mother - walks into the dining room where people sit, they carry the birthday cake ahead of them, ceremonially. Perhaps the lights have been dimmed to exaggerate the spectacle as - with their movement through the air - the flames dance and jig even more than usual. If they could sing, surely they would accompany the loud and variously tuneful renditions of 'Happy Birthday to you!' or 'For he's a jolly good fellow!' that might endorse such processions. There are smiles now, the reflection of narrow flames glinting in excited eyes as a face comes close; then, with an exaggerated expression, cheeks puff and a solid blow attempts to quell the flames. Cheers for those who succeed in a single attempt!

But the candles have already been victorious. Their malevolence has gone unnoticed. While they are sung to and heralded, they whisper amongst themselves that another year has gone, another year that cannot be reclaimed. They revel in their secret knowledge, marking the next step on an invisible countdown, aware that the honoured guest will be so overwhelmed by their celebrity role that the questions 'Will I see a cake with candles next year?' and 'How many more candles are going to dance for me?' are never asked.

As he sat on one of the pale green plastic chairs arranged in rows before the semi-private booths, he thought back just two weeks. The party - ostensibly for him - had really been for the children. Or, more accurately, for the grand-children. How they had cheered when Lizzie bought the cake in! How excited they had been to see him try and extinguish all those flames with his first blow - and how they rushed forward to add their own breath when he failed! He wondered if all revelations came at such moments of general excitement.

He shifted on the seat. There were three rows of chairs, each chair close to its neighbour, and each row firmly fixed to the floor. It was impossible to be comfortable. Looking around, there were only two others waiting: an elderly man with a long, sad, worn out expression, and a younger man in a white t-shirt with the number '6' in bold red stitching on the front. He wondered what it meant, if anything. He wondered what they might think of him, sitting in his needle-cord trousers and short sleeve shirt. Adjusting his glasses, he was suddenly thankful that the place was not full.

"Mister Bolton," came a disembodied voice. "Cubicle six."

It should have been the young man in the t-shirt, number six, but it was his name - for now at least. He rose. The small booths were partitioned by dark panelling set at such an angle the from a distance they might have been mistaken as forming a single wall. A number - green like the chairs - was fixed at the entrance of each booth, and as he walked forward to his allotted cubicle he discovered another chair (free-standing this time) facing a cream-coloured table. On the other side of the table a man in a white shirt and loose tie sat waiting for him; he looked as if he might have been there for hours. On the table in front of him, various papers of different colours were neatly arranged. A number of them he recognised as being the forms he had filled in a week ago, his handwriting - executed with the wide-nibbed

Mont Blanc he had received last Easter for twenty five years' service at 'Mason's' - bold and certain.

"Mister Bolton?" the man in the tie said somewhat flatly and without rising or offering his hand, "please take a seat."

'What else was I going to do?' he thought as he sat down. Looking behind him, he could see nothing of the others who were still waiting. There was a pause.

"I've never seen an application quite like this," said the Clerk, obviously feeling the need for some kind of opening gambit.

"Is there something wrong?"

"Wrong?"

"Have I completed all the necessary forms correctly? Do you have everything you need?" Bureaucracy was one of the things he feared, just as it was one of the things he now desired to be free from. He knew he could not ignore 'the system', that he had to work within it, with it, if he was going to achieve his goal.

"Yes, yes, of course" - he wondered what it was about Civil Servants that made them so obvious - "it's just that your request is a little unusual."

"But it's all right? I mean, I'm not breaking any laws or anything like that?" He tried to sound a little subservient; he wanted to give the Clerk the feeling that he was in a position to help him. Conflict would be counter-productive right now; this ex-youth sitting across the desk from him held the power to grant his request and send him out into the world afresh. Even in the depths of petty bureaucracy, in the end it still came down to individual people.

The Clerk tried to smile reassuringly.

"Indeed no. Your deed poll application is absolutely correct. In fact, I've seldom seen one filled out quite so accurately. So completely."

"So there's no problem then?"

"Well" - an awkward pause - "I think I really just wanted to confirm that you were sure about the name you had chosen."

"Sure? What do you mean, 'sure'?"

"It's just a little - unusual." He fingered through the papers in front of him as if offering 'Mister Bolton' a chance to step back from the brink. Perhaps he thought that some reflection might lead to a change of heart. "Sometimes we get people who realise at the last minute."

"Realise what?"

"That it's too big a step, I guess. Too much of a change. Maybe that they even like their old name more than they thought." The Clerk tried a small laugh to accompany his small joke. Both failed.

"But my name isn't me," he said with certainty. Indeed, he might have added (if this had been a philosophical debate) "how can it be me? It was given to me; something that I have had to live up to, grow in to, be burdened by. And now, now I know who I am and where I am going, isn't it right, proper, fair, that I should be given the opportunity to say 'This is who I am. This describes me now'?"

"Mrs Bolton?" the Clerk offered, vaguely.

"Yes?"

"What does she think about this?"

He refrained from answering. There had always been the possibility that someone would try and complicate matters, to bring external influences to bear which - in his own mind at least - were irrelevant. He wanted no debate. He had wanted no debate with Lizzie, so he had simply refrained from telling her. She knew something was afoot, of course. You don't get to live with someone for forty two years without gaining some degree of telepathy.

"Is there anything wrong with the application?" he asked again. After all, what business was it of this once-spotty Clerk whether or not he had engaged in extensive consultation about his plans? What had it to do with anyone other than himself? 'It's my name', he thought to himself, as much now as he had many times before in the past two weeks. 'I can do with it what I choose. If it is the thing that defines me, that identifies me, then why should it not be more - relevant?' But he said none of this; the Clerk could only have picked it up if he had been naturally telepathic, and looking at him - seeing his bored eyes and lifeless lips - he knew this was not possible.

"No sir," said the Clerk, peering at him almost with an air of confusion.

"What do I need to do then?" He had completed all the forms; he had supplied all the requested information, proof, witnesses. The Clerk had been right about one thing: he had indeed been scrupulous. And devious too, like when he subsequently doctored the forms after their signing and before they were submitted.

Following a final pause - and, if he was not mistaken, a slight sigh of resignation - the Clerk explained that he would read aloud the declaration from a document in front of him. It was obvious that this must be carried out correctly; ritualistically, almost. It felt like a marriage ceremony. He was going to be joined in matrimony with his new name, his new identity - 'let no man put asunder...' The Clerk told him that once the declaration had been read, there was a requirement for him to verbally state that it had been understood prior to the final form being signed by them both. 'Do you take this name...?' 'I do'.

"And that's it?"

"You will receive formal notification in the post that all the necessary governmental records have been changed. This usually takes around five working days. Apart from that, you are basically free to start using your new name."

"Shall we get on with it then?" he said, aware that he was smiling slightly - after all, this was the first step in his plan to thwart the candles.

How Does It Start?

ONE

How does it start? Perhaps with something inconsequential; with something that excites our emotions or triggers a memory. Perhaps - in the way that it assaults or caresses us - it begins with our senses; is sensual in the most profound way. The sound of a bird in a tree, the rush of the breeze, or warmth on our skin; the taste of lemons that takes us back to Madeira, or the Brunello that is Tuscany, pure and simple; the reflection of the sun, sparkling and dancing on the lake near the bandstand; cut grass, fresh bread, pavements after rain; an alarm, a church bell, the cry of a baby deprived of milk; haze on the horizon, the magic of a rainbow, an unexpected reflection in a shop window; spices, the coldest ice-cream; coffee - the smell of, the taste of, the sound of percolation.

And then perhaps it starts with an accidental touch. Fingers brushing, momentarily; a fraction of a second too long. But long enough to dwell for more than an instant, and in that moment is sufficient time to scribe volumes greater than anyone could ever imagine; whispers of hope and longing, foretelling of regret, sounds of crying, the most bitter taste, the indescribable tingle that sets forearm hairs to attention, hearts racing - not one, but two! - and pulses quickening, and in the eyes...! A whole lifetime. Or then again, is the trigger the absence of those things. Is it the desire for that accidental touch, a burst of sun, the need for rain, the silence in a church?

But start it does. Quickly or slowly, but inevitably. Painfully or joyously it will assail us, teach us, enliven or depress us, inspire, move, motivate, crush, destroy. And all we need is to be aware and awake, sensible to the certainty of its coming, of that moment when things freeze, the world shifts, and we must move on with a different reality. 'All we need'…? The sensibility and intuition of a poet, the openness of a saint, the naivety of a child, a willingness to discover, an acceptance that we do not know enough - that we cannot know enough. And above all else perhaps, to embrace risk, and change, and the courage to make things different.

Is that it? The undefinable? Is that how we migrate through our lives and take our small steps towards a seemingly unending infinity of steps? If we could trace our lives, backwards through such moments, would we be surprised by what we found or lost, or by how little we knew? Would our ignorance astound us, or our lack of bravery and ambition, our absence of courage, bravado, morality - immorality! And surrounding all of this, our inability to describe, articulate and make tangible anything and everything that has happened to us?

When he thought of language, as he did now, some of these things might have come to him. Drip-fed or in a rush, he might have attempted to unravel or rearrange them, to create a picture that might make sense of things. Above all, he wanted to understand, and for him understanding was about articulation, for only then could he manage to grasp the unknowable; yet even as he desired this, clumsily working with the tools of his trade - words, paint, pastel, manufactured 'things' - he somehow became further removed and thus more desperate. It was as if every desire he had ever known had been crystallised into a single, simple goal: to describe - *something* - to perfection.

*

Somewhere else there is a bed, its white metal frame suggesting history, something clinical. It is the kind of bed which evokes Nightingale wards and Matrons and crisp blue uniforms, dark stockings, and clipboards for charts. There is a tension in the air arising from doubt, from the clash between life and death and the struggle of mortality. Whispered conversations, closed curtains, the sombre mood of the visitors bringing flowers that no-one really wants; a gift from the dying to the nearly dead. And there is a rattle in cries and words. "Who are you?" shouts a cancer patient almost gone, left with dementia as a parting shot. "Nurse! Nurse!" On the window sill or a vacant chair, yesterday's paper with a half-finished crossword; in the waste, the cardboard cup from the café on the second floor, still warm with the dregs of the undrinkable tea that was consumed to fill the time.

And beneath the crumpled linen, almost hidden now, the patient - patient in both senses, waiting as they are, though for what they can no longer remember. There was something - once. It had been important, but now… A failing synapse makes an almost futile attempt to salvage something, and in the dimness that is less than a glimmer, comes the fragment of a thought that wonders, perhaps for the last time, how it all started.

TWO

" 'The hands are wrong.' "

" 'The hands are wrong.' Is that what she said?"

"Word for word. Exactly that."

There was a pause. Outside, through a mottled window that was supposed to suggest age, history, permanence, the sky was darkening. The tables in the garden which had, not long ago, been packed with those taking their Sunday lunch - and in an act of defiance almost, braving the early Autumn in doing so - were now deserted. It seemed inevitable they would soon be barraged by rain, and Oscar knew he might need to run to the car. The uneven window panes distorted the image somewhat, generating edges of abstraction on the scene outside. Was that an idea? Was that something he could use?

"And were they?"

He dragged himself back to Simon, released for a now rare excursion, sitting there in full focus, HD-ready, his pint nearly bereft of liquid, a smile not on his lips but in his eyes.

"Wrong? Of course they were! You know I can't paint hands very well…"

"At all!"

"Very well," Oscar insisted playfully. "She knows I can't do hands very well. She knows that. So why did she mention it? What was the point?"

"Maybe she was disappointed. Maybe she felt you were letting her down." Simon drained his glass. "Maybe she was really asking why you bother to try at all."

Everything was suddenly glass. Simon's pot, the faux seventeenth century panes; over the bar, more glasses, bottles, jugs. All glass; all reflecting, fragmenting; all taking the reality that lay beyond them and twisting it into something defying depiction.

"Maybe."

Oscar finished the last of his ale and rested his hand back on the table. From over his shoulder, somewhere a clock chimed. Perhaps he could use that idea - of glass - somehow. If he could mimic the blurring (pastels would be good) he might be able to come up with something new.

"Breasts."

He looked back at Simon.

"Breasts. You paint great breasts."

"Yes, thanks."

"No, I mean it!" Was Simon being serious? "I bet she's never complained about your breasts. I mean, how you paint hers…"

"Correct. Funnily enough, she hasn't. But then she can't, can she? It's easy to complain about hands and fingers and feet (remember Hockney!); but to complain about how I paint her breasts… Well, that's too close to home, too personal. No woman will really care if their fingers are slightly less than ideal, but…"

Simon stood up. Oscar allowed his mind to photograph him. Tall-ish; slim-ish; handsome-ish; wealthy-ish… He always seemed like a man on the verge of something, of attaining a peak but then failing in the final ascent. If it had been Everest, he would have made all the camps but got stuck at the last one. His failure had not been terminal, far from it; but Oscar wondered exactly how satisfied his friend really was being so close to - what? - and yet so far away. Thwarted almost. And he knew part of the blame lay with Simon himself.

"Of course, you can't take all the credit?" This as Oscar also rose.

"For what?"

"Your skill in painting breasts. After all, you've got such great material to work with. Rachel has the most exquisite tits!"

Oscar laughed, in spite of himself.

"Now there you are not wrong."

They paused in the small lobby by the front door, examining the now falling rain, each of them silently judging the need to make a dash for it. After a moment, Simon stepped out, evidently deciding not to run. Oscar pulled up the collar of his jacket and walked beside him.

"Have you ever been tempted?"

"What? Rachel, you mean?"

"Yes. For her perfect breasts - and in spite of her imperfect hands..!"

Oscar waited until he had unlocked the car and they both got in. His hand paused on the ignition.

"You know, I haven't. Not really. No. And after all this time. No; not after all this time."

And the car growled into life.

＊

A spot of paint. Round, perfect, dropped onto an unblemished canvas. In its gloss meniscus, reflections; mainly of light, of sources of light, and depending on where you were, how you tilted your head, moved, there were different things. And the light, those reflections, changed the colour. It had been just blue as it waited to fall from the tube, dropped slowly and deliberately so that its form would not be adulterated by interference - at least not yet.

But what was it now, if you looked from here, or at this angle, with that reflection? Azure blue? Or Brandeis blue? Or Cambridge, Carolina, Cerulean, Cobalt, Cornflower, Denim, Egyptian, or Electric blue? Indigo, Iris, Majorelle, Maya, Midnight, Navy, Oxford, Persian, Prussian, Sapphire, Sky, Steel, Ultramarine? There was a blue called 'True blue'.

"What the hell's that?" thought Oscar.

Perhaps this one spot was all those things and none of them, simultaneously. He became drawn not to the colour, but to the words internally incanted as if some mystical spell. In some bizarre way the colour became the words, and yet the words had no meaning. Did that suggest the colour had no meaning? Was it somehow just itself, imperial, impervious, impossible?

He teased at the spot with the edge of a small hog brush, destroying its symmetry and smearing an edge unevenly. As the shape changed, its mirror-like quality dissipated, and then the colour lost its lustre and ability to morph, and it returned to that which had originated from the be-smeared tube. Oscar paused and picked up the tube again. 'Royal blue' said the label.

"That's sorted then," he thought - and with new-found aggression, smashed into the small spot before squeezing more paint onto the medium before him.

This was the most liberating time: taking a virgin canvas and destroying its whiteness, violating it in such a way that he could become its redeemer and free it, give it new life. It was destroying to allow him to create. But that was not what liberated him. The idea that he was preparing for some noble endeavour was fine, romantic, and - superficially, at least - the public argument. But what freed him the most at moments like this when he was starting out, laying down a wash, some crude outlines, was precisely that he was *not* trying to create or depict; precisely because he was not yet aiming to give birth to something perfect; because what he did now failed to matter. It was of no consequence; in itself, it was not an important product. Or end product. So he could squeeze and brush and stroke, he could be rough or smooth, harsh, gentle; in the inconsequential nature of his actions - the fact that they were somehow 'worthless' at the end of the day - he became liberated. He could rejoice in the unfinished.

"That's interesting".

Simon had been standing in a corner of his studio one day looking at a canvas.

"What?"

"This." Simon held up a rough sketch, monotone green, the raw canvas still showing through rough outlines where the rapidity of his strokes had left some unsullied fabric exposed.

He had tried to capture that initial experience of freedom, of liberation, and - paradoxically - to paint something before he had finished it. To try and regenerate that sense of being unshackled and capture it, the dynamic life of it, within an image. Of course he had failed. The unconscious rough strokes which would normally fail to matter suddenly became final strokes, became something that *did* matter; it became consciously important how thick the paint was, how long the brush strokes were, how close they came to draughtsmanship.

"That's shit," he had said to Simon. "Something that didn't work."

"It's interesting though."

And Oscar knew that it was interesting. He knew that there might be something there if he could only harness it, if he could only stop being himself and somehow forget his deepest motivations. After that attempt, and for a while, he started to experiment further - not with his painting, but with himself. It seemed logical. He felt he needed to find a way to take himself out of the equation, to sever the link between thought and action, to allow instinct dominance over calculation.

Drink was the easiest place to start. He tried getting drunk, really drunk, and only then picking up the brush or the pencil, the pastel or the crayon. But there was a fine line. Not drunk enough and he remained in control, and became angry and even more frustrated. Too drunk and he would hardly be able to stand, or hold anything; more than once he simply fell over and threw up. The experiment was a failure. He produced nothing of interest, everything was bereft of talent. And it cost him a month of his life.

After that he tried sleep deprivation. The idea was that he would still be in control to a degree, but that he would be too tired to care, to seek perfection, to calculate. He was banking on his subconscious taking over and looking after him, delegating responsibility for his art to a part of him he could not control, that he hoped was always there, a constant no matter what his mental state. The output was better, but this was far harder on him in many respects. He felt helpless in a completely different way, and it was not comfortable; indeed, it felt dangerous, risky. And it took time to be ready - at least two days - then time to recover, often longer.

Simon had some dubious friends. For his third - and final - experiment Oscar turned to drugs. "Nothing extreme or addictive" he had told Simon; it had to be safe. And so one day he was given three small pills and told to take them only one at a time, and then at least two days apart. It turned out to be a week he couldn't remember and which produced not a single tangible thing to show for it.

"How was it?" Simon had asked, smiling. He knew of these experiments, and had already expressed his view that Oscar was 'off his trolley'.

"You know, I've no idea," this a few days later over a Starbuck's coffee. "There were some dreams, I think. Some really weird dreams. Maybe they will come in handy one day, I don't know."

"But that's it?"

"It?"

"I mean, you've finished," Simon paused, fractionally, "playing with yourself? These experiments of yours."

Oscar smiled back.

"Finished, yes. I can go back to being the frustrated, neurotic, incoherent sod you know and love!"

"Good," said Simon, "because I've missed that guy for the last few weeks. And to be honest, we have been worried about you."

"We?"

*

If you stood at the end of the platform, just after it had begun to curl to the right and just before the 'Do Not Cross Here' sign, and if you leant slightly to the left, you could see the tunnel mouth perhaps three hundred yards away. The twin tracks merged together between here and there before the single line disappeared into the blackness. It was, in many respects, a perfect construct: the symmetrical smoothness of its curvature (there wasn't a straight line to be seen in the rails as they bent gently away); the brickwork that seemed, from this distance anyway, immaculately pointed with russet bricks edging the stone-coloured ones; and from somewhere, and at certain times of the year, the vine that climbed up one side of the tunnel mouth and was just beginning to reach the top of the opening, particularly charming when it was beginning to flower.

He remembered, many years ago, standing in that same spot as a child and waiting for the steam trains; trains long gone now. When they were approaching, sometimes - depending on the direction of the wind - you might get a sense of the smoke from the tunnel before the engine emerged; but most often you saw the iron monster first, then a huge billow of smoke chasing it out of its cavern. Perhaps to some small children it might have seemed like a dragon, or a machine being chased by a dragon. It seemed strange that the sound came later; but even then, it was the sound of the steam first, and then the sound of the engine. It was difficult to reconcile that the noise made by the most insubstantial and temporary element was more assertive than that from the locomotive itself.

And when he watched a train leave - a much rarer occasion as he was usually on the train - it was a picture played in reverse, and in so many ways. The sound went, and then the engine; the coaches followed, and finally, like the remnants of a promise, a wisp of smoke swirling at the roof of the tunnel before being sucked away. But steam trains, except for the odd Bank Holiday 'special', had not run there for many years now. They had kept the fabric of the place in good order, modelling it against some image of an idealised country station, and the tunnel mouth still retained its claim to perfection. But something was missing, something had been taken out of the experience; not ripped out exactly, but the sense of loss suggested that violence had been exercised.

Turning back from the 'Do Not Cross Sign' and his habitual validation that remnants of the past still existed in the present, he knew this might be his last time standing here waiting for the train back to town. He also knew - as if this were mutual or causal confirmation - that he had probably seen his uncle for the last time. It had been a meeting of little consequence and no satisfaction. He had spoken of the past, remembering things, even talking about the station, and his uncle had said things too; but there had been no conversation, no dialogue. It was as if their words had missed each other in mid-air; as if they were occupying the same physical space but had arrived there in different times or from different realities.

He had hoped for more. He had intended to stay longer.

"I know it's hard," said the Nurse as he left, clearly embarrassed about the excuses he had made to leave early - so early, in fact, that he had forty minutes to kill at the station, "but that's how it is. If it's any consolation, he was on quite good form today. Some days there's nothing there. I'm afraid we're seeing more of those."

"Yes; the Doctor told me."

She had paused, thinking about something to say, to reassure.

"I'm sure he was pleased to see you. I know he was looking forward to your visit - after all, he did leave you that present."

Involuntarily he looked down at the somewhat awkward bag he was now carrying in his left hand. It was large, rectangular, and the plastic handles cut into his fingers. He had swapped from right to left and left to right at least five times since he had arrived at the station, loathed as he was it put it down on the ground. At some point - and he did not know when - he would open the bag, loosen the brown wrapping, and examine it. On the train? Perhaps. He had not yet decided.

❈

So what happened next? He knew people would come to visit him and that they would talk to him. He suspected there would be awkward silences and various attempts at joviality; laughter, he knew, would not be at a premium, but honest laughter would be scarce. He didn't feel the need to be helped to remember; he was sure that he could manage that. After all, weren't there events enough, landmarks, achievements? Did he not have a record of all this, in various media, to help him?

And people did come, at first in a great wave; some of them he had not seen for a long time and, he suspected, might never be seen again. They crashed in on him like a wave on a beach, and he felt himself being sucked back by them, losing parts of himself to their undertow, as if all they achieved in attempting to help him was to help themselves and leave him less that he had been before. In a strange way their sacrifice had turned into his sacrifice, and he could feel himself becoming restless, angry, resentful. And then most people stopped coming and those that did spent less time with him. It was as if the tide had finally gone out and all was calm.

Of course there were conversations in the beginning - and good ones too. Ones that actually carried meaning, with all the pretence and fluff stripped away because time was precious. These he would engage in earnestly, fervently. But soon enough it became difficult to concentrate; he listened but seemed to hear only half the words. He found himself speaking but his speech elicited no response, as if they had stopped listening too. That was when he stopped trying. What was the point if they failed to listen? If he failed to hear? He still had his version of events, his history. He didn't need anyone to help him travel back in time.

THREE

The first thing he noticed about her were the lines she made through the air as she walked. She seemed to have the surreal quality of being able to bend light. As she came through the door, past the counter behind which the Barista worked, then between the tables towards them, reality - or at least his perception of it - was somehow shaken. It was as if she had an aura to which all light was subservient.

She smiled warmly, first at her sister and then at him.

"Rachel!" Mel said somewhat unnecessarily as she rose to greet her.

Oscar rose to his feet and, once the sisters had hugged, shook the hand that was offered him. It was only at that point he became aware of her beauty. He noticed it first in her hand, its taut, perfect skin, and then - perhaps again - in her smile. Close up as she was now, taking the seat next to him, she no longer bent the light about her and he was able to focus. Mel had warned him that Rachel was beautiful - and that the two of them were not alike. He could see that now, both aspects. Had Mel not told him they were sisters - and had she not been the kind of person whom Oscar believed was incapable of lying - he would have assumed that they were just friends; or perhaps more than that as they sat across from him, still holding hands on the table.

"I've seen your work", Rachel said immediately. It took him by surprise.

"Really?! Where?"

"At the little gallery just off the Finchley Road, near the tube station. You know the one?"

"Yes, of course. They still have some of my stuff in there?"

She smiled. He noticed she had released her sister's hand so that she could use both her own to gesture subtly while she talked.

"You're surprised? Because you're amazed that they rate it highly enough to still be selling it - or because you expected it to all be gone by now?"

"Don't tease!" Mel admonished gently.

Oscar laughed.

"If I had to choose between the two, it would have to be the former rather than the latter."

"Don't be so modest", Rachel said, "it's very good. I prefer the portraits to the landscape I saw."

"Which one was still there?"

"It was of the sea. A long, wide beach. Looked English, not foreign."

"The Gower", Oscar confirmed. "Welsh, but close enough. I'm not surprised they haven't sold that one. I've never liked it much."

"Well you may just have to take it back home…"

The waiter came over and took their order. It was mid-morning, so just coffee except for Rachel who ordered some shortbread.

"Why did you prefer the portraits?" he asked.

She had not taken her eyes from him since they had sat down. He could see she was being more serious now.

"I don't know. They seemed more honest."

"Honest?"

"Not just in the way you depicted your subjects - though clearly you were able to get inside them somehow. But the painting itself, in terms of the technique I suppose, seemed more authentic, genuine."

Oscar tried to weigh her words, assess their truth not only in terms of the way she said them (did she actually believe what she was saying?), but also from his own perspective. Was that what he thought too? His brief musing was interrupted by Mel. Rachel now looked at her as she spoke.

"Would you paint Rachel? For me? I would very much like you to do so."

It was a question that might have been posed to an old friend, not someone you were meeting for only the third time. It was a question delivered in an even, measured way, packed with honesty - as Oscar had already come to expect. So, he thought to himself, this was the reason Mel had wanted them to meet.

He thought back to his impression of Rachel from just a few moments earlier: her entrance, the lines she made as she moved through the air... Would it be possible for him to capture that! What a challenge it might prove! How such a sitter might transform a canvas!

"Of course," he said. "I would love to."

How could he say otherwise?

FOUR

People used to say it ran in the family; that there was, genetically passed on and then further enhanced, an ability - to some degree - to be creative. Josh had been too young to remember other than vaguely the dinner table debates about Nature and Nurture, debates usually triggered by a quorum of the appropriate adult family members being in attendance, and the spark of some event or exhibition to act as catalyst. As he grew older and better able to both understand and then contribute to the conversations, simultaneously they became more irregular. For various reasons it became a rarity for the prerequisite combatants to be in a room together at the same time, all of which made those blue touch paper moments considerably less frequent.

He could recall, as a precocious teenager, more than once trying to ignite such a conversation "between the pear and the cheese" as the French might say, but almost always to no avail. Without an even spread spread of advocates either Nature or Nurture would win an uncontested victory, and there would be no satisfaction in that, no matter which side you took. Josh inclined towards Nature. It was attractive for him to do so. For one thing, it allowed him to romanticise about his family - both immediate and tangental - and for another, it meant that he didn't have to think about things too much; there was little need to openly consider practice, training, or whatever the correct or fashionable phrase for related workmanlike endeavours happened to be.

"Let Nature take its course", he might have said, as if that were his motto; a get-out clause that would, on certain occasions, have sparked a domestic riot. On balance, he believed it, but failed to be dedicated, diligent - even though he had his own regime for practice, as if he were secretly trying to back both horses.

In the end he had to give it all up. No matter how hard he tried - in private or in public - by the time he reached his late twenties he knew in his heart he just didn't have that magic 'Nature' ingredient which could elevate him from being an 'also ran'. Josh could see the leaders simply galloping away from him and now matter how much he cajoled and whipped, he just couldn't keep up; this despite the fact that there was a large part of him both fiercely independent and competitive. More Nature again, though without doubt primarily from his mother this time. The prospect of being second-best was unappealing. Even encouragement from his uncle and promotion of the idea that 'second was still pretty good, and better than 99% of everybody else' wasn't enough, especially as it rang hollow from his uncle's lips even as he spoke the words. An uncle who was never second-best.

Once he was established in an 'honourable' profession and proving himself at home in the offices of the City of London - more Nurture than Nature - his tight and undeniable connections to the ethereal world of the Arts still managed to confer upon him some degree of uniqueness; a soft glow he was happy to bask in from time-to-time and to use to his advantage.

"Is *he* really your uncle?!" the wide eyed girl might have said in the bar after work.

"Yes, he is. I've got some of his stuff back at my flat if you'd like to see it some time..."

It was a shallow but reliable ploy.

He had become independent - and thus forced to find his own way in the world at a truly fundamental level - earlier than he might have wished; certainly earlier than was the norm. Just before he enrolled at Keele University, his father went off to a football match one Saturday and never came home. His visits to Craven Cottage were infrequent but not unheard of. In that context, his decision to go and watch the local derby with Chelsea raised few eyebrows. It was clear to all of them - Josh, his mother, and his uncle - that things in the 'Fathership' (as opposed to the Mothership) were not all they could have been. Work had been tough recently; hours unquestionably long and draining; enthusiasms sapped or gone altogether. Even those rare evenings where life conspired to throw them all together - perhaps with one or two reliable sparring partners - failed to blaze like the old days, and they endured embers devoid of any glow.

Later, he would recall that there had been no panic when his father failed to immediately return. The fact that Fulham had apparently done well (Josh never could remember the result though) was sufficient to suggest that some kind of celebration may have ensued. And later, when he had still not returned, the default hypothesis was that he had become ensconced with some of his 'football friends' and was probably sleeping it off in one of their flats. Even now, Josh could not resurrect any call to the police. His mother had made enquiries with known acquaintances, but they were understated, factual questionings, untarnished by a sense of panic - or even emotion it seemed. The two of them seemed to quickly accept the disappearance as if it had been inevitable - and simply a matter of timing. A month later, it was as if he had never even existed.

And then, half way through his final year at Keele, his mother died. He knew she had not been well for some time; there had been a recurrence of an old illness, but it was, she assured him, nothing to worry about. And so he didn't. Instead he did what most third year students traditionally try and do: knuckle down and attempt to scrape an extra grade from exams which, had application been even and appropriate throughout the previous two years of study, would have been a breeze. Her death not surprisingly derailed him emotionally for a brief period; but it was the practicalities of death and the mundane and real-world procedures through which he'd been forced to go that impacted him most of all. At the time he wondered if he hadn't been preparing for her death for some while - indeed, since his father's departure - and, as such, was effectively just playing out a scenario for which he had been unconsciously rehearsing over the previous two years.

This was a theory that briefly exploded some months later when, sitting alone in the Chiswick house he had inherited too early, he was suddenly seized by a raging depression that saw him lurch violently off the rails, and whose outcome was the recognition that he was never going to make it as 'an Artist', and that he needed to forget his bequeathed ambitions and get himself a proper job. Thus, the 'honourable profession'.

FIVE

He had never painted with an audience in attendance - not that Mel could see what was going on from where she sat reading by the large window that occupied almost half of one side of his attic studio. Almost at right angles to her, Oscar could sense her presence rather than her. He felt as if he were being chaperoned on a first date. Or rather that Rachel was being chaperoned.

Not that there was any need. Rachel was fully clothed. That first sitting was for a portrait - 'a quick sketch' Mel had called it - and she had come armed with a large, wide-brimmed yellow hat for Rachel to wear. Oscar had objected. He complained about the hat blocking out the light, the compromising of skin tones, the deadening of colour - indeed, anything he could think of. But it was, Mel reminded him, 'just a sketch; nothing important'. Oscar had therefore begun to work in a rather poor frame of mind.

The afternoon had started well enough with him showing them around his modest studio, Mel and Rachel pulling canvases from behind other canvases and passing polite, enthusiastic, supportive comments. Rachel was drawn to one or two of his portraits, their models posing nude.

"Who's she?"

"That's Val. Valerie. Professional sitter, before you ask. It's what she does in her spare time. Some people get a kick from doing things like that."

"She's pretty," suggested Rachel.

"Good bone structure," Oscar said, trying to remain detached and non-committal.

But now, irritated by having to compromise his judgement and method, he worked on the 'sketch' with unusual vigour and speed. After a while though, he became absorbed. The hat provided a play of shade across Rachel's face he had not anticipated, and when exaggerated a little it suddenly became ambiguous. The shade thrown by the hat accentuated the red of her lipstick, and the way the background lamp was placed, he was still able to bring out the blue of her eyes. He worked carelessly, quickly. He failed to notice when Mel had appeared behind him, standing motionless, watching.

"That's perfect," she said.

And then the spell was broken, and Oscar was forced to stand back. Rachel's face, though vigorously drawn, stared calmly back at him, her eyes - mysterious under that hat - penetrating and fearless. There was a vibrancy and celebration about the picture that surprised him. Oscar realised three things. The first was that Mel had, in her matter-of-fact way, interrupted him at precisely the right time. He knew, instinctively, that one more brush stroke would have been one stroke too many; that he would have been taking away and no longer adding. He also realised that the strange notion he'd had of Rachel 'bending light' when he first saw her in the coffee shop had now manifested itself onto his canvas. The background, which he believed he had tried to depict in a realistic - if 'light' way - was fragmented, blurred, smudged. It appeared as if Rachel had - by imposing herself upon reality - taken command of it, almost broken through it and forced it to her will.

And thirdly…? Thirdly, he knew that he must paint her naked.

❋

"What are the pills for?"

Simon and Oscar were driving back to Simon's flat having just had dinner with Mel and Rachel. For Oscar this had seemed the next logical step. They had got on well enough; the evening had passed pleasantly and there been appropriate degrees of laughter and seriousness. Once Simon had become accustomed to them - Mel's disarming direct honesty and Rachel's beauty - he relaxed. Oscar had sensed him trying too hard.

"I don't know; she hasn't said."

"You haven't asked? Why not?"

Oscar was ready for this.

"Because I've only just met her, and it feels - well, a bit too private somehow."

"But you don't know?"

"I don't."

"Shall I tell you why you won't ask?" - this after they had pulled away from a set of traffic lights, Simon changing up through the gears.

"Sure thing, Einstein."

"Because you know she will tell you. She's bound to. How could she lie?"

"How indeed?"

"So you don't want to know. QED, you're afraid to ask."

"Wow! Einstein and Freud in a single conversation! You'd better go and have a lay down when we get back to your place!"

Simon turned the car into his road, coasted past the first three houses, then rolled into his drive.

"Is it because you're not interested? Or because you are interested? In her I mean. And maybe you don't want her to know that you're interested - or not..."

"Beats me, Sigmund," Oscar got out of the car.

Two glasses of whiskey later: "I'll ask her for you."

Oscar turned away from the bookcase where Simon kept his extensive vinyl collection and moved back to his armchair. Simon was lying, eyes closed, on the sofa.

"You'll ask for me?"

"OK," Simon confessed, eyes still closed, "I'll ask for me. Because I'm interested. Why does a remarkable woman like that need pills? And take them in public? What are they for? What's wrong with her? And before you say anything, she's remarkable because she's the purest person I've ever come across in terms of honesty, self-knowledge; the whole ball of wax. And I'm interested because there's something there I don't know and I want to. OK?"

Oscar sank back in the chair cradling his drink.

"It's your funeral."

SIX

Abandoning Chiswick was inevitable after his collapse there. After all, it held too many memories for him: memories of a happy childhood and of his mother - but also of her death and his father's abdication. When latterly it had come to symbolise his recognition that he could never - at any level - follow in enlightened familial footsteps, it was as if his simply being there was a sham, and he had no desire to feel like an impostor.

Leaving proved surprisingly easy for Josh. He had nothing to tie him there any longer and had established nothing in the way of a local coterie that would pine for him once he had gone, nor one that he would miss. In any event, he told himself, London was London; it was just a big village, as Estate Agents were fond of saying, and anywhere was accessible from anywhere else as long as you had patience and stamina. The money helped ease him on his way. His parents had bought the house for a song and, when prices began to rise and Chiswick became even more desirable, his mother continued to resist temptation and sat tight. Her defiant logic and pragmatism held firm, never really tempted by the potential windfall that a quick sale would have brought her. Unlike him, she did have a coterie on hand, and one which needed her as much as she needed it. Growing up in her presence, Josh had nothing but the vaguest inkling of the scale and depth of her realm beyond his father (for a while) and his - famous! - uncle. Indeed, it was not until her funeral that he experienced the breadth of her reach, made real by the scale of the crowd determined to pay their respects; one so large indeed, that the start of the ceremony was delayed by a few minutes to allow the Vergers time to settle all the mourners.

In some ways the sheer scale of her network demonstrated to Josh just how 'wrong' Chiswick was for him - and reinforced the notion that his sense of failure, now edging beyond the artistic, was somehow complete.

So he did take the money and run. The sum was considerable. Enough for him to acquire a small flat near the river and closer to town; a central and somewhat bijou residence with an address that seemed to match the image of a young professional making his way in the world. Some might have argued purchasing the flat was a shallow act - it had a showy postcode to boot - but Josh could live with that. He needed time to think, to reorientate himself, and if his flat and its location gave him a partial character and identity for free - at least for a while - then that was fine. It would be something else he didn't have to worry about just yet.

His mother would have scolded him roundly. "Josh, how can you?! That's dishonest, and you know it! It's also lazy, taking the easy way out. It lets others define you in their eyes rather than you define yourself in theirs." And when she said this to him - sometimes in dreams - he knew she was right, and he could not counter her argument nor push back against it, in part simply because she wasn't there.

Work, when it arrived, came surprisingly easily. Lacking any real idea as to where he should be focussing his efforts, Josh enquired at a Management Consultancy about an internship allied to their graduate programme. He discovered that, because he was just a little bit older than their usual applicant - and because he had 'something about him' - the company bypassed the internship part of their programme and took him on immediately as a junior consultant. That there was nothing he could actually consult in didn't stop them. Later he would tell others 'being well-groomed, articulate, and able to look pretty good in a suit' was qualification enough. There were lots of young, ambitious people who started in his intake with exactly the same set of qualifications; a group of driven youngsters beginning their strenuous three month training programme, each aiming not to be in the fifty percent who would be dropped at the end of it.

Josh wasn't particularly driven, and when he started on the programme his focus was just getting through the next day. He didn't bother to look six months into the future. Whether he made it or not was of little concern to him - especially as rebuilding himself was the primary goal.

But he did make it. "Maybe," he suggested to his uncle once, "I looked better in a suit than anyone else!" People liked him. He was unspectacular, but reliable. His assignments were always on-time, of decent quality, and usually led to further business. He had a disarming honesty about him, and the clients liked his soft but firm clarity. That was his mother then - though perhaps with some of the more abrasive edges rubbed off. One quarter, thanks to two big retail assignments, he earned more in pipeline income than any other junior consultant, and for a few weeks he was known as 'Josh the Dosh'. A few weeks after that, he lost the 'Junior' prefix to his job title.

SEVEN

"I told you the hat would work."

Oscar was standing alongside Mel by the fireplace of her living room where his portrait of Rachel now took pride of place. She had chosen to frame it simply - 'not to distract from the picture' - and the neutral colour of the wood was entirely subservient. The hat leapt out of the picture, drawing the viewer's attention to Rachel's eyes. Looking at it again, now in situ, Oscar was both surprised and impressed.

"It works well; I'll give you that," he concurred.

Mel momentarily rested her hand on his arm.

"*You* worked well," she said. It was a simple but loaded statement.

Oscar laughed lightly and turned away.

"Rachel should take all the credit, of course. After all, how I could I fail with a subject like her?"

"Because she is full of beauty?" Oscar noted how she had not chosen to say 'because she is beautiful'. "Because she has those perfect eyes? You still had to capture those; you still had to have the craft and guile to do so."

"Thanks," this as he sat back down on the sofa and looked back towards the portrait. "But it's not that. She has some kind of quality about her. It's difficult to explain. As if she forces light to focus on her and her alone, and so everything around her becomes - I don't know - second rate, inconsequential."

"Hence the background?"

"What do you mean?"

She moved towards him.

"The way you've given it no definition at all - even thought there was definition to be had in abundance. Is that why you painted it that way, to emphasise her superiority over everything else?"

He shook his head.

"I just painted what I saw. Honestly. I saw no definition. I saw nothing but Rachel."

"And you want to paint her again?"

"More than that," he suggested.

"You *need* to paint her again?"

"I have to. Simple as that. You've seen some of my other models. Val, for example. She's a pretty enough girl, but she's nowhere close to your sister. She lacks Rachel's kind of quality. I didn't realise it before because I've never seen anyone quite like Rachel - at least not from my 'artist's perspective'."

Mel smiled and sat next to him on the sofa. Her shoulder brushed his.

"I'm not sure I can allow my pragmatic sensibility to agree with you."

"You're teasing me!" Oscar said, a little tremble appearing from somewhere in his voice.

"Yes, of course. I may not understand," Mel affirmed, "nor see things the way you do, but I still manage to get a sense of them. And if I were you, I know what I would want now."

"Which is."

"To paint Rachel naked, of course. You need to see her unencumbered, unvarnished as it were. You need to see the full effect of her; to be challenged by the maximum she has to offer you - as a painter, I mean."

Oscar allowed her assertion to remain unanswered for a few moments. She was undeniably correct - and Oscar sensed that she knew that.

"I can deny none of that," he said, giving in. "What does Rachel think?"

"Why should she think anything?" Mel challenged.

"Because I suspect you will have already asked her, Mel. I may not have known you very long, but from what I do know I'm sure you will have already posed the question. You are direct, thorough, honest. Clarity is your byword in many ways - and you will have wanted to get this clarity from Rachel. Not for me, but for yourself."

She laughed suddenly, differently, allowing her hand to rest on his knee. It felt like the gesture of victory, or of some kind of prize.

"You are right, of course. I did ask her, because I needed to know. And yes, as much for me as for you. Partly because if she said 'no', then I wanted time to think how best to break the bad news to you."

"And did she?"

"What?"

"Say no?"

Mel allowed a pause to build. She was teasing him again. Oscar knew he might have had the answer instantaneously, but Mel was keeping it in check, restrained on a leash until she was ready to release it.

"She did not say no - but", Mel heard him catch his breath at her first words, "but she said it was my choice. That I could have the final say. She trusts me; trusts my judgement - especially of people. She has no problem with your talent - how could she have?! - but in many ways she is still so naive..."

"So, do *you* say 'no'?" Oscar asked, the smile gone from his face but the tremolo still there in his voice.

"I say 'yes'. Yes, you may paint her again. You may paint her for yourself, not for me. You may keep the painting; I won't want it. She is away for a few days, but then she will be back; you can make the arrangements then."

Oscar sensed that there was something else; a 'but' that had yet to be voiced. He prompted it.

"But?"

Mel smiled again.

"You are a very bright, Oscar. Yes, there is one precondition; one small thing I want you to do for me first..."

EIGHT

He had lost all sense of what day it was. It didn't seem to matter any more. Morning, afternoon, evening; all had become undefined, a blur punctuated by being told what to do, what pills to take, and the somehow reassuring interruption of bodily functions. Had he been able to rationalise it, he would also have noticed how the intense concern and care afforded him by the nursing staff on his arrival had subsided into the casual monotony of process. Yes, they still were gentle and caring, attentive to his needs, but that initial celebrity had worn off. He was just another patient waiting to die.

It was fitting perhaps. Occasionally, when he felt strong enough, they would ease him out of bed and wheel him to the large window at the far end of the room where he could look out onto the private grounds below. It was a room which faced the rear of the building, so no natural thoroughfare. Occasionally he would catch glimpses of a gardener or two tending the shrubs; sometimes he would see people huddled together, arm-in-arm perhaps, their bodies close, walking too slowly. He had given this a name. What was it? The nurses had told him once this was where people - usually patients with relatives - were allowed to walk in private after they had seen one of the consultants and where the definitive bad news had been delivered. 'The Death Walk'. Yes, that was what he had chosen to call it. He assumed that nearly everyone would have one such walk - unless death had come upon them unexpectedly or they were totally alone in the world. He almost was. There was no-one to mourn for him, not really. Indeed, there were few people left who cared.

He had not allowed the consultant to do his dirty work for him.

"It's bad news, Josh", he had said, having taken the young man out through the rear door and onto the lawns himself, "but you're a bright lad; I expect, like me, you saw that coming."

It was a memory which visited him less frequently now, just like all his memories. They had become his oldest friends, who, in their own way, had decided to drift away like old acquaintances, less enamoured of and responsive to his fame. And why should they not? As they gave him less time, he imagined that same time being shared and enjoyed with others elsewhere. Was this then what dying was all about? You lost more than just your physical life; your friends went next, followed by memories - perhaps the embodiment of your soul - slowly fading away, betraying you, as much as the days did too. If so, then it was a cruel end. Occasionally he would feel angry for no reason and a tear would escape his eyes.

"Your mother was beautiful, Josh," he said once, "in her own way. Remarkable woman. I was very fond of her you know."

"I know uncle."

Later, it was "How is she, by the way?" and Josh would humour him with the same old stories - little knowing that Josh's sensibilities refused to permit reminding his uncle that she had been dead for many years now.

"Did you ever paint her?" he asked once in response.

"Paint? Who?"

This was a conversation that had stung him - but now he struggled to remember why.

"My mother. Did you ever paint her?"

Outside, a man in green overalls appeared pushing a wheelbarrow. It was filled with detritus from the garden: weeds, leaves, clippings. He wanted suddenly to be a flower, so that he might be cut back - 'dead-headed' - and then allowed to grow again. He wanted another chance, another ride on the roundabout. But then, in a moment of lucidity, he recalled he had never been able to paint flowers. Just like he couldn't paint hands.

NINE

"I still think this is one of the best things you've ever done."

They were standing in the smallest of the gallery's modest exhibition rooms; on the wall ahead of them a large portrait of a naked woman dominated the entire space. From another room, the murmur of staff and the sounds of final preparation could be heard: the fixing to walls of briefing cards containing titles, dates, prices; against the gentle hum of air conditioning, the punctuation of the gallery owner issuing instructions. Tim had been good to Oscar, and this was the grandest gesture yet - though clearly he was in it for the money too!

"'The original and best', as they say," smiled Oscar. "I've come to think that there can be nothing better, more honest, than that first attempt. The most raw one. After that, any knowledge and experience you've already gained tends to colour your approach. What you want to pick out - or leave out."

"If you say so, Professor," Simon didn't move. Oscar noticed something abstracted about him, but at this precise moment he was too wrapped up in the promise of the show to give it any further thought. They would open in the morning. He knew there were unlikely to be fanfares, but it was his largest solo exhibition to-date and if you knew where to look, there would be reviews the day after.

"Mel never liked this one, did she?"

"I don't think she ever said," Oscar replied. "After all, she said it was for me; a personal endeavour. After the hat portrait, it seemed as if she had all she needed. Well, almost all." He glanced at Simon. No reaction. "At any rate, I don't recall her saying anything about it. Or even if she saw it come to that."

"Oh she saw it," Simon affirmed. "Maybe when it was kicking around your old studio before you moved. I think this is the first time you've ever actually had it on the wall, isn't it?"

"Now who's turn is it to be the Professor?! You're right. But you say she didn't like it?"

"That's what she said to me. More than once. Don't get me wrong, she didn't say it was bad or anything - she would never say that - but rather that it wasn't her style I guess. There were other paintings of Rachel she preferred. Even the one with the wonky hands!"

Oscar turned momentarily. There were three other paintings of Rachel in this room. On the opposite wall, she lounged on a sofa, her gaze directly at the viewer. Oscar had placed a television in front of his easel and just asked her to watch it. It had worked well.

"When was the last time you saw her?" Simon's question brought him back.

"Who? Rachel?"

Simon nodded.

"I don't know, maybe a couple of weeks ago. In passing. She sits for me less often now."

"Making her own way in the world on the back of the publicity you gave her."

"I wouldn't say that. She was always a bright enough cookie. Had enough of her sister's genes in there somewhere to ensure she'd get on okay."

Simon turned and walked over to the television portrait.

"This one's, what, about thirteen years ago? Eight years later on from that first one? After you met her?"

"Nearer ten," said Oscar joining him. "Does it show?"

"We all get older," said Simon, somewhat cryptically. Then, after a pause: "She didn't say anything about me?"

"Rachel? No. Why should she?"

"No reason."

The spell of preparations suddenly broken, Oscar followed Simon back through to the other room and towards the front door. After thanking Tim one last time, he joined Simon on the pavement outside.

"What's wrong, Simon?"

"Wrong?" Simon paused, then started walking. "Drink?"

"Just a quick one, then. I need to be back here bright and early."

✻

"I'm thinking of going away for a while."

They had been sitting at a table tucked away in the corner of the pub (Simon's choice) and Oscar had let the silence hang long enough for his friend to break it.

"I *am* going away for a while."

"Anywhere nice?" Oscar tied to keep the mood light, but he knew he had misjudged it as soon as Simon looked back at him.

"America. Probably. For a while."

"I assume that you're planning to go on your own?" No answer. "What does Mel think about it?" Again, no answer.

Oscar took a long pull on his beer. The positive anticipation of his exhibition was now little but a recent memory. He reminded himself that he still had tomorrow; that would be his day.

"She doesn't know, does she? Mel? She has no idea."

"Things have been…" Simon searched for the right word for a moment, then gave up; "rough. Recently, things have been rough. I'm not sure what it is; me probably. I don't know."

"She hasn't said anything to me."

"No? When did you see her last?"

Oscar couldn't remember.

"And why should she say anything to you anyway?"

"Come on!" Oscar protested. "We were pretty close, remember?"

"It's her idea." Simon allowed the words to hang in the air, as if he were listening to them via some kind of echo. "Well, not exactly; not in so many words. But she won't be surprised. I mean you know what she's like: robust, resilient, independent…"

"But she's also a mother," Oscar cut in, "and she wasn't well not so long ago. And may not be again, who knows? Yes, she's tough - but she's also fragile and vulnerable at the same time. She needs you, Simon."

"Does she, Oscar? Does she really?"

"And maybe you need her. More than you think. Maybe you need them both."

There was a sudden blast of music from behind the bar, swiftly followed by a "Sorry!" from the Landlord as he adjusted the volume down. It was still a little louder than it could have been. Simon picked up his glass and drained what was left - nearly half a pint - in a single draft.

"I can't keep up with the boy any more. He's changing. The differences are too great."

"Its puberty. He's nearly a teenager. Don't all kids change when they get to that age?"

"You've seen him?" There was something of a challenge in Simon's voice.

"Yes. Of course. Last week I think; after his art group at school. As usual."

Simon made to stand up. Oscar put his hand on his arm.

"Can I help?"

"Not this time, uncle. Maybe the wheels were always going to come off at some point - for one of us. But I never thought it would be me. Somehow I'd assumed it would be someone else. Not Mel. How could it be Mel? She would always manage to resolve things, sort them out, dissect and reconstruct them in a fashion that suited her purpose."

"You make her sound almost Machiavellian." Oscar observed.

"Sometimes she is. Haven't you noticed how she can manipulate people? Manipulate us? Oh, she does it in a charming, disarming way of course. We are taken with her 'style' I suppose." Simon paused. "When was the last time she *didn't* get what she wanted? Tell me that. She wanted the hat painting; you gave it to her. She wanted you to paint Rachel naked; you did. Ok, maybe that's not a great example… She didn't want you to sleep with her sister; so you didn't. She wanted me. She wanted - some impossible things… And we always said 'yes'. Always. And now this. Maybe she wants me to go away. How the fuck do I know? I'm not sure I know anything any more, Oscar. Except that it's suddenly just become too hard."

"Wait," suggested Oscar, trying to buy time for his friend - and for his own thoughts to catch up. "Wait until after the weekend. Why not go to the football tomorrow? For a change. Just to get out somewhere you can scream and shout a bit. Let your hair down. Might make you feel better, who knows? Then talk to her."

Simon stood up.

"Chelsea," he said.

"Sorry?"

"Chelsea. That's who Fulham are playing tomorrow. I've already got my ticket."

"That's good," said Oscar, trying to sound encouraging.

Simon was suddenly by his side and moving.

"Good luck with the show," he said, and then was gone.

TEN

There is a special kind of silence that pervades hospitals; almost a non-silence. As if sound is absorbed and then, later on, leaked out slowly to fill the vacuum. As she walked along the corridor, it seemed as if she was only hearing a part of the sounds of her heels made; half of it was being sucked away for later, to be embellished by the shadowy echo from previous walkers. The sound felt embossed.

It also felt sad. Or perhaps that was simply her overlaying mood. She had been given her briefing by the Doctor; she had been told what to expect, how different he would be compared to her last visit. "Now when was that exactly?" "I've been away" she had said to excuse herself - and she knew that the Doctor had recognised her and would therefore believe her white lie.

The door to his room was open. She stood outside and looked in. He appeared to be asleep. She wondered about turning and walking away, but instead found herself going on again, through the door. She said nothing, but headed for one of the two chairs that had been placed towards the end of the bed, facing the window. Outside she could see the trees moving and remembered with a sudden shiver that it was cold, autumnal. It seemed fitting, somehow.

A nurse stepped into the room, smiled at her encouragingly, and then withdrew closing the door behind her.

She sat down.

The patient in the bed shifted slightly.

"I can still see things, you know," he said. His voice made her jump. Partly it was the suddenness of it, and partly its complex hollowness. It seemed both bereft of meaning and yet full of portent as if the very sound of it carried all the message, irrespective of the words uttered.

"You have always been able to see things," she said, almost involuntarily.

Oscar shifted again.

"Once upon a time...", he started, and then paused. "I used to know how that story went."

"There were lots of stories," she said, attempting to be comforting, "and lots of people in them."

"Only one. Only one. Mine was the only one that mattered. Ask me."

"Ask you what?"

There was a pause as he shifted again.

"I hope you haven't brought me any more of your medicines; your poisons! Just leave me and my friends alone. And tell the doctor he walks with a limp."

Simultaneously there seemed both logic and the absence of logic in what he was saying; both anger and pity. She could not tell if he was responding to her at all, even on a subconscious level.

"Which friends?" She tried to keep up with him, just in case.

"Rachel."

"Yes?"

"Rachel was my friend. I think she was. I remember some things about her. I remember when I first saw her in the café. I had never seen anyone like her before. What she did to light... It would be nice to see her again."

"I'm here Oscar. It's me."

"Who's Oscar?" he said, agitated. "Never met him, Nurse. Heard about him, of course. Never met him. Not one of my friends. Someone liked him, who was that?"

"We all liked him."

She realised she was sitting on the edge of the chair, leaning forwards. She tried to relax, but could not.

"Who? Is Simon back? I think he was my friend once. He went to watch football - in America, I think? Is that why I lost him?" There was a low, short, rasping laugh. "He used to buy me beer," he said conspiratorially.

Rachel stood up, turned her back on him, and went to the window. Outside a couple was walking slowly arm-in-arm. She raised her hand to her face and found that she was crying.

"'Do me a favour', she said to me once. It was a demand, a bargain, an exchange. 'Do me a favour and you can paint Rachel naked.'"

She turned around to look at him. He hadn't moved. His eyes were closed, but his hands were working feverishly at his covers. She knew she should call the nurse - but not just yet.

"Who? Who?"

"That was the deal. Ha! Our little secret. What were they called? Once upon a time…"

Outside the trees swayed, and the walking couple had disappeared. Rachel tried to sift what he was saying, filtering things out, excluding things, to try and make sense and certainty out of it. The picture was clearing, but how true an image was it? Even now, in this final state, was Oscar unwittingly playing with words as he once played with colour and lines and shadow?

"I think I might have loved her."

"Who?"

"But they're all gone now. Visiting Winter somewhere. All except Josh. Joshie."

Suddenly he was still, his hands motionless. She waited just a moment, then went to the door knowing she should find the nurse.

"My boy", she heard him whisper as she stepped into the corridor.

ELEVEN

The painting had remained unopened, leaning against his bedroom wall. Josh had found the visit to the hospital so draining that his first instinct on getting home was to simply put the package down and try to forget about it. His fingers had stung from the pressure of the bag ties, and he was glad to be free of those.

Knowing that his uncle was about to die (the Doctor had been very clear about that), meant their relationship was suddenly in limbo. Josh knew he had seen him for the last time, and all that was left now was to wait. He also knew his aunt was due to see him soon after his own visit; perhaps she would bring some news. Josh had been surprised by his increasing closeness to his uncle over recent years. Normally where such relationships worked well for children, the fragile familial bonds tended to weaken; grown-ups just didn't need uncles and aunts in the same way.

The news when it came - via a somehow unexpected phone call the Sunday following his final visit - hit him hard. He had been expecting Rachel to be the bearer of the final news; instead, it had been the professional, caring - if slightly acerbic - tones of Dr Wilson. The message had been a perfunctory one, but Josh did manage to establish that his uncle's passing had been a peaceful one. And that Rachel had been there.

The weather was good that morning; bright and just a little on the cool side. Josh decided on a walk before lunch. He found himself on Putney bridge and, for a few moments before returning, paused. Up river, he could make out the stands of Fulham Football Club. He had never been there.

Once back in his flat, he went into his bedroom to change out of the heavy jumper he had chosen to wear on his walk; it was then he caught a glimpse of the brown-wrapped oblong against his wall. "Now is the time", he told himself. After all, there were no further questions to ask or interactions to be had. His uncle's present was now a bequest, a status that seemed to suit it.

Josh sat on the end of his bed and looked at the package. There were few things it could be. A portrait of Rachel, perhaps - after all, she had been his favourite subject. But then, what relevance could that hold for him? Josh knew that his uncle would not have given him just any old painting; that was not his style. It would have to have meaning. On that basis, Josh's second guess was that it might be some kind of landscape, even though that was not Oscar's preferred subject. But of what? A view of Chiswick, perhaps; that would have some resonance with him. Or of the idyllic little station that had occasionally been the starting point of their family holidays when they had been younger? But Josh dismissed that too. He could not see his uncle sitting, painting en pleine air. And some what ironically, that very same location had become the arrival and departure point for visits to the hospital.

Unable to decide what it might be, Josh leant forward, picked up the painting, and loosened the strings.

It was more drawing than painting; a rapid, freehand mix of charcoal and pastels. Judging by the freedom of it, the pastels were probably a later addition. And it was a portrait of sorts. The subject was reclining, apparently asleep in a bed. Apart from the partial covering of a sheet or duvet, they were clearly naked. There was a feverish quality in the work; a suggestion of panic engendered by knowing there was a deadline to be hit, that time was running out. This was not typical of his uncle - nor was the fact that, in his obvious haste, he had managed to capture the hands to perfection.

But it was not Rachel who was asleep on the bed. Not Rachel, who had fallen into a pose so relaxed that it appeared to epitomise complete satisfaction.

And at this, Josh's head had begun to spin. If his uncle had decided to leave him something with meaning, a message, then the painting offered few possibilities. Indeed, there was only one.

Josh was staring Mel; at a portrait of his mother.

A Strange Kind of Map

i)

I had not expected to fall in love again. Not after all this time. I had assumed those days were long behind me, replaced by sporadic episodes of ultimately ineffectual flirting leading nowhere in particular. And yet, here I was - and as old as I was - displaying the annoyingly enthusiastic and naive tendencies which are usually the purview of the young and the innocent. If I recognised them for what they were it was simply because I had been there before; memories dredged up from when I had been unformed, from when passion and focus were one and the same thing, from when days simply weren't long enough. Being able to see all that now gave me options, of course. I had choices: whether I embraced this new love or not, and if I did, how far I might take it and at what speed. My age allowed me to regulate my response in a manner I had never previously enjoyed; choices which gave these new 'old' emotions weight and substance. There was a degree of gravitas in what I felt now, a sense of purpose.

If you asked me what triggered this re-ignition, then I would struggle to find an answer. 'How do most things start?', I might challenge. We like to think of cathartic or cataclysmic events, episodes of chance, luck - danger even - which suddenly and uncontrollably propel us from one state to another. Incidents that spawn some kind of seismic shift from there to here. In consequence these events always seem the more profound when we realise that the 'here' to which we have travelled was a destination about which we were ignorant, or an outcome didn't think possible. There is, within most of us an element which thrills at being out of control. We look back on such step-changes and recall the frisson of electric excitement, as if all the atoms in the world had been rearranged, just to sweep us from A to B.

Not that it was like that for me. Not only was there no sudden magical moment which caused the transformation, but my new 'here' was somewhere I'd been before. It was known territory. I'd like to think that foreknowledge made my conversion seamless, and was the platform on which my 'knowingness' could be based. I had, you might say, a solid foundation.

But then again, I might be lying. Or at least not telling the whole truth.

The basic facts relating to my past were indisputable and wholesome enough. Decades previously I had entered the hallowed halls of University life only semi-bent on a course of study that - depending on your point of view - might be variously interpreted as suitable or easy or complex or a complete waste of time. From my own perspective, perhaps I travelled more in hope than expectation, as the saying goes. Embarking on the study of literature was s decision supported more by logic than instinct, more common sense than divine inspiration. And maybe I was lucky. Perhaps the stars did all align for once. I had only been there a few short weeks before I was in besotted.

I found I loved to read. I loved books. I loved their feel and smell; I loved the abstract way words stared back from their pages when you glanced at them. And it was - unlike so many relationships during those fuzzy emotional years - a love that was totally requited, totally giving, without exception and without boundary. It was like embracing a partner who could hold many forms, being by degree dangerous, inspiring, melancholic - a whole panoply of emotional engagements ready to fit to my mood.

But the innocence of it led to an uncontrolled devouring, and instead of being satiated I was always left wanting more. More in terms of volume, in terms of variety. I wanted the dangers to be more extreme, the highs to be higher, the lows lower. If I burned through the fabric of this passion over those academically-led months and years, then perhaps that was inevitable too; the only possible consequence of total freedom and zero restraint. After I left University, unshackled from the structure of course work and study, I should have been able to renew my vows, to re-embrace my love; but instead I floundered. I didn't know what to read next. I tried and failed. It was as if both I and all the books in the world - that vast limitless promise before me - had been hollowed out; as if our relationship had suddenly run its course and neither of us had any more to give. Looking back, I suppose the demands the University syllabus imposed had paradoxically forced me to explore beyond the boundaries I might otherwise have set myself; offered both encouragement and safety net. In a way, the course had been the muse. Perhaps the love I had embraced - the love of books - had been somehow surrogate.

All of which - nonsense or not - perhaps helps to explain how being in love again now feels more mature, profound, controlled, satisfying. All those things. It has come upon me for and of itself, not tied to some other priority or motivation. This is my freedom in the 'here' of today.

But if I lied about the single all-consuming, triggering event, I apologise. It actually had less to do with books and reading; perhaps that is what I meant to say. There was no magical moment when I picked a novel up or re-read a poem from my ancient past. Nothing like that to flick the switch; indeed, there may not have been a switch that needed 'flicking'. But there was one thing.

The day I suddenly went deaf.

ii)

The house we lived in was remarkably idiosyncratic. An 'architect designed' 1970's chalet-style detached, on one side the roof began about three inches from the ground, a feat whose repetition on the other was prevented only by the presence of the garage. From certain perspectives out on the road, the house looked like a slab of Toblerone with a small slice taken off one corner. Perhaps nibbled, just to try it out.

Inside, the result was that, apart from one of the major rooms on the ground floor - a large kitchen-diner - all the ceilings boasted jaunty angles; in some of the upstairs rooms, the ceiling started at the floor. Most of the first floor windows were Velux, set into the pitch of the roof, and it was only in the main two bedrooms where the presence of dormers allowed for windows set to the vertical. As a consequence, ours was a house more of blinds than curtains; a restriction that led my then wife to threaten moving - and sometimes divorce! - just so she could allow her creativity with fabric free rein.

The toilet - an extra one, set apart from the main bathroom - occupied a traditional location 'at the top of the stairs'. How many times do you visit other people's houses where your enquiry about the loo is met with that stock phrase? But in our case, that was where the similarity ended. The roof sloped (of course!), and the loo seat itself was positioned in such a way that when you sat on it, the ceiling rose immediately in front of you. We had installed a low shelving unit at its shallow foot, just to try and make the most of the dead space. There were lots of similar dead spaces upstairs. The window in the toilet was located so that when you were sitting down, you could look up and out at the sky. At night-time, you could sit and stare at the stars if the sky was clear. That side of the house, facing away from the town on whose edge we sat, was protected a little from the city's glow; just here the sky could appear particularly dark.

I used to read in the toilet of course, once I'd fallen back in love. Initially just almanacs or collections of witty quotes or facts; the kinds of books that were light and fluffy, and contained appropriately sized morsels to see you through your ablutions. We called them 'toilet books'. It was, I suppose, one of the reasons we put that shelf in. At night, when I struggled to sleep or needed the loo, I sometimes sat in there, reading and looking up at the stars. Bizarrely it became a place I loved.

Of course, there were certain things I couldn't read in there. Novels, for example. Novels were for the bedroom primarily, and occasionally the lounge. I found relationships established themselves between the types of thing I was reading and the rooms of the house. The conservatory - set on the 'alps-side' behind the lounge - had a remarkable glass roof that extended from about six inches off the floor almost to double height. In the winter, it could be a haven on sunny days when its heat radiated into the lounge and beyond. I loved to read biographies and histories in the quiet there; they seemed to fit somehow.

Mind you, when I say quiet…

I had suffered from tinnitus for years - though for exactly how long it's impossible for me to say. When do you first notice it? An insidious background hissing that is initially so subtle as to be imperceptible, yet which day by day increases in intensity by the merest fraction until suddenly there it is. When I first noticed it - and when I realised that it wasn't some external background noise - it was only mildly annoying. It didn't seem to have any effect on me being able to hear well, which felt slightly contrary. Later it became intrusive. In every room I went, every shop in which I browsed, every restaurant that fed me, the hiss was a constant companion; the metaphorical monkey on my shoulder, always there, always nagging away at me.

And then one day it stopped. I was in the toilet - reading, of course. It was the middle of the day. I can't remember what book I had open at the time, but I was suddenly conscious that something was different. I looked up through the window to see if it was raining, or if the clouds were now racing across the sky blown by a sudden wind. It took me a while to place the discomfort I felt, a discomfort generated by the sensation that something profound had changed. And then I realised that my whispering had disappeared. Gone completely.

Suddenly excited, I dropped the book, finished up, washed my hands and opened the door. Belying my years, I flew down the stairs and headed for the lounge where I knew Lou was. Simultaneously, I tried to speak, saw the television, saw the smile on her face, her mouth making the shapes of words - all together, a combination of events that should have generated a minor cacophony. But there was nothing. Absolutely nothing.

iii)

When Lou left me less than six months later people most wanted to express their reaction to her going. The word they used was 'unfair'. I missed the inflections in their voices when they said it - I missed their voices! - but the notes they wrote to me were plain enough. "That wasn't fair," I would read, or "I don't think that's fair". Variations on a theme. Some comments were less restrained. Soon enough I found that without their voices layering inference and meaning onto whatever they said, the words in the notes they wrote were effectively stripped back to the bone. Communication became raw, black and white; words leapt from the page towards me with a new and harsh power - a violence almost! - that surprised me. A pink Post-It note on which "Was that fair?" was written in a rapid, hard to read hand, often carried more accusation or meaning than the erstwhile speaker might have been able to invest in it had I still been able to hear them. Of course, when the notes were written in my presence, their faces still told a story.

Occasionally they would spin the words around and ask me the question; did *I* think it was fair? I remember being alone sitting at the kitchen table. I took a slip of paper and wrote my own question on it, wanting my words to be as stark as everyone else's so that my reaction would be in balance. "Was it fair that Lou left?" That was how I chose to phrase it. Perhaps it took me twenty seconds to decide that the answer was "yes".

She had tried of course. Tried and cried. The first few minutes and hours were panic-stricken really. We rushed around, she made phone calls; we hurried to the Doctor's, to the hospital. I was prodded and poked, scanned and then scanned again. Between the tears she smiled a lot. On reflection that now seems strange, but I know she was trying to keep my spirits up - and probably her own too. We quickly evolved a way of communicating that seemed to work. At first she just kept on talking, forgetting herself. They she would read aloud what she was writing as she wrote it. Perhaps she was hoping for some miraculous return of my hearing and her continuing to speak was an insurance policy of some kind.

And then she stopped speaking, and after that the volume of her notes began to fall away. The odd bits of whimsy or off-the-cuff thought just disappeared, and we were left with only the limited communication needed to function and get through the day. The palette quickly became basic and bland. It was evident that not being able to express herself as she wanted - and be understood as she wished - was killing her little by little. I guess none of us realise how important something we take for granted is, until it's taken away.

I suppose I stopped talking too, and probably a little quicker than Lou. I tried to carry on at first - it was certainly important to do so during those hospital-bound first few days - but then I found that - unable to hear what I was saying, not knowing how I was saying it, what it sounded like, what meaning my voice might have been carrying - I began to mistrust myself. I recalled seeing and listening to deaf people speak and finding the experience hard. I wasn't sure back then if I found it difficult for them or me, but now I knew well enough. I had been embarrassed for both of us (even the listening was challenging) and so probably didn't want to put anyone else through that.

So was it fair that Lou left me? How could it not have been? I was no longer what she had signed up for. She was still young enough, vital enough. She had enough of her life left - even being in her fifties - for a chance to find happiness elsewhere. Now I could give her nothing other than painful memories; memories of how things used to be - and a reminder of how they might have been in the future. When we cancelled the long-planned holiday to America, perhaps that was a sign; a tangible coffin nail. And there were no children to worry about. There had never been any children to worry about.

Some of my friends, finding communicating with me difficult - struggling to write out notes in my presence - found ways to leave their comments and questions where I would discover them later. Smuggled into my coat pockets perhaps, or left on odd pieces of furniture around the house. The cistern in the loo became a favourite noticeboard for a while! From time to time I used to uncover small missives whose words would shout out to me suddenly and unexpectedly, divorced from their authors. It didn't take me long to recognise handwriting, and I caught one or two people out that way. Then they started writing in super-neat capital letters when they had something they wanted to say anonymously, out of sight as it were. They and I started to become invisible in a strange way.

"WAS THERE ANOTHER MAN?" took me by surprise one day. I found it underneath a magazine on the little shelf beneath the coffee table. I had no idea how long it had been there. Although cowardly, I could understand why someone had not wanted to 'say' that to my face. I sat and looked at the note. The answer was that I didn't know; I didn't think so, but I didn't know. But part of me hoped that the answer was "yes", for Lou's sake.

Without any premeditation I began to collect some of the notes people had written. I didn't have very many visitors really - I was never that sociable on my own, so most of our friends transferred away with Lou - but nevertheless I took to ensuring that in the rooms downstairs (and in the loo!) there was always a supply of Post-It notes, pens and pencils. I also discovered that having a supply of ready-made messages for the questions and observations that seemed most popular allowed 'conversations' to flow a little more readily. When someone wanted to ask me how I was or if I needed them to get me anything (as if I was some kind of invalid!) all they needed to do was to point to the relevant one I had made earlier. Because I had also prepared some standard responses - for when I wanted to avoid speaking - often we could pass the first couple of awkward minutes just pointing and not writing. Maybe it helped those who came to see me.

Over time, one of the consequences of this approach was that when people wrote something down their notes tended to carry more weight. I didn't have to throw away any more yellow squares demanding "How are you?" - at least not in my own house. I think that was one of the things that drove me to start collecting. "WAS THERE ANOTHER MAN?" meant something; it was important. Even if I didn't know who wrote it (though I had an idea!), it represented a fixed point on my journey; the journey post-hearing and post-Lou. I kept the notes in a small folder, much as a businessman might keep business cards. The only thing I did to them was to add the date they had been written - exactly where I could, approximately where I could not. It was a strange kind of map.

iv)

"DID THEY FIRE YOU?!" - I ended up with more than one version of that one; similar words, echoing each other, phrased slightly differently yet all essentially asking the same question.

The answer to which was "no". If pressed, I would tell people that it was "emphatically, no" - though I suspect they believed that less than they should have. The firm had been very decent about it, of course. They gave me as much time as I needed to get sorted, to work out how permanent my changed medical state might be, and to 'get my head together'. Then they had me back in the office - part-time at first - to see what we could work out. But it was immediately obvious that I was hopelessly ineffective. In spite of the brilliance of modern technology without the bedrock of conversations, being credible and making efficient contributions in meetings - being able to answer the phone, for Christ's sake! - I was transformed from a reliable, dependable delivery-oriented guy to a passenger. And worst than that: a passenger who made just about everyone else feel bad.

Within what seemed like days (and maybe it was just days) the HR process kicked into motion. I was consulted, Lou at my side, about my options. Turned out that there really was only one. I would be retired on health grounds. That was part of the benefits package; the insurance they provided for their staff and themselves. It was generous enough, looking at it dispassionately; an early retirement with sufficient funding to not have to worry about ever working again.

At face value, great. But then I was going to be kicking around at home all the time, a real physical presence with all my failings permanently on-hand, nagging away, to be dealt with constantly. Lou put a brave face on it, but it was just another one of those 'big things' that made the situation impossible for her. We tried to kid ourselves that I could put all my new-found free time to good use: in the garden, decorating, getting fitter, being 'creative'... But these weren't things you can just switch on and off; not for me, at least. Lou started working longer hours, just to keep out of the house. "WAS THERE ANOTHER MAN?" was a question I could have written out for myself in the weeks before she left.

You find out a lot about people when faced with such a traumatic situation. Not just Lou - or me, come to that - but the people you had tagged as your friends. There's a sliding scale isn't there? Acquaintance, colleague, friend - something like that. I was surprised by some of the people who slid down the scale from 'friend' when I had them pegged as the people who would stand by me - and by others to whom I had given almost no time yet who travelled in the other direction. Take Jake. A youngish lad who worked in my section but with whom I'd had little contact. He was into sport and girls and drinking, boasting something of a reputation in each field. I never really paid him the time of day, yet suddenly there he was, concerned, helpful, visiting even. Oh, he didn't turn into a saint overnight, but I saw him in a new light. I hope others did too. I think he might have been the one to write the "WAS THERE ANOTHER MAN?" question. It fitted his modus operandi.

They threw me a retirement party, partly because they wanted to show either their appreciation or concern; but I always suspected that the motivation for doing so was driven by relief and self-interest as much as anything else. Everyone knew we were getting a little 'top heavy' organisationally; too many of the older, senior guys around, blocking opportunities for the young 'Thrusters'. Rumours had been bouncing around for some time that some of the old guard would be eased out. Losing me made their thinning-out job easier by a count of one.

v)

"ISN'T THERE ANYTHING THEY CAN DO?" - Whenever someone says 'they', the association is most often a negative one; like the 'they' of my old company. Of course, when people were asking about Doctors or the medical profession generally, there was really only frustration; a second-hand frustration, on my behalf. And again the answer was 'no', at least not initially.

After the scans and tests and being variously poked and prodded (the camera tube up the nose was the least pleasant of all the things I had to undergo), the consensus was consistently in the negative. I think they were stumped but never wanted to admit it. In the very early days I seemed to be meeting my consultant, Dr. Rodgers, weekly - and each week he would want to try out another of the gadgets he had to-hand. All variations on a theme really. Essentially flavours of hearing aid, each working in some subtly different way. It became evident quite quickly that they were just hoping one of them might miraculously connect with my brain somehow.

They didn't, and as the few options they had were exhausted, so the appointments became more sporadic until they were monthly and then quarterly. In a way it was something of a relief. Preparing for those first few sessions would put us through the mill of hope (rather than expectation); of crossing fingers and wishing - maybe even praying in Lou's case, who knows? Each time we went to see Rodgers our hopes ended up crushed, and when this started to coincide with us beginning to feel the strain in our personal relationship - well, it just didn't help. The first time he said he would 'see me in a month' I'm sure I must have smiled inside. I didn't know how many more times I could get myself 'up' for the visit. It wouldn't surprise me if Rodgers wasn't just a little relieved either. I don't think I'd given up exactly; I'm not sure I ever did. Perhaps I was just a little more pragmatic than Lou. Perhaps Rodgers gave up within the first few weeks - but if he did he never said or let it show.

When I next went to see him - after the first of our monthly interludes - I ended up going alone. Perhaps in part freed by the move to a less frequent commitment and what that signalled, Lou had left the previous week, so at least I could show up without having to go through any preparatory ritual with her - and without having to create any false sense of expectation.

"WHERE'S LOU?" had been the first thing he had written down - though I didn't need to see what he had written as I could partially read it on his lips as he spoke, and certainly see it in his eyes. "IT'S COMPLICATED" I wrote back, and to his credit he left it at that.

I was beginning to get a little better at lip reading by this stage., and I think we learn it to a degree even when our hearing is impeccable. It was an invaluable skill to be able to at least partially master; essential in public situations, like shopping or getting the bus. The primary way people try and communicate with you is through speech; not many carry round a stock of sticky yellow squares and a pencil just in case... And I found that for the mundane practicalities of life people don't vary what they say that much. Oh, they might flex the specific words they use, but the core meanings are all too often the same. Like the old jokes about the English only talking about the weather - but a little bit more profound than that. Though not much.

vi)

"WOW!!" - That one was mine.

It was almost a year since my hearing had started its sabbatical and I was due another check-up with the Consultant. To be honest, I almost phoned in to cancel it. I had long since reached the 'what's the point?' stage, I guess; after all, Rodgers had tried nothing new for maybe six or seven months now. In fact, during that time I don't think he'd tried at all. We went through the motions: the same examinations, the same questions, the same shaking of the head. We could have scripted it and saved time: I could have slipped him my bits of paper in advance, he slipped me his. Bingo; all over in five minutes. Our relationship was spent.

Maybe I had given up, but I'd established a routine of sorts and this helped me to get by, resigned to my fate if you like. I'd eventually got over Lou's leaving, established the sense of internal 'quiet' I needed to live alone with myself. I had become more domesticated than ever, managed to keep myself and the house clean, and feed myself without ever coming close to salmonella or botulism. I'd even begun to make some better use of all the time I now had, and not just by reading (though I had needed to invest in a whole new series of bookshelves along one wall of the sitting room). So to all intents and purposes, I was sorted. Under those circumstances I'd gone to the hospital to tell Rodgers that was the situation and that it was the end of the line as far as he was concerned.

Except it wasn't Rodgers.

It was a Dr. Watson (no honestly!), and Watson was different from Rodgers on a number of fronts. First and foremost, she was a woman. Secondly, she was lively and talkative. During that first session I don't think she wrote a single thing down, she just talked to me as if I was able to hear her perfectly well; the fact that I couldn't meant I had to work hard to try and keep up. Later she confessed that was part of her standard practice - partly because that's how she was personality-wise, but more importantly because she wanted her patients to work at it, she'd seen too many who'd given up too soon. And she wanted her interaction with them to be as 'real world' as possible. "No lifejackets in my consulting room" she said - or I think that's what she said…

Thirdly, she was prepared to try something new. It was the smallest ear insert I had ever seen; a little crude and unfinished but "new from the States" and she wanted to try it. She put one of the little devices in my right ear and handed me a small fob that looked like the key of an expensive car. "Try it", I saw her say. The buttons - there were four of them - were conspicuously marked: on, off, up and down. I pressed 'on' and nearly leapt out of my chair. A sudden screaming noise blasted through my head. I dropped the fob, then dived to the floor to switch it off as quickly as I could. The whole episode lasted maybe two seconds.

When I regained the chair - and my equilibrium - she was sitting on the edge of her desk smiling. "That went well!"

vii)

I saw her every day over the next four days. That first session - lifejacket free - lasted so long and was such a mental effort that I was drained when I left. As soon as I got home I fell asleep. When I woke a few hours later (it was early evening by then), I felt as if I had lost something - or gained something. It was difficult to articulate. Perhaps both.

She spent our appointment on the second day adjusting and calibrating the devices. She explained where she could, and I took in what I could assimilate. Gradually that loud blast began to be replaced with more muted tones varying in pitch and duration. By the end of the third day I was able to distinguish - now in both ears - some of the things she was saying. She said she wanted me to wear the implants home, to try them out in the hustle and bustle of the outside world; and while I shouldn't have them switched on all the time - the newness of it all might be too daunting - I should do so sufficiently to be able to see if I felt comfortable hearing again.

She was sitting on the edge of her desk facing me. It was her favourite spot. For the first time in over a year I was conscious of a silence having descended. It was the most bizarre sensation.

"Why are you still looking at my mouth?" she said, breaking into the moment.

"Because you have wonderful lips" I replied, without hesitation. And it was true. I had spent the last year focussing not on people's eyes, but on their mouths. Doing so had needed to become my default if I was to try and read them. The eyes were no longer the windows to the soul as far as I was concerned. So I had seen a lot of lips, believe me, and Dr Watson's were peerless.

I looked up at her eyes as soon as I had spoken, uncomfortable that I was now blushing like a schoolboy. Luckily - but slowly - her smile returned.

"Thank you," she said, "though one thing I think you may want to work on is not to immediately say exactly what you think. For the last year or so you'll still have been responding to things instantly but *internally*, without any safety net. Getting your hearing back means getting your voice back too. If your thoughts start going straight to your mouth without the application of that filter we all have in place... Well, you could get into all sorts of trouble."

I waited a fraction of a second. Trouble sounded appealing.

"Can I buy you dinner - to say 'thank you' for all your help?"

"Did you think about *that* before you said it?"

I nodded and she laughed.

At the end of the fourth session both implants were fitted as snuggly as they were ever going to be. The tuning was finished. When I removed the devices to recharge them I went back to being deaf, but that didn't matter; at those times I staggered battery charging to ensure there was always one ear I could hear out of. There was something slightly 'electronic' about the sounds I was getting, but that could have just been my imagination. I guessed it was a little bit like people who are slightly colour blind seeing different shades in the same objects. Whatever colours they see, the same physical things are still there.

The "WOW!!" post-it is now in a small frame and hangs on the wall above the bathroom loo. I wrote it when I went home after that final appointment. It was a 'wow' to represent both the miracle of my new hearing and the miracle of Viv. She *did* have dinner with me the following week. And yes, I guess going out with a patient was probably in breach of some kind of code of conduct. But where else was the poor woman going to meet new people if not at work? I even managed a proper introduction to those lips of hers...

There are no piles of virgin notepads lying around the house now. My map, such as it is, is finished; my little collection complete. Well, almost complete. There are a few rogue dayglow squares stuck on the fridge with ideas of places to visit and things to do when we go on holiday to America - but that's another story altogether.

Stanley Grice

On what turned out to be Stanley Grice's final Christmas Day he decided to shun electricity to demonstrate just how far his life had declined. It was a symbol, and Stanley liked symbols. If he chose to measure the merit and meaning of his life through his experience and enjoyment of Christ's birthday (and clearly he did to a degree), then his decision was only fitting. And so it was that he filled his living room with candles to see him through the evening, their somewhat soft and romantic light in strong juxtaposition to how he actually felt. What was perhaps more surprising - and certainly less premeditated - was that, when he accidentally kicked one of the candles over and it ignited the newspaper he had recently been reading, he let the paper burn and passively submitted himself to the conflagration that quickly ensued. Not only had it been his last Christmas Day, it had been his last day. Period.

Stanley Grice hated his name. It offered him no comfort and no acceptable alternatives. The usual sobriquets failed to inspire him. If asked "What do you prefer: Stanley or Stan?", over time his response became the same: "Grice". And that was how he became known, by that single - if unusual - label. It was a harsh word, 'Grice'. It escaped from your mouth a little like a curse, and seemed to lack any kind of warmth or positivity. You spat it at people in a challenging, almost aggressive way. Yet this was in no way a parallel to the man himself. Indeed, far from it. It was simply his reaction to the curse which had been placed upon him - and from which, sadly, he lacked the imagination to extricate himself.

On the face of it, Grice was an ordinary man. Where he varied from the norm, he did so by the smallest of degrees: he was slightly taller than the average male, slightly bulkier; he was slightly more intelligent (at least as measured by matriculation and examination results) but never an outstanding student; his voice was softer, his hair longer, his demeanour more passive; and where his physique might have lent itself to great sporting achievements, this latter trait - passivity - scuppered such prospects early in his life. Therefore none of this marginality of difference, even in the most sophisticated of combinations, led to his being extraordinary in any way. From a very early age - certainly since his father abandoned he and his mother, followed by her slow decline into alcoholism - the only claim he ever felt he could make was that he could 'carry a tune'.

Of course, this alone was not something which facilitated his standing out from the crowd. After all, what boy in his right mind would choose to boast to his classmates not only that he could sing well, but that he could also execute a pretty reasonable impression of some of the classic crooners of the 60's and 70's? There was no kudos, no merit in that. Indeed, the only possible consequence of doing so would be to face ridicule; and so he kept his one and only minor talent hidden, toned down his voice during the prescriptive visits to church with school at Easter, Christmas and harvest time - and then belted out popular classics in the privacy of the bedroom or bathroom with the door locked.

It would have been something perhaps if Grice's singing talent masked an innate musical ability, but it did not. Despite at least two attempts, he failed to learn how to read music; and rather incongruously, his fingers were too short for the guitar or piano, and any attempt at woodwind raised hell with the neighbourhood cats.

None of this panoply of mediocrity (nor his secret vocal ability) prevented progress through life however. Like all boys, he discovered puberty in an accidental way and then went on to explore its then limited extremities in a cloak-and-dagger fashion (again, mostly in the bathroom with the door locked). He took and passed his examinations; he considered his options; he choose an unprepossessing and unambitious 'new' university; he meandered on. And for most of this time he was his own sounding board. With his father gone and his mother increasingly unable to look after herself never mind act as some kind of Oracle for him, he had no choice. His friends were never close enough to help - and boys at that age (some might say at any age!) are rarely capable of dispassionate, rational, and un-self-serving advice for others.

If you wished to challenge Stanley Grice on the grounds of 'not being very interesting', you might have had a point (although an academic might argue that every individual is interesting and complex if you just take the trouble to look). One thing that did seem slightly off-centre about him was his choice of degree at that somewhat anonymous university. He chose Art and Philosophy. Although he just managed to attain the required grades for the subject, on reflection it's easier to elucidate the reasons why he didn't choose that course rather than the reasons he did. It was *not* chosen because he was especially artistic (his drawings were once described as 'naïve' when a tutor was trying to be polite); neither was he passionate about art history. Similarly he did not appear to have the mental capacity to be any kind of 'thinker', and so his approach to the more abstract elements of his course was to learn as much as possible by rote. But what *did* trigger his interest was the combination of the two, the application of the abstract part to the execution part. He was, he discovered, interested in what things meant, what they represented, how they could be interpreted; 'symbols', if you will.

When looking back, he was never able to explain how, from the relatively sparse pages of a university prospectus, he was able to define exactly what the combination of Art and Philosophy might yield, nor how its potential (even if plainly visible) could have any interest for him. Perhaps it was no more than a happy accident that he was to find himself in a class of just nine, and one of only two males. Such an imbalance in the close proximity of lectures, study groups and tutorials, inevitably led to embarkation on an extended study of post-puberty life and, more specifically, to do so with Rosemary Martin.

That she was almost diametrically opposed to him in every way seemed to hold little terror for him. She was popular, gregarious, intelligent, indiscrete, immodest and something of a predator. Perhaps that combination held Stanley Grice in thrall: she was everything he could never be. It made her reckless and dangerous, unpredictable and mildly threatening; he was powerless against her, even before that remarkable evening when, just a little drunk, she managed to unzip his fly and slip her hand inside his trousers. For her part, Grice was a little more than a conquest, a trophy. He became a safe port for her many storms; someone she could return to, certain in what she would find and how he would be. He offered her quiet stability when she needed it most. There was almost a sense of commerciality about their relationship, in what she gave him and what he provided her in return. But for all his commitment, she treated him badly, abused him mentally, and almost never changed. Almost.

When his mother died, Grice was the only one at her funeral. Still at university, he had asked Rosemary to go with him, but she was in one of her 'distant' moods and her response - "Christ, no! People will think we're married!" - allowed for no debate. His leaving home had triggered a rapid and unsurprising decline in his alcoholic parent. Within months she was failing to return his calls. From a friend of the family he heard that she had been admitted to hospital, and then, before he could visit her at the end of term, came the news of her suicide.

He tried to contact his father using the last few addresses of which he was aware, hoping that someone would forward his messages. On the day, he loitered outside the crematorium hoping to see him suddenly appear, but the only other people there were either from the service before or awaiting that which would follow. As he finally gave up and made his way into what turned out to be a short and antiseptic ceremony, he realised that even if his father had made an appearance, there was actually no guarantee that he would have been able to recognise him - other than via the presence of a second person.

For him there was no discernible emotional response to his mother's death. Indeed, his second Christmas at university morphed into one of peace and contentment. Rosemary, who had rebounded back to him in mid-November, was still there, calm and at least temporarily attached (something that would dramatically change after New Years' Eve). To many who did not know them, they would have appeared just a normal young couple; it was a sensation he was to know rarely.

Earlier that year, Rosemary had told Grice to join the University choral society. It had probably been more dare than constructive suggestion, but he had complied nonetheless. He discovered that all the bathroom practice from his earlier years had paid off, and he was developing an interesting, if unexceptional, tenor. Then, during a break in one practice session a week before that year's carol concert, Grice - who seemingly never did anything on a whim - stunned his fellow singers with an impromptu rendition of 'Good King Wenceslas' in the styles of Presley, Crosby and Bennett. Perhaps doing so was a reflection of his contented status with Rosemary. A week later, in the university hall, he had his moment of glory when, backed by the entire choir, he performed his one and only solo in the same fashion, its content and delivery made all the more sophisticated by the choirmaster, Mr Thomas, who - it later transpired - was a closet Bing Crosby fan. Weakened by the approbation heaped on her man, Rosemary became - for just a few short hours - the doting minor player in the relationship. Grice was probably never happier.

Intellectually he was making some progress too, and in many ways this was as tangential to his formal studies as Crosby and Presley were to being a chorister. His particular amalgam of art and philosophy was increasingly leading him towards a study of 'meaning', and whilst this was not a formal strand of the published course (in Grice's interpretation of it, at any rate) his tutor allowed him to progress the interest on the premise of volunteers being better than pressed men. Over the last two years of his studies this translated into a dissertation on 'Meaning in Dali'. He was not, of course, breaking new ground; there was a wealth of material to research and - as is traditional - to plagiarise; but Tim Johnson, his tutor, was happy to encourage Grice, even if he occasionally strayed from the strict academic boundaries of both Art and Philosophy.

Inevitably, he found himself taking this interest in symbols - what did something 'mean'? - into his own life. There were some big topics Grice found he needed to unravel. Why, for example, had his father left? Not in the mundane and practical sense of being out of love, or tired of a relationship, or of needing to 'move on'; but what did his departure signify at some 'deeper' level? In his mother's case he had a wealth of material to mine. And Rosemary? However, at that precise moment in time he lacked the maturity to do little more than scratch the surface. His conclusions were of the superficial variety more suited to the saloon than the library, and he became frustrated that his endeavours to uncover 'meaning' bore little fruit. Later he would understand more, and by his final Christmas his comprehension of his mother's decline seemed total.

One of the theories he developed over time was that maturity and experience were simply fancy words for scars. In Rosemary, Grice had the perfect subject to help him expand his knowledge in this area. Indeed, when she disappeared mid-way through a New Year's Eve party (just a few days after his triumphant solo performance) and then failed to materialise again for the best part of three weeks, she delivered a double dose. His challenge was not in the disappearance itself - after all, it wasn't the first time! - nor, having heard about sightings of her from others, that he was concerned for her safety; no, it manifested itself in the sudden and dramatic jump from one state to another, from bliss to solitude. Although he had trained himself not to hope, not to look forward too much, there was part of him that had entertained the notion that Rosemary's affections for him had finally turned a corner that Christmas, and that perhaps she was a changed woman. Grice had submitted to that greatest of scar-givers, possibility.

Of course she do return to him later, and, in the usual mix of condescension and contrition, re-established the switch-back norm of their relationship. It remained his way for the rest of their time at university. In his pursuit of meaning, their relationship remained a lid Grice refused to lift until he was certain that Rosemary could not return to haunt him.

That she did change would have been something of a surprise had he not been able to look back armed with the knowledge of the tragedy that left her no choice. There were many people across the country who had accidents that winter three years after they left university. The snow had fallen early and the thaw remained an unfulfilled and stubborn promise for many weeks. She had been a passenger in a car that was travelling through Slough on its way towards Hampshire and a friend's house near Aldershot. There had been no speed involved, just a patch of black ice hidden in the darkness near a set of traffic lights; that the road was running downhill at that point did not help, nor did the young driver's lack of experience. Coming to a red light, he braked too hard and the car started to slide. Rather than steer into the skid and release the breaks momentarily, both opposites were taken. The lorry coming across the road from the other direction had nowhere to go. The impact was mid-car and square on to where Rosemary sat in the rear passenger seat.

Grice had not seen her for two months when he walked into her room at the Paddington hospital. She had already been there for nearly three weeks and the medical staff were finally in a position to confirm her waist-down paralysis. A nurse warned Grice just moments before he walked through the door, but to him it felt like something he already knew.

She burst into tears when she saw him. Later, partly driven by his quest to understand, they would discuss the trigger for such a response given the historic nature of her relationship with him. Many words would be used, mainly by her, to explain away her tears: guilt, relief, realisation… Guilt was the one she returned to most. When he visited her the next day she seemed more prepared to see him and there were no tears - at least not until he sat on her bed, took her hand in his, and asked her to marry him.

He would later wonder if that was not the one moment of callous calculation in his entire life; as if he was finally in a position to take advantage of her as she had taken advantage of him for years; as if, in her debilitation, she actually had no choice, he was now the best she was going to get. Who else would want her? If she saw it that way, to her credit she never said so. She always described it as the most selfless act she had ever witnessed, and the perfect statement of his love for her. She did not deserve him; she was worthless, she said. But at no point did she try to dissuade him from his chosen course. They married five months later.

Perhaps inevitably there were no children, though it was not her paralysis that prevented procreation. Early on they agreed it would be 'difficult', 'unfair' - to both of them. Whenever they discussed the option in those early months words always came in quotation marks, as if they actually stood for something else. Symbols, perhaps. Although on balance he wanted children, Grice was happy to accede, assuming the greatest unfairness would probably have been on her, not because of her physical incapacity but because she was pathologically unsuited to be a mother. He might have taken the risk - and the burden - but chose not to do so.

Given the practical constraints that her disability imposed, they enjoyed a relatively normal life: normal in the sense that he worked, she remained at home; normal in that they went to the cinema, entertained friends, took holidays regularly. By the time she began to falter, they had visited Africa, America and Asia; Grice had changed jobs just once and been promoted many more times (his lack of flair and imagination, and dire reliability seemed to have commercial value). They had moved houses too; further out of London and higher up the ladder (the latter phrase always made Rosemary laugh with its inappropriateness). Their cars got larger; their celebrations smaller. Once a friend had described them as 'the perfect couple' assuming Rosemary was out of earshot. She hadn't been.

In contrast to her university days, Rosemary's consequent faltering was not mental but physical. She did not become wayward or unpredictable (in many ways, how could she?), but weaker and sickly. Not at all related to her accident, she had been dealt - she used to say - a 'double whammy': her cancer was formally diagnosed just before Christmas some twelve years after they married.

This was perhaps the only time Grice wavered, not that it lasted long. Assuming she had paid her price, Rosemary's illness was, to him, unfair in the extreme. Indeed for a while she needed to be the strong one simply to see him through the trough into which he fell; it was a burden she took on just as she was becoming incapable of doing so. He simply did not know how to cope. Having nothing to fall back on (because the centre of his world was to be taken from him), he edged toward breakdown only to be thwarted in achieving even that because he suddenly realised Rosemary was falling faster than he. He had to arrest his own slide to take care of her.

By Easter she was dead. Her funeral was the antithesis of his mother's: packed, vibrant, joyful almost. Most of the people there he knew well. There were one or two he vaguely recognised from their college days; one or two who looked as if they had simply walked in off the street to stay out of the wind (it was a bitterly cold spring). Later, as he sat alone searching for meaning in her death, he had the strangest sense that, in spite of their life together and the things they had done, Rosemary had actually begun to give up the day they married. He wondered if accepting him - being forced into accepting him - represented the greatest defeat she could possibly suffer, because of what it meant to her. Was it as if he, Grice, had become for her an icon for the very thing that he had spent years trying to decipher. In their lives *he* was suddenly a symbol; *he* pointed to meaning. He knew how demeaning that would have been for her, and could only see himself as an effigy for defeat and disappointment.

Was that when he gave up, when he arrived at that damning interpretation? Or was it when he waked away from the crematorium? Or on their next, now empty anniversary? Or that first Christmas after she had finally left him? Perhaps it had been the first time he had known true loneliness since he'd been a child. He worked on for a few years any passion he retained simply leaked away, the promotions stopped. The car stayed the same; he remained rattling around their last house; he holidayed nowhere.

Sometimes at night he would lie awake and try again to process all those symbols, those conundrums of meaning, that he had failed to solve: his father's disappearance, his mother's suicide, and just about everything that was Rosemary. And still his hardest puzzle was trying to get meaning from himself, from his life, from how he had lived it. Where was the meaning there? What was it all for?

It was a short list yet too complex to comprehend, a puzzle too hard to unravel. He might have been gifted many lifetimes and still be unable to answer even the simplest of questions in relation to himself. A final question - "what was the point?" - loomed large. Perhaps it was inevitable that acknowledgement of it would come at Christmas time, sitting in a room illuminated by candles.